'For readers who crave going deep int
My Brilliant Sister is pure pleasure. Th
about sisterhood, creativity, who shou
what makes a good life – while staying firmly grounded in the compelling voices of three strong women. I was spellbound by each of these subtly interlinked narratives. Amy Brown is a shining star!'

EMILY BITTO, AUTHOR OF *THE STRAYS*

'*My Brilliant Sister* is a work of such beauty and truthfulness. It's also a sustained poetic and political enquiry, which moves effortlessly from the smallest to the largest and poses irresolvable questions of being and language, with a melancholic lightness of touch.'

MILES ALLINSON, AUTHOR OF *IN MOONLAND*

'Gorgeously alive to both the smallest and biggest elements that make up a life, and a nuanced, moving and compelling exploration of the necessary compromises that accompany any woman's attempt to find meaning in work, whether domestic or creative, or – sometimes, somehow, magically – both.'

CERIDWEN DOVEY, AUTHOR OF *MOTHERTONGUES*

'*My Brilliant Sister* is truly that – brilliant. Amy Brown's writing is superb, and the story is wonderfully told. This novel speaks to both our literary past and our sense of who we are now.'

TONY BIRCH, AUTHOR OF *THE WHITE GIRL*

'A searing, multi-layered book that not only reflects on female authority and a queasy balance between family and ambition, but also perceptively prises open the ways in which we live our lives through others.'

ALICE MILLER, AUTHOR OF *NOWHERE NEARER*

'A rich, playful meditation on art, domesticity, wildness, and the struggle to be understood – I loved it.'

EMILY PERKINS, AUTHOR OF *LIONESS*

MY BRILLIANT SISTER

ALSO BY AMY BROWN

Neon Daze
The Odour of Sanctity
The Propaganda Poster Girl

MY BRILLIANT SISTER

AMY BROWN

SCRIBNER

SCRIBNER

First published in Australia in 2024 by
Simon & Schuster (Australia) Pty Limited
Suite 19A, Level 1, Building C, 450 Miller Street, Cammeray, NSW 2062

Simon & Schuster: Celebrating 100 Years of Publishing in 2024
Sydney New York London Toronto New Delhi
Visit our website at www.simonandschuster.com.au

10 9 8 7 6 5 4 3 2 1

A catalogue record for this book is available from the National Library of Australia

9781761424359 (paperback)
9781761424366 (ebook)

Cover design: Sandy Cull
Cover image: Heritage Image Partnership Ltd/ Alamy
Typeset in Adobe Caslon 11.5/16 pt by Midland Typesetters, Australia
Printed and bound in Australia by Griffin Press

The paper this book is printed on is certified against the Forest Stewardship Council® Standards. Griffin Press holds chain of custody certification SCS-COC-001185. FSC® promotes environmentally responsible, socially beneficial and economically viable management of the world's forests.

FOR NICK AND ROBIN

Contents

The world thus
appears as it truly is:

twinned, or twice
as deep and large.

MAGGIE NELSON, 'TWINNED'

One

IDA

To Swim

I pretended I'd learned not to drown in the lagoon at Ocean Beach. I walked my hands along the sand, kept my chin high like a dog's, and the rest of my body floated behind me.

'I'm swimming!' I knew I wasn't but said so anyway. My earliest memory of comfortable dishonesty chosen over honest discomfort.

Now I swim as often as possible, at least twice a week these past summer holidays. Once the thermometer gun at the Brunswick baths had beeped at my forehead, I was ushered to the slow lane and permitted forty-five minutes of submersion. I like everything about swimming slowly: the tactility of the water on my body, the repetitive rupturing of the surface, the straight lines in the gawdy blueness crazed by movement. But the holidays are over and I'm back in the dark staffroom for the first day of term. It's just past eight and the place is filling with masked chatter, anxious platitudes.

There's a briefing before the first lesson. The principal's words as she reiterates policies are muffled by her N95, and the tide of stress is already coming in fast; I'm not listening well. They're teenagers I'll be teaching and yet speaking to them terrifies me. Speaking to any group of people does something to my blood. I'm obviously in the wrong profession.

'This is my twentieth first day of term one and I still couldn't sleep last night,' a maths teacher whispers in my ear, kindly but too close to my face. I smile and then realise she can't see it.

Every classroom is properly ventilated, confirms the principal. If a room is found to be without sanitiser, this should be reported. The bell cuts her off. Bodies, so many bodies, flow into the corridors and join even more bodies, with unlaced shoes, haircuts that haven't been professionally attended to in months, faces with noses and mouths exposed, masked chins.

I'm breathing shallowly and fumble with the key in the classroom lock, while my students wait, apparently patient. When the door opens I remind them to spread around the room.

They are quieter than I'd expected. On the back wall is a timeline of literary movements that my Year 10s made at the start of last year, one of the first activities I successfully set as a secondary school teacher. It resembles a criminal investigation board: writers' names and pictures are pinned to the board and linked to significant dates and places with red thread. What was once taut is now loose, dangling to the carpet. Mary Shelley is missing a pin and has spun upside down. Someone has drawn hearts with pink highlighter around ROMANTICISM. When I have a spare five minutes, I'll take it all down.

'How are we feeling? Bit weird to be back?'

Nods.

No one has been anywhere other than Melbourne. Many have family overseas. Some have family in hospital. Most would like to sit close to their friends, arms entwined or around shoulders. But most also care about not getting sick. They are surprisingly compliant for seventeen-year-olds. I begin the literature lesson with talk about what we've read over the break, what we'd like to read, what we recommend, then I move on to the set texts.

'Our first unit will involve studying this wonderful novel,' I say, pulling Miles Franklin's *My Brilliant Career* out of my tote bag as if it were a magic trick, a little too hammy. 'What's your first impression of the title? Of its tone?'

Scarlett, a girl I taught last year, as bright as she is earnest, raises her hand. Light catches the badges on her lapel as her blazer stretches.

'It's impossible to tell without having read the novel,' she says. 'But I have read it, over the summer, and I think the title is ironic and ambivalent. It establishes the ironic, ambivalent tone of Sybylla's narration throughout Franklin's work.'

'Well put.' I pause. I'd forgotten how Scarlett speaks. Not a 'like' or an 'um' anywhere. Each sentence an opportunity to rehearse for an essay. Each sentence spoken in class a chance to intimidate the competition.

'What do you think Sybylla is ambivalent about?'

'Marriage,' says Scarlett immediately. 'On the one hand, conformity to please her mother, and on the other, eccentricity, the desire to please herself.'

The lesson is fast becoming a dialogue between us. I turn to the rest of the class. 'Please make reading *My Brilliant Career* your priority.' It was set as holiday homework, but I sense few have finished it.

The rest of the lesson passes without disaster, the next is spent with excitable Year 9s. Then a teabag dangled for a few seconds in water from the Zip heater, a splash of milk, burnt lips, reapplied mask, and off to a philosophy elective titled 'How to Live a Good Life'. Lunch, a salad, I eat on the front steps of the school, alongside a severe succulent garden out of bounds to students. I smile amiably at passing colleagues but fail to speak to anyone. I am yet to make a real friend here. I don't think I'm disliked particularly, but nor have I proven myself to be warm or entertaining. I am socially distant.

After lunch I have a free period, during which the staffroom is blessedly empty and silent. I should be preparing lessons and unit plans, reorganising my notes from last year, but instead I sit and rest, meditating on the painting pinned above my desk. Swathes of royal purple, deep green and crimson writhe in a loose figure 8 (formally known as a lemniscate, Scarlett tells me). To my eyes, it's perfect. I know that the plump little fist which held the paintbrush to make the lines is a large part of the pleasure I take in the work, but I also objectively like it. I make a note to bring it to the philosophy class when we study aesthetics.

The afternoon drags, and as soon as it is acceptable to leave, I go. Sulphur-crested cockatoos are cracking pinecones under the trees next to the carpark. Something about their grey claws behaving like paws is delightful.

There's still not much traffic on the streets. I drive past the defunct ferris wheel, the Eureka Tower, artificial markers instead of natural landmarks in this flat place. Past the Queen Victoria Market's empty carpark, past the busiest part of the city – the hospital. Past the university, where I know very well that no academics or students are working, and then the restaurants on Sydney Road where we order food to be delivered to our doorstep on Friday nights.

At the childcare centre, I put my mask back on and rub more sanitiser over my hands before pressing the doorbell. The door used to be left open, and parents could wander through to the backyard to find their children playing. Now the children are escorted in and out by educators. Parents must stay behind the line.

'Mummy!' Aster runs and grips me around the thighs. I bend and kiss her head through the mask. Her bright pigtails are lopsided, and smell of barbecue rice crackers. She looks tired after nearly ten hours of childcare for the first time in months. I hoist her up and carry her to the car.

'Remember,' I say, when we park in our driveway, 'try not to disturb Daddy. He's still working.'

'Okay. Can I watch a show, though?'

'Yep.'

'With a snack?'

'Of course.'

'Sweet, savoury and healthy?'

'Sure.'

The house is quiet and cool. The study door is closed but no voices are coming from it. So, no meetings. Still, Aster and I go quietly to the living room, where I put a sheet over the couch to catch crumbs and she kicks her sandals off, lies back with her legs in the air. 'Can I watch *Bluey*?'

She knows her way around the remote, so I leave her to it, put my bag on a chair and assemble apple, crackers and a biscuit on a plate. Her glazed-eyed smile at the satisfaction of the situation is pleasing. A bit like watching cats tangled together in a knot of loving sleep.

To Burn

We're having stir-fry for dinner. I slice whatever I can find in the vegetable drawer of the fridge – a slimy spring onion, flaccid courgette (which I've learnt to call zucchini), withered red pepper (which I now know as capsicum), a shrunken thumb of ginger, garlic cloves ridged like fingers that have been in the bath too long. This meal reminds me of a very short story I love titled 'Stir-fry', in which the narrator takes everything she doesn't want any more, throws it in the wok, lets it sizzle then slides it into the bin.

The rice cooker broke last week, so I use a saucepan. Absorption method. One cup of water, one cup of jasmine rice, flame up high to start with. I crack three eggs into the hot wok, slosh in soy and drag the bubbling liquid up the side of the pan until it's a solid – this is the only part of cooking this dinner that I enjoy. The sudden transformation of the egg. I flip it out onto a paper towel on a plate.

'Can I watch another episode?' Aster asks.

'Yes,' I say, and remember the washing I put in the machine before leaving for school. Her undies are in there and she's out of clean ones. I pull the damp, unravelling body of clothes out into the basket and carry it on one hip out to the courtyard. There are never enough pegs, so I double up the socks and edges of T-shirts.

The efficiency gives me a quiet sort of pleasure, which is swiftly overcome by the smoke alarm.

Aster runs outside, hands over her ears, crying. 'I can't hear and it's my favourite episode!'

'It's okay, I'll fix it.' I run in to the stove, put the hissing saucepan in the sink and turn off the gas. I grab the broom and use the handle to prod at the button in the middle of the smoke alarm until its bellowing stops.

'Ah,' Aster sighs. 'That's better.' She returns to her dead beetle position on the couch. 'Can you put it to where it was?' I pull the dot back along the line until the cartoon dogs are where she wants them to be, then press play.

There's a bitter smell, so I open all the windows and doors. A blowfly arrives, circling my head as I try to salvage the rice. If you scrape the top gently and don't disturb the black crust, it's sometimes alright. But in this case the white grains on top are still crunchy.

'Fuck.' I take the saucepan to the bin, using a butter knife to lever out the steaming mess. It's the only suitable pan for rice. I scrub the bottom as best I can, until there's only a faint stain of black, pitted with oval dots.

'Is everything okay?' he asks, suddenly at my shoulder.

'You gave me a fright.'

'You should wear gloves, you're destroying your hands.'

He looks like he's just woken up, but I know he's rising slowly from the depths of thought, eyes not quite focused, hair and beard a dishevelled cliché in the same copper colour as Aster's curls.

'What happened?'

'I was boiling the rice.'

'You're meant to turn it down to a simmer once it's boiling.'

'I got distracted.'

'Do you want me to help?'

I do, but he sounds like he doesn't want to. 'You could finish hanging up that washing?'

'Okay.'

I cook more rice, carefully this time, and throw everything else in the wok with soy sauce and mirin. No recipe. No pride or joy. A bit like the way I apply make-up.

'Do I have time for a run before dinner?' he asks, holding the washing basket, which still has a few wet socks in the bottom.

'It'll be ready in five minutes.' I stare at the basket.

'I ran out of pegs.'

'Clothes horse?'

He sighs.

'You could go after dinner.'

The three of us sit together at the table and eat, none of us with much pleasure.

'Do I have to have this?' Aster asks, holding up a bit of zucchini.

'Try it at least.'

'I have. I hate it.'

'Okay, well, eat everything else instead.'

'No phones at the table,' Aster tells him. He doesn't hear at first, so she yells. 'No phones!'

'What?' He looks up at me, as if I've said it. 'Is this a new rule?'

'It's her rule. She'll do her best to stay seated and eat if we're not on our phones. It's a good rule.'

He frowns and puts it screen-down on the table.

'How did you go today?' I ask him.

It isn't the project that's the problem, he tells us. It's the administrative hoops he's being made to jump through. He'd rather be working on his monograph than chasing up ethics approval. Aster starts to sing, chant – insistent nonsense – as she does when she doesn't know what we're talking about.

'Quieter please, darling, I'm trying to listen to Daddy.'

She looks me in the eye and continues her song. 'Fill me in later,' I tell him.

'How was school?' he asks.

'Tolerable, I suppose.'

'Oh dear.'

'No, it's fine really. The kids are good. And at least I'm not teaching from home.'

The workstation I made for myself in the corner of the living room, TV behind me, window to the courtyard in front of me, bookshelf to my right, is still there, just in case. I picture myself sitting in the old leather chair, staring at my face on the screen, the only person with the camera on. A three-year-old sitting on my shoulders, banging my scalp and chanting, 'Mummy's a drum, Mummy's a drum, Mummy's a drum.'

He goes for a run while Aster watches another episode of *Bluey* then brushes her teeth, hops in the shower. I sit on the floor, watching her fill a plastic cup with water and delicately crumble fingernail-sized lumps of soap into it.

'Guess what it is?' she asks.

'Soap soup?'

'No!' she laughs.

'I don't know then. What is it?'

'Marshmallows on a campfire.'

'Of course.'

When I turn off the tap, she orders me to leave her campfire in place. I promise not to disturb it, wrap her in a towel, ignore her howling as I rub her tangled hair dry and spray it with something that smells of bubblegum and has a unicorn on the label.

In her bed, we snuggle together and I read *The BFG*. My eyes keep closing.

'Stay with me,' she pleads.

'Okay.'

When I wake, groggy, it's dark. I ease out of the bed, close her door, and finally change out of my work pants with the too-tight waist. I get straight into pyjamas.

There's a line of light under the study door. The shower smells of his shampoo. Aster's cup has been kicked over and fragments of soap are scattered across the floor. I kneel on the damp bathmat and reassemble the campfire.

To Mother

'I've got to go, Mum, sorry.' I don't look at my mother because I'm beckoning Aster back to the laptop. 'Shall we say goodbye to Nana now?'

She keeps reaching for 'end call for everyone'. She refuses to say goodbye. Something about the screen causes her to regress to a chaotic, furious, wordless state. She hurls herself at the keyboard and rolls on the floor.

'Not goodbye!' she calls at last. 'Bad bye!'

'That's the best we'll get. Sorry, Mum,' I say, glimpsing her perhaps frozen face, with the familiar vase of roses behind her, the framed photo of me on the wall next to the framed photo of Aster. Then a small hand returns and this time hits the red button. My mother disappears and my four-year-old daughter smiles. 'End call!'

I dislike her behaviour but I must admit that I can't stand seeing my face on the screen either, or my mother's face. Is that how I look? Is that even how she looks?

Are you okay? she texts later. *I don't think you're okay.*

I'm okay, I reply, thinking I'm probably lying, then deciding that, no, this is in fact what okay means given the context. I have food, water, shelter, an income; my family are alive and well.

Your accent's changing, she writes, and I don't reply.

Most of my literature students are, like me, new to Australia. Even if they were born here, their parents in many cases were not, so I don't assume their background knowledge. We are back in lockdown again, and I share my screen to show the slides: here is Goulburn,

New South Wales, where Franklin grew up and her novel is set; this was the year of federation, 1901, when the book was first published. Here's a photo of her holding a monkey as if it were a baby.

'*My Brilliant Career* reads like an autobiography – a diary, really. A yarn, to use her own word, but —'

I see Scarlett's microphone unmute. 'Do you have a question, Scarlett?'

'When you say "her" own word, do you mean Franklin's or Sybylla's? Because Miles uses "yarn" in the introduction. Is the introduction narrated by the author or the protagonist?' Her breath is heavy through my laptop speakers. She seems to be leaning close to her microphone, though I'm not sure as her camera is off.

'Excellent question.' For a moment, I don't know how to answer. I have a weary feeling that I'm about to ramble and obfuscate.

'An introduction is usually paratextual – outside the main text – in which case it would be Franklin herself declaring the work a yarn, but ...' I pause and open my copy to page one. An answer presents itself and I'm relieved. 'But if you read the letter starting "My dear fellow Australians" you'll see it gives an address of Possum Gully, which is Franklin's fictionalised name for her family property – that property was actually called Stillwater. So we can assume that the narrator here is Sybylla.'

I have been misplacing my energy, reading far more than necessary about the life of the novelist. Curriculum documents and textbooks agree that students should not be encouraged to conflate narrators with authors: biographical details should not hijack analytical discussions. Essays that veer into speculation about authorial intent will be marked down. And yet I recently bought a 432-page 'short' biography of Franklin, a collection of her letters and her diaries.

'It looks like you're doing research,' he said when we were in bed the other night, both sitting up with glasses on, reading matter balanced against our legs, pens in hand. He said it with some pity in his voice. Or caution.

'She's just interesting,' I said.

'Really? I had to study her book when I was at school. Thought it was rubbish.'

'Remember she wrote it when she was a teenager. And she wrote other novels.'

'I think *Frankenstein*'s rubbish too.'

'Well, I think Sebald's rubbish.' Sebald is his favourite novelist. He gave me *The Rings of Saturn* the year we first met, when we were working together on a contemporary fiction subject back in Wellington. Initially I pretended to be impressed, or I believed I was impressed, I'm not sure which. Later I confessed that I found the long meditations on herring fishery tedious.

'Sebald's a genius,' he said, almost whispering.

'Agree to disagree?' I leaned over and nipped his shoulder gently.

'That hurt.'

'No it didn't.'

We both have a break at lunchtime and walk to the hole-in-the-wall cafe to get bagels and coffee. Past front gardens of native flowers – grevillea, callistemon, happy wanderer – attracting native birds: rainbow lorikeets and honeyeaters, much gaudier and more confident than New Zealand species. It's the closest thing we've had to a date in eighteen months and I take his hand for a bit, but it feels contrived so I drop it. He's telling me about his former PhD student who's trying to contort her thesis to fit the requirements of the grant she's applying for.

'So, to make it relevant, she's framing Badiou's politics of love as an antidote to the climate crisis: "a truth is not constituted in a garden of roses"!'

I am distracted by real roses – a wall of mutabilis gloriously mottled with pink and peach. 'Sorry, I zoned out. What were you saying?'

'Never mind.'

We walk the rest of the way silently, each, I assume, thinking about our work. He is currently a cultural theorist, having been a poet, literary critic, and philosopher. I am currently a schoolteacher, having been a poet and a university tutor in English literature.

'Can you order?' he asks when we reach the cafe. He prefers not to talk to people if it can be helped.

'The usual?'

'Please.'

I order two long blacks and two avocado and tomato bagels. We take them to the playground and sit in the shade of the oak tree, watching the equipment that our daughter usually plays on. Being here without her is peaceful but also faintly melancholy. It prompts a thought I have several times a day – what would I do if she died? I routinely rehearse the reactions and conversations, never getting further than an image of myself sitting on her bed and being unable to move. There's a scene in Jenny Erpenbeck's *The End of Days* in which a mother who has just lost her baby assumes a culturally enforced position – sitting on a grieving stool in the middle of the kitchen, consuming only what is brought to her. When I read this I thought it a kind idea; a frugal solace to be held in place by such a rule. As we eat and watch other people's children playing, I tell him what I've been thinking.

'You have these thoughts often?' he asks.

'Quite often.'

'That sounds unpleasant.'

'It is.'

'Poor biddy.' His pet name for me.

I lean my head against his shoulder, breathing in his parsley and honey scent.

To Marry

I'm not married to him. We had a celebration rather than a wedding, in the summer of 2016 in Wellington. I wore a vintage purple silk suit, cream silk blouse, and green heels. We exchanged poems, not vows. People brought gifts, but that was more due to our imminent move to a larger rental. Nesting gifts, not wedding gifts. A friend acted as pretend celebrant, wearing a dog collar and black gown. 'Let us begin with Kierkegaard,' he said.

He'd slid a tab pulled from a beer can as far up my pinky finger as it would go, up to the first knuckle. We were wonderfully drunk. 'How about it? We could be Ted and Sylvia.'

I'd made a face. 'I'll be Sylvia,' he said, sending us both into hysterics. What could be funnier than deciding to spend the rest of our lives together?

When I first saw him, he was sitting alone on the lawn outside the Hunter Building, reading Ted Hughes's *Birthday Letters*. I was on my way to the International Institute of Modern Letters for a meeting with a colleague. His hair was short then and he was clean-shaven, but not boyish. Freckled cheekbones and a jaw that resembled an actor's, though I couldn't decide which. I didn't notice this all at once, I don't think, mostly just his red hair and book. I must have looked for too long because he looked up. We were staring at each other.

I smiled and slowed my pace. He took off his sunglasses and smiled back.

'You won't believe this,' he said, 'but I think I'm reading about you.'

I didn't have a clever reply. I imagine I just looked confused, even blushed.

'The poem's called "A Pink Wool Knitted Dress".' He turned the book around to show me the page.

'Mine isn't wool,' I said. 'It's velvet. A Pink Velvet Dress.'

He told me his name then and held out his hand and asked mine. We shook hands and I told him. If I hadn't had that meeting to go to, I might've sat down next to him, on the grass. As it was, I lingered anyway.

'Odd coincidence,' I said, and pulled Ted Hughes's *Birthday Letters* from my bag.

'Ah, so you're taking Literature and Cultural Politics next semester?'

'I'm tutoring for it. Are you taking it?'

'No, I'm lecturing.'

And then I realised I'd heard about him. The handsome, talented Australian who'd been appointed as the new English literature lecturer, a job I'd applied for, with little hope of getting it so soon after receiving my PhD.

'I'm giving a guest lecture,' I said, sounding pathetic.

'Which week?'

'Five, I think – on Plath.'

'I'll be there in the front row.'

'Are you going to finish that?' he asks, looking at my bagel.

'No, you want it?'

'I shouldn't. But I will.'

I pass it to him. His cheekbones are still freckled but his jaw is hidden by a beard now. 'Can you eat and walk? I need to get back.' I look at my watch. Twenty minutes until the next Zoom.

'I might stay here a bit longer,' he says.

'In the playground?'

'I might walk for a bit. I need some fresh air to help me think.'

I walk faster alone, past the clinker-brick bungalows, the gelato shop, towards the city, pale in the distance. My bra is sweaty by the time I unlock our front door. I change it, and my T-shirt, brush my teeth and my hair before sitting back at the workstation.

The philosophy class is smaller, more voluble and relaxed. All the cameras are on except for two. This afternoon we're talking about meaning in life and why it matters. That is, in fact, the title of our reading. The philosopher Susan Wolf has questioned the meaningfulness of the life of the gamer who sits in a curtained living room all day, playing. Since this playing does nothing to benefit others, is a pleasure solely for the gamer, can it be meaningful? Wolf asks.

'Oh my god, she's such a boomer,' says Millicent, one of my favourite students.

I play the class a video about a thought experiment, Sisyphus Fulfilled, in which the man cursed to roll a rock up a hill for eternity has been given a serum that makes rock-rolling satisfying to him. Millicent says, 'That's a life I'd like to lead. Is that bad?' By the end of the lesson, the class agrees that Sisyphus Fulfilled is the best life scenario anyone could hope for.

'Are there any final questions?' I ask in the last five minutes.

Harriet, one of the more erratic students, unmutes herself. I fear I won't have time to answer what she asks. 'Miss,' she says, 'why is it that whenever you play videos online the same suggested video comes up?'

'Which video?' I ask unwisely.

'It's called,' she giggles, "Why you'll marry the wrong person".'

I am relieved not to be in an actual room with the laughing class, glad that they are mostly muted. I laugh too. 'Because it's a talk by a philosopher, Alain de Botton.'

'It's not because you married the wrong person?'

'No,' I say drily. 'If that's the only question, then you're all free to go. See you back here tomorrow.'

'That was a bit impertinent,' he says when I've ended the Zoom. He'd snuck into the kitchen, out of my camera shot, to get a glass of water.

'Harriet generally is.'

'I was surprised at what you said.'

'Why?' I ask, standing to stretch my back.

'Would you actually call de Botton a philosopher?'

I laugh. 'You're such a snob.'

The last period of the day is free and I use it to prepare literature lessons. We are analysing chapter six of *My Brilliant Career*, 'Revolt'. The heroine, Sybylla (who is not Franklin herself, I will remind the class, but is reminiscent of her), fights with her mother. The family is poor, and as the eldest sibling, Sybylla could be earning her keep. But she has no feminine skills whatsoever; she doesn't sew or cook, she loathes the notion of teaching, and she refuses to marry. In contrast, her younger sister Gertie is demure and dutiful. 'I am capable,' Sybylla declares, 'of more depths of agony and more exquisite heights of joy in one day than Gertie will experience in her whole life.' The arrogance of this sentence propels me along the corridor to my bedside table to retrieve the biography and letters, to read about the real Gertie, Franklin's sister, Ida, nearly two years her junior. Ida was for some reason known as Linda.

When Stella Franklin sent her sister a copy of *My Brilliant Career*, Linda replied:

> That is a *lovely lovely* present you sent. I can never thank you enough for it. You will *never* know how much I prize it (simple minded as I am). It wasn't altogether a surprise to me, as you said you were sending me something that I would never be able to send you & of course I guessed then. No such luck as ever being able to send you such a thing. I wish I was only clever enough to do it … I am so proud to be the sister of an authoress …
>
> I have read a good bit of it. You are pretty hot on me in places not to say anything of poor Father … What a proud girl you must feel. You will be able to walk along the street & see *My Brilliant Career* staring you in the face from all the booksellers & shop windows … I must go & gather in the clothes. I think I have told you all …
>
> Tons of love,
> from
> LLF.

Below the top notes of Victorian virtue – pleasantries, self-deprecation, humility, gentle chastisement, generosity and industry – I detect sarcasm. What, I started wondering, if Linda had in fact been 'clever enough'? What if it were only those bullies propriety and conformity that had stopped Linda, who adored hearing her sister's stories, from telling her own?

A year after Linda wrote this letter, I read, she became engaged to Charles Graham, the model for Sybylla's love interest – Harold Beecham. Charles continued to write intimate missives to Stella months after becoming engaged to her sister. In 1904, Linda and Charles were married. Stella's opinion about the wedding itself – or perhaps her role as principal bridesmaid, or her sister's choice of husband or her friend's choice of wife – is written on her face in a gelatine silver print. She looks far from impressed, elbow leaning on a chairback, cheek leaning against her white-gloved hand.

The wedding coincided with the first New South Wales election in which women had the right to vote. Both the wedding and the election featured prominently in Linda's letters to Stella during 1904. Having moved into Montrose, the marital home, Linda found her circumstances abruptly altered; she warned of the horrors of marriage and hoped that her sister would never have to endure such a thing. I wonder at what might have caused this depth of agony, to use Franklin's words. Violence on Charles's part? Or ignorance on hers? Or both, or neither?

In 1906 Linda gave birth to a son, Edward, whom she called Teddy. One year later, she died of pneumonia in Queensland, where she, Charles and Teddy were to make their new home. Stella Miles, having left for San Francisco, never met her nephew.

To Work

When we are locked down I, like everyone, long to be out of the house. But when leaving is required again, I tire easily. Using my eyes to compensate for a concealed face and forcing my voice through the mask is tiring. Only two more weeks of term, I think, rinsing my face. It is evening now. Aster is tucked up asleep and I can almost feel her comfort, radiating like warmth through her closed bedroom door as I tiptoe past. Just knowing she's there, in her seashell pyjamas, snoring softly, is enough to slow my pulse.

He is behind the study door, working. I have work to do too, and will, must, but my eyes keep watering, and the floor seems to rise and fall as I walk, as it did when Aster was a baby and I was feeding her every three hours. More sleep is the answer to most problems. But first I must mark the literature essays closely analysing Franklin's style of writing. I skip to Scarlett's first, because while it's the longest (seven pages), it's also likely to be the most fluent and entertaining. I'm not disappointed. At the end of each of her sentences I mark a tired green tick, the written equivalent of nodding to show you're listening, when really you're falling asleep. Competent, controlled sentence after sentence observing the youthful vigour of the narrator's grandiloquence and the paradoxical desires between which she oscillates. To marry the handsome landowner, tall and broad-shouldered and who flatters her, or to avoid the dusty path of domesticity and become instead an authoress. These two things, according to Sybylla, are mutually exclusive. Scarlett has written that Franklin 'portrays her heroine as a mercurial force of her own conflicted nature'. My pen hovers as I decide whether to tick or not. Instead I scrawl: 'elaborate'.

It's eleven o'clock. My alarm is set for 5:45 am. Aster has been waking at two for the past three nights, with a nightmare or needing a drink or wanting to get into our bed for a cuddle. I should try to go to sleep now, but there are fifteen essays yet to be read. Maybe if I get up even earlier, I can read them before she wakes. I can't remember if we have any bread in the freezer. We're all out of Weetbix.

I make two cups of chamomile tea and take one to my bedside table, the other to the study. I open the door and see him sitting at his desk typing aggressively, as if the keys are to blame.

'I brought you tea.'

He keeps typing.

'Shall I just put it here?' On last week's *Saturday Paper*, next to his mousepad. 'I'm going to bed now.'

'Okay,' he says stiffly, still typing.

I never could manage a full all-nighter. Once or twice I wrote until after midnight, but the results were never successful. This might have something to do with the fact that I'm no longer an academic. Instead I live a diurnal life governed by bells, traffic, mealtimes, bathtimes and bedtimes. Nocturnal waking is, for me, deeply unpleasant, accompanied as it is by the worst of thoughts. They've visited the past three nights: after I've soothed Aster back to sleep and returned to my bed I have lain awake closely analysing every shameful, weak and selfish thing I can claim to have done or been. All the ways in which I am a bad teacher, mother, wife, daughter, woman and human parade about the bedroom for me to scrutinise. When I weary of the lambasting, I replace it with wistful speculation, replaying scenes that might have gone differently. For instance, the day he came home jubilant and told me he'd been offered the position in Melbourne.

We had a cottage in Wellington then, by the beach in Lyall Bay. I'd push Aster in her pram along the waterfront each morning, or meet a friend for coffee, or take the bus in to the city library. Most weeks there would be a book launch or readings. I was in a writer's group. I didn't have work at that time; it was too costly and difficult to put the baby in childcare just for casual tutoring, and we lived four hours' drive from my mother's house. As her only grandchild and her only daughter, Aster and I could never visit often enough.

The postdoctoral position I'd been verbally offered in early pregnancy somehow evaporated after I gave birth. I thought that once Aster was bigger, I could find my way back into the university. After all, I'd studied or worked there for twelve years – it was my community. Or so I believed.

Then he came home with a bottle of Lindauer and news. 'I didn't want to tell you until I knew for sure, because I thought it was a longshot, but I got it!'

'Got what?' I was hopping from foot to foot, jiggling Aster and patting her bottom, trying to stop her wailing at imminent new teeth.

'Senior Lecturer in Cultural Studies – in Melbourne!'

'Oh my god.'

'I know! I'm stunned too.'

'Congratulations.' An awkward hug with screaming red tears between us.

'Are you okay?'

'I'm just taking it in. When do you start?' I wanted to sit down but Aster wouldn't allow it, so I kept jiggling and pacing, looking out the window at a plane coming in low over the sea, aiming for the runway next to the beach.

'Next semester.'

'In two months?'

'Yes, I think so.'

And so we moved. For him, it was going home. For me, it was leaving. I was so bitterly angry at the time that I applied for a lecturing position of my own, in Auckland. The week before we flew out, I was offered an interview. I thought about it for a day before withdrawing my application.

To Meddle

We have been invited for Easter to a property ninety minutes' drive from Melbourne, belonging to one of his colleagues and old friends, Heidi. She's an anthropologist and her husband, Piotr, is a doctor. They have two daughters, one about the same age as Aster and one two years older.

The last time we visited their off-grid mudbrick home was the summer after we arrived in Melbourne. Black Summer. The sun was a coral-coloured pupil in the smoky iris of the sky. It was an overnight New Year's Eve party, an elaborate tradition of Heidi and Piotr's, which went ahead despite temperatures of over 40 degrees. I remember camping in a borrowed tent with Aster. We had all the windows and doors open, just gauze between us and the land. But there was no breeze. Even at four am, when the bush doof had been turned off and slowly replaced with the rustling of creatures – wallabies or echidnas? – we were still damp and flushed. I remember my bottle running out of water as I sat awkwardly on a corner of the inflatable mattress, trying to breastfeed and feeling faint.

As soon as the sun rose, I put our bright little mammal in a new nappy and light cotton dress, tied her into the sling and walked alone down the driveway, then along animal tracks towards the dam, past tents of sleeping adults I'd barely met. The dam, edged with wattle and eucalypts, was low, Heidi had explained apologetically, after years of drought. Crouched in the mud were three kangaroos. The largest rose from drinking to its full height – taller than me – and stared with dark, horsy eyes, twitching its ears. The other two, as if instructed, bounded off up the bank and into the bush. I stood frozen, holding Aster against my thumping heart.

This Easter, the dam is as it should be, apparently. A small lake, large enough for playing with a rowboat or swimming lengths.

'The waterfall's impressive too,' Heidi tells me. 'We should go for a walk there after lunch.'

We're sitting on the deck, drinking in a view vaster than anything Melbourne could offer. 'It's a strange relief to be on a hilltop,' I say vapidly. The layers of distance are somehow soothing on the eye. In the foreground, grevillea and a bird bath, blue with superb fairy-wrens; in the midground, the neighbours' racetrack for training their horses; and in the far distance, the almost hidden Hume Highway and the blurred horizon, which I (embarrassingly) initially thought was the sea.

'Do you miss home?' Heidi asks.

'Yes. Especially when I can't go back.'

'It must be so hard,' she says, beginning to clear our plates, 'not having family here during all this. I don't know how you two are coping.'

His family are in Perth, mine are in Hawkes Bay, New Zealand. We are just about exactly in the middle of those two places. But the issue is not the four- or five-hour flight, it's the closed borders.

'This is helping,' he says, 'being here. It's good to mix things up. Have a break from our little house. Have some new company. She's loving it.' He gestures to Aster, deep in a game of cubbies with the two other girls under the trees.

'I'm glad,' Heidi says. 'That's exactly what this place is for. Mixing things up. Sharing. Having a break.' She inherited it, she tells us, from her aunt, who had set it up as a retreat.

After another plunger of coffee, we put on gumboots (there are spares for visitors) and venture to the waterfall. The girls skip ahead at first, but quickly tire. He and I take turns piggybacking Aster as the terrain gets rougher.

'This land is terrible for farming,' Heidi says, 'with all the granite. But it's become a beautiful sanctuary for wildlife.'

'We should cut back the undergrowth before next summer, though,' Piotr says. 'And do something about the wattle taking over the driveway.'

The further we walk, the less sure I am of the way back to the house. There is no path. Or rather, there are many narrow paths made by wallabies or roos.

'This is the under-over tree!' says Marta, the eldest of the girls, running ahead to a trunk that's fallen across our way. 'Kids walk under, grown-ups climb over. But I can climb over too!'

'I can walk under it too,' I say, crawling through the gap.

'You're a little grown-up!'

I laugh. 'I suppose so.'

'There's always this moment, about here,' Heidi says, 'when I'm not sure whether to turn left or keep going down. What do you think?' she asks Piotr.

'Honestly don't know either,' he says, putting his arm casually around her waist and rubbing her back. 'Down a bit further?'

'I think maybe left,' she says.

So we turn, and cut across granite boulders slippery with emerald moss. Every stick seems to be a snake to me, and there's a surprising number of delicate white and purple wildflowers that might be native lilies. If we were in New Zealand, I'd know the species.

Heidi's instinct was right. We hear the water before we see it. 'Listen,' we all say to the children and each other. 'What do you think that is?'

'Aeroplane?' Aster asks quietly.

'No, it's better than that. Waterfall!'

It appears between the trees unexpectedly, white bodies striping the cliff. 'There are two!' he says, sounding as I imagine his child self would have sounded, his intonation similar to our daughter's.

'Wow, I haven't seen it like that before,' Heidi says. 'Look, they're joining together at the bottom. We must have had so much rain.'

Rain, I am learning, is revered in this country. We don't have the same relationship with water in New Zealand. Nor with fire. He was pleased to be leaving the earthquake-prone capital, and feels safer in Melbourne, away from fault lines. But there are other dangers.

That evening, Aster is excited to be sleeping in the big bed with her parents. We're not in tents this time, but even the strange shadows and scuttling forms of huntsman spiders on the ceiling don't bother her. The day of fresh air and play lets sleep come easily.

I return to the kitchen before Heidi, who's still persuading Lucy, her youngest, to go to bed. Piotr is at the bench mixing whisky sours.

'Cheers,' he says, passing me a crystal tumbler. On top of the stiff white foam, he's drizzled a flourish of rust-coloured bitters and dropped in a maraschino cherry.

'Thanks, that looks professional,' I say, clinking glasses with him.

Eventually the four of us are sitting around the open fire, sipping sours and eating cheese and baguettes. No one feels the need to cook. Heidi muses about trying to introduce fireflies to the property. Piotr deems this wrong.

'You think introducing more insects would be harmful?' she asks, incredulous.

'I don't know if fireflies are native to this area,' Piotr says. 'I think it would be meddling with the ecosystem to introduce anything that's not.'

'What's wrong with mixing?' Heidi asks, starting to sound drunk. 'We must mix. We are a part of the whole.'

'But is it our part to move fireflies?' Piotr asks.

'I don't see why not.'

He – my he, the most familiar person to me in the room – looks to be about to say something, possibly ironic or provocative.

'Is it hubris,' he says grandly, 'to ask these questions? Shouldn't we do all we can to propagate our survival, as any other species would?'

'But —' Heidi begins. He cuts her off. I try to predict where he's going. The skin on his face is flushed.

'Perhaps the obvious next stage of our species' purpose is deliberate and controlled self-destruction?'

'Cheery conversation,' Piotr says. 'Who wants another drink?'

'I don't know what that had to do with fireflies,' I say quietly when Heidi and Piotr are in the kitchen.

By the time we go to bed, I'm feeling desiccated and headachy. Two paracetamol, two ibuprofen and I drink a whole bottle of water. I rub moisturiser into my cracked palms and pawpaw ointment onto my cracked lips. Almost as soon as he crawls under the blanket, he joins Aster in a soft chorus of snores. She nestles into me when I lie down and I kiss her forehead and reach across her to stroke his shoulder.

But I don't sleep. The mindfulness app recommends letting thoughts float like clouds across a blue sky. Notice them passing but do not try to hold onto them. These are the clouds that pass that night: animals, it has been argued, are incapable of suicide because they lack an understanding of their own mortality. The philosopher Thomas Nagel, in his essay 'What is it Like to be a Bat?', famously questioned the accessibility of any consciousness beyond our own. An article I read this morning pointed to many cases of non-human beings appearing to commit suicide. A terrier that refused to be fed by anyone other than his deceased owner and appeared to die of grief. A stag that threw itself off a cliff rather than being eaten by pursuing hounds. A wild-born orca in a Seaworld that attempted to beach herself on the edge of her tank. A researcher speaking about the orca's case explained the behaviour as a stressed response to human intervention. Most cases of apparent animal suicide or suicide attempts take place in captivity.

To Play

'Play with me?' Aster asks. It's still school holidays, shortly after our Easter trip, and we're both in our pyjamas at ten am, sitting in a patch of sun on the rug. He is out for a run, a coping strategy after receiving disappointing reviewers' reports on a paper he submitted to a prestigious journal. Come back when you're calmer, I didn't say directly, but implied with my eyes.

Aster wants to play Lego. There's a tip's worth of pieces covering the rug. Searching for the ones you need is the largest part of the game. Or trying to turn what you find into what you need. I rake slowly with my fingers, duller with the Lego than she is. I find a flat rectangle and attach a wheel to each of its corners, then press a steering wheel near the front to prove it's a car. My daughter's creations involve hinges, skis, fulcrums and chains. On the rare occasions when he plays with the Lego with her, he builds spacecrafts with exhaust pipes and flames.

To play is to pretend, but it is also real. The more realistic the pretence, the better the play. To play is to trick yourself into entering the real by appearing to escape from it, though the best games don't give you time to think about them in this way. An online professional development day I attended instructed teachers to scrutinise the language used in the classroom, to be intentional about our vocabulary. Should we set homework or homeplay? posed the well-known Harvard pedagogue. I thought of how 'homeplay' would be received by my Year 12 students, the majority of whom seemed to view their school years as the top of the chute down which they'd slide into medicine or law. They wanted work, believed in work. Complex, highly paid, well-respected work. Play made no money. Play would therefore be a waste.

I wonder how the class would react to the novel I'd read recently in which a climate scientist is asked how to prepare a child for future weather. Make sure the child is rich, advises the scientist. Survival skills are secondary to wealth. Wealth is the only effective insulation against rising temperatures. Money will also buy consolation. A therapist to ask gentle questions and to soothe; a soft-timbred yogi coaxing her to love herself.

To Lie

I am lying in bed too long. The mornings are getting darker and colder. Would ten more minutes here be refreshing or enervating? I need to get to work. He is still sleeping. She is still sleeping. Best to get in the shower before anyone wakes. If I can wash away the night sweat, get my hair dried, my blemishes concealed, then dress and get coffee under way before anyone speaks to me, the day will be easier.

There's something the colour of the dress I wore when we first met growing around the plughole of the bathroom sink. I wipe it with a piece of toilet paper and flush it away. Dust is gathering softly in the corner of the bathroom, behind the toilet brush. I sweep it up with another square of paper and flush this too. My housekeeping is becoming streamlined and wasteful.

Aster sleeps so late that I've finished my coffee (and put his share in a thermal bottle), eaten my fruit, yoghurt and cereal (and placed a portion for him on the table) while she's still in bed. We need to leave in fifteen minutes, I should wake her, but I sit for a little longer, scrolling through photos posted by friends in New Zealand. There are attractive piles of books just read, dogs off leash on beaches chasing driftwood, freshly baked sourdough, babies, flowers, and women touching flowers.

'Hello,' he says, bleary in his sleeping T-shirt and thinning pyjama bottoms. 'What are you up to?'

'Torturing myself.'

'Delete the app. You'll feel better.'

'Fuck, I'm late now. Need to wake her.'

I leave the table as soon as he sits; I bundle her out of bed and pyjamas, into clothes and the car. ('Quick goodbye to Daddy.') Her temperature's checked at childcare and she's permitted to enter.

'She hasn't had any breakfast yet,' I call down the corridor as the educator takes her hand and leads her to the back room.

I drive through the empty CBD, park next to the pine trees where the cockatoos roost and run to the staffroom. First period is Year 9 English. We're reading *Romeo and Juliet*. I ask stale questions: are they really in love? Are they in control of their actions? Who is to blame? How do you know?

'Are you okay?' asks Priya, a science teacher, at lunchtime. We're sitting at opposite ends of the staffroom table, both eating leftover pasta. 'You look a bit tired.'

'I am tired,' I admit. 'But otherwise fine. How are you?'

'Honestly, over it.' She tells me about a prac that didn't work.

I'm glad I teach English and only have to deal with words, not real-life, dangerous things – mercury, Bunsen burner flames, sheep's hearts. 'I don't know how you do it.'

'Neither. Somehow it gets done, though.'

The afternoon is cool but still and clear, so I take the literature class out to the picnic tables to read Plath's *Ariel*. Priya's Year 9s are watching something fizzing in a bucket on the basketball court. I wave to her, smiling behind my mask. Maybe we could make a Year 10 science fiction elective together, in which I teach a text and she conducts relevant experiments. I picture students reading the scene in *Frankenstein* when the monster wakes, then touching the school's Van de Graaff generator, hair on end. I scribble a note on the back page of *Ariel*, reminding myself to suggest this to Priya.

In the car to pick up Aster, I listen to a radio journalist interviewing the new director of the Australian Space Agency and am reminded of my pervasive fear while pregnant that one day our daughter would move to Mars. An aspiring Martian spoke to the students at school last year; she was comfortable with the idea of leaving Earth and her family, had no colonial qualm about imposing herself on an environment that isn't hers. The new director is asked about the prediction that by 2030 there will be remote mining on the moon, just as there's remote mining in the Pilbara right now. Australia, I learn, is a world leader in remote asset management.

The word 'asset' comes from the Latin for enough: *satis*, satisfied. Referring to the moon in this way reduced it for me, to an enormous distant arse.

Virgin Galactic, I think as I lather shampoo into Aster's hair, suggests immaculate conception. A goddess spraying mythical milk across the sky. Breastmilk isn't counted as part of any country's GDP. Recalling this, I feel the movement of something lying dormant, a seismic flexion so deep it's barely detectable.

To Comfort

First Aster gets ill, then he does, then I do. It's *a* virus, it turns out, not *the* virus.

There's a long queue at the drive-through testing station in the hospital carpark. Aster watches *Bluey* on my phone and I amuse myself by drawing on the back of a photocopy of Mercutio's Queen Mab speech. I have a black pen and an orange highlighter in my bag. In the rear-view mirror, her pigtailed head is bowed to the screen, and out the back window are road cones and temporary fences made of plastic tape. My own face bears a blue surgical mask just below dark shadows and bloodshot eyes.

There's a Kinder Surprise on the front passenger seat. Aster knows it's hers if she cooperates, but when the nurse opens the door, holding a swab, there are still screams. She unbuckles her seatbelt and tries to wedge herself in the footwell. I coax, then threaten, then coax again.

The nurse is professional but running out of patience. 'Can you hold her down?'

I try. My daughter is twisting and thrashing so much that I worry the swab will go in her eye or up into her brain somehow, but the nurse eventually gets what is required from us both.

After the ordeal, Aster is instantly composed. 'Can I have my treat?'

'Do you think you deserve a treat?'

'No.'

I try not to laugh. 'Why do you think it was so hard? Were you very scared?'

'Yes.'

'But you know it's all over quickly and doesn't really hurt.'

'But I still don't like it.'

'Neither.'

The next morning, Aster is still playing with the plastic giraffe that came inside the chocolate egg. She assembled it herself, and the neck doesn't bend as she believes it should. 'Fix it!' she cries, hurling it across the room.

I can't help her as the groceries have just arrived in a box on the doorstep, in the nick of time for breakfast. We were out of everything. I unpack the cold things into the fridge, then adjust the giraffe's neck and make her a bowl of cereal and sliced banana.

'I like the banana next to my cereal,' she whines.

'I know you're not feeling well but please don't whine,' I say.

'I'm not whining!' she yells.

I hear our bedroom door slam shut.

'Daddy is trying to sleep. He's sick too. Please don't yell.'

She silently picks the banana out of her bowl, puts it on the tablemat, and then starts whimpering.

'What's wrong now?' She looks properly sad and raises her arms for a hug. I pick her up and carry her to the couch, where we lie together for a bit instead of eating breakfast.

'It's miserable being sick, isn't it?' I say.

She sniffs and nods. 'Read to me?'

'I just need to do fifteen minutes on my computer, then I'll read. You choose some books.'

While she's in her room, I leave hasty lesson plans for the teachers who are taking my classes. I am on carer's leave today but can feel something unpleasantly familiar beginning in my right lung. When I inhale there's a dragging rasp of fluid moving underneath my ribs. I cough to clear it. Moving and talking prompt coughing. I should probably be lying still.

She returns to the couch with a book that belonged to me when I was her age: *My Naughty Little Sister*. Despite being published in the 1950s, it enchants her. He refuses to read it to her, deeming it tedious rubbish. Lying with her under a blanket, reading the stories that were read to me when I was sick, I am doubled, tripled; I am my mother and myself and my child. I don't know if it's empathy or narcissism that spreads me so thin.

'You're coughing a lot,' she says, not criticising so much as observing.

'Yeah, sorry. I'll just get a drink of water.'

When I was sick my mother would make me lemon and barley sugar cordial, or dissolve cubes of chicken stock in boiling water. When I had my tonsils out I got ice cream and jelly. When I had pneumonia I don't remember what I ate.

The following day, after waking from a night of coughing and febrile dreams involving road cones and tigers, there's something sharp and insistent under my right breast. Like a shard of rib.

As I'm unpacking the dishwasher I double over.

'Maybe if you try not to cough that'll help?' he suggests.

I stare at him.

'Or maybe you should go to the doctor.'

'I think I should. Can you look after her? She's still not well enough for daycare.'

'Okay.'

First I phone school, then I make more lesson plans for the relieving teacher, then I make an appointment with the GP.

'Because you're symptomatic, please wait in your vehicle until the doctor is ready and then use the side gate to go to the respiratory clinic,' the receptionist says.

In the car, I notice my teeth are chattering. In the rear-view mirror my skin is greyish. Knowing it will be a long wait, I've brought my laptop with essays to mark, but keep reading the same sentence without absorbing anything. My phone rings, calling me in.

First there's another PCR test. Then my temperature is taken (39.4). Then my heart rate checked (high). The cold stethoscope is driven across the bones of my back and front.

'Breathe in,' she says. 'Now cough. Are you always this thin?'

'I'm not sure.' It occurs to me only now that I haven't been eating as much lately.

'Have you been feeling generally unwell for a while?'

'I suppose. I don't know. I'm generally tired.'

She writes something. It's hard to tell under her PPE but she seems about my age, maybe a little older.

'Do you get asthma?'

'No.'

'Have you had pneumonia before?'

'Yes, several times as a child.'

'You've got it again, the lower lobe on the right side. You're not well.'

'I thought so.'

'And my guess is also pleuritis, based on the pain you describe, but you'll need a chest X-ray to confirm. Usually I'd say go and get that done straightaway, but I don't want you to catch Covid as well.'

She gives me a script for two kinds of antibiotics and a medical certificate for two weeks of leave from teaching, including Zoom lessons. 'Rest,' she says. 'You need to *really* rest.'

To Conform

I email the head of English and the assistant principal, explaining my diagnosis, apologising for the inconvenience. They each reply within half an hour, reassuring me that my classes will be taken care of, particularly the seniors, and that I need not feel concerned. I should rest. The assistant principal, it turns out, has had pneumonia in the past. 'If you don't rest properly now,' she writes, 'it's likely to drag on for months. Take care of yourself.' The head of English asks me to send her the essays that need marking and says I am not to worry about a thing. Just like that, I am redundant. I take my cough and pleuritic lung back to bed intending to read, but instead I sleep. I can't remember the last time I slept in the middle of the day; it must have been back in New Zealand, in our flat in Lyall Bay, with pōhutakawa petals blown against the window and a baby Aster on my chest.

As he and Aster recover, I sleep away the days, waking to take pills, gradually feeling better. This time when I wake I hear the washing machine beeping at the end of its cycle. Then I hear the study door open and the squeaking of the clothes horse unfolding. He took her to childcare for the first time ever this week. There's a *Bluey* episode for that, called 'Daddy Drop-Off'. There's a *Bluey* episode for most things. He's also collected her in the evenings and cooked dinner for the past three nights. Although I'm still coughing, I no longer have a fever and the pain is easing. I can get up slowly to go to the toilet now.

There are fresh rolls of toilet paper stacked on the shelf under the bench. I put on my dressing gown and slippers and go to the kitchen to see what else has changed.

'Hello,' he says. 'Do you need anything? I can bring you a cup of tea in bed.' He looks different, his actions are faster and surer, as if he has a mental list of things that must be done.

'It's okay, I want to try being up for a bit.'

'How are you feeling?' He looks at me. We look at each other. The sides of the bridge of his nose, where his glasses sit, seem shadowed. His hair is almost long enough to be tied in a ponytail.

'Bit tired and sore still, but much better.'

'Remember what the doctor said. You need to really rest.'

I must've told him this verbatim before I put myself to bed. I dreamt the discussion too – road cones, me hissing *I am not well. I need to really rest.* Him slinking away like a tiger at the zoo. Blending into the bamboo.

Thanks for letting me, I want to say but cannot quite yet. Not sincerely at least. Not without it sounding forced and odd. Instead I ask him about his work.

'I'm taking a break this week from teaching. One of the sessionals is covering my tutes. The only urgent job is the grant. I've got a meeting shortly. Just wanted to get this load hung out to dry first.'

'I can do that.'

'No, you go back to bed. You still look ashen.'

I take his advice, and my next round of pills with an attempt at food – a peanut butter sandwich and a mandarin. In bed, I prop myself up on two pillows to ease my coughing and open the biography of Miles Franklin that's been sitting on my bedside table. I turn to the glossy pages of black and white photos in the centre of the book. My favourite picture of Stella Miles Franklin is the one taken just after *My Brilliant Career* was published. Her wavy black plait reaches her bottom, which looks like a bustle due to the cinching of her corseted waist and her severe posture. Her hands are elegant in black leather gloves, and under her left arm she holds an umbrella. My second-favourite photo shows an older Stella in evening dress. Bare upper arms; hands and forearms gloved and holding a small monkey. The monkey's right hand rests on Stella's breast. Her face is close to the animal's; she has a subtle, thin-lipped smile and a steady, faintly amused gaze aimed directly into the camera lens.

There are only two photos of Linda Franklin in the biography. One fair, delicate portrait in which her profiled face is haloed with flyaway hairs catching the light. The other is her wedding photo, the bride at the centre of a stiffly composed scene. I look and look and find few clues about this woman's short life. She probably expected to live as long as her mother, to give birth many times, run a farm household. And yet she died of what I have in my lung, a long way from her home, when her son was only one year old. For the conventional daughter, allegedly incapable of the depths of feeling of her novelist sister, this end was dramatic.

'Does everyone have a tragic flaw?' one of my Year 9s asked me earlier in the term.

'Do you mean in *Romeo and Juliet* or in life?'

'I mean in the play.'

'In the play, not every character is complex or important enough to have a tragic flaw.'

'But that's just the way it's told.'

'Exactly. Put anyone, or any character, at centre stage and watch them for long enough, and they'll reveal their flaws and suffer the consequences.'

To Buy

Having taken yet another course of antibiotics, I eat yoghurt and kimchi to replace the gut flora killed by the medication. The day I'm scheduled to return to school another lockdown is announced. Being online is a relief. Much easier to teach without a mask. To not have to walk from room to room. To keep warm and largely still.

In the evenings, once Aster is asleep and he is writing, I am too tired to read, so I indulge in online searches for items I will need for re-entering public life.

I could spend twenty-two dollars on ethical socks that save cheetah habitats. They have an embroidered cat on the ankle and are patterned with spots. One dollar of my purchase would be donated to a conservation fund. Or I could buy a unitard made of recycled drink bottles and be conscious of my contribution to planting trees.

Promotions in my inbox: Entropy Elves (new fat brain toys), Bed Threads (floral paradise inside alchemy), Kowtow (new blue-collar workwear), Etsy (express yourself), Girlfriend Collective (post-sweat. post-surf. post-bonfire). *London Review of Books* (The Peterloo Massacre), Halcyon Nights (Congratulations! Order #HN-30363 confirmed).

Sleeping and shopping mentally, I dream that he marries Rachel Cusk. 'She's going to be my mother-in-law!' I scream to friends, whose expressions tell me I've made a mistake. I wake exhilarated and wet with sweat.

My mother might have darned the threadbare heels of the socks I binned; I could've been irritated by lumpy stitches and found penance in the itch, like that hair-shirted masochist Saint Elizabeth of Hungary. Darning is work nobler than making new or, worse still, buying new. Better to buy nothing at all. Better to eat only carrots you've grown yourself. Best not to move. Movement stirs up carbon; each breath heats the air.

'I'm going to wet your fire!' Aster yells in the morning before daycare. We are playing elemental warfare.

'What if my fire is as wide as the ocean?'

'What if my water is as deep as the ocean?'

'What if my fire is as hot as the sun? What if it *is* the sun?'

'Then I'll put your sun out with my big cold moon!'

As a child I would play at coughing into a handkerchief until my mother asked if I was sick. I'd gaze gravely at a pretend bloodstain and say, ''tis tuberculosis, is it not?' I wanted to be taken up from under by an illness – like Katherine Mansfield, I learned later, when she became an idol. I wanted to waste away, but never knew how to pronounce *phthisis*.

One evening, I join a Zoom event organised by my friend Ana in Wellington, at which writers read aloud their feminist erotica. The first reading is not about female pleasure. A narrator goes home with a softboi. She strips down to naught but her apathy, slides a condom onto his penis, rides as if galloping away from the burning city of Patriarchy and squints until his face blurs into oblivion. He tells her he feels seen. She says that's rare.

I ought to be on her side, and am, but find myself sympathising with the hapless man who has no idea he's been reduced to shape and colour. It's his turn to be objectified, I might have said at a different time. But tonight it seems tragic.

The next reader's protagonist meditates on boiled eggs, and magnolia petals out the window, describing the labial pinks and membranous textures in a politely English sublimation of what she'd like to do with the woman across the breakfast table. Then a memoirist describes a mistress administering a menu of BDSM to a client.

'What turns you on?' Ana asks the writers when the last reader has finished. Even via Zoom, there is a frisson of something.

'Confidence,' says the memoirist. 'I don't mind admitting it. Anyone who says confidence doesn't turn them on is lying.' The confidence with which she makes this claim turns me off a little. It triggers an image of Trump.

The magnolia and egg fancier blushes and lowers her eyelashes as she mentions colour wheels. 'Creatively,' she said, '*creatively*, colour wheels turn me on.' I slide down to another friend's rectangle on the screen and beam at her muted laughter, right hand over her heart as if the comedy makes it ache.

Ana ends the session by answering her own question. 'People who buy books turn me on,' she says. 'When I sell someone a book and it's a book I love, I get turned on imagining this customer taking the book home in their bag, opening its cover, breaking its spine, and reading the same sentences I've read; I get turned on thinking about their thoughts entwining with mine, having read what I've read. I get turned on imagining meeting this customer again and talking to them about what we've shared. That really turns me on.'

I believe her. It is the only part of the event that seems to be unequivocally erotic.

To Walk

'I have tired legs but I don't need to be carried yet,' Aster says on the way to the playground. 'Because, at community kinder I don't get carried. I keep walking. And I carry a heavy bag.'

Community kinder involves leaving the daycare-kindergarten centre to explore the suburb. For this, the kinder has issued her with a drawstring backpack designed for resilience training. Each morning I stuff it with her drink bottle, a snack, her jacket and a change of clothes. With this tied firmly to her shoulders she walks as far as she's instructed to. This is preparation for school, which is preparation for life. Not expecting anyone to carry you. Continuing on despite sore legs. Accustoming oneself to discomfort. I am not at all sure that this is what adults, who have the means to avoid discomfort, actually do.

The playground is as far as I have walked in more than a month. On the slight incline past the gelato shop, my chest tightens. 'One foot in front of the other,' I say to her. She holds my hand and we match each other's pace nicely. When we arrive, she throws me her bag and runs to the spiderweb, climbing the ropes confidently. I sit at a picnic table, holding my side and smiling at her. It's sunny at least – thin winter sunlight warming my scalp.

He's back from his run by the time we get home, drinking water at the kitchen sink and radiating heat and elation. 'I'm up to ten,' he says.

'Well done! That must feel good.' I sit at the table and try to deepen my breath.

'It was very slow, though.'

'Still, it's ten kilometres more than I could run.'

'You'll get there. Just be patient.'

I laugh. 'I haven't run ten kay in about six years.'

We used to run together, around to Island Bay and back, then into the freezing sea, our young skin mottled with extremes. It felt as though we couldn't help being fit in Wellington. Every walk or run involved a steep hill or a headwind. This city is flat and sedentary in comparison.

After the walk to the playground, I need to lie down. Aster and I watch *Paddington* together. When my eyes close she tugs my sleeve. 'You're missing a good bit,' she whispers.

This is the week we were supposed to spend visiting my mother in Hawkes Bay but I'm not well enough to fly, so I've rebooked the trip for the September holidays. If we aren't locked down again then. I have just started my fourth round of antibiotics. If I'd caught pneumonia in 1907, like Linda Franklin, I suspect I wouldn't have had much hope either. I don't tell my mother this thought when we Zoom. She's sitting in her usual place in the living room, vase of roses and photos behind her.

'I hope you're resting,' she says. 'I wish there was something I could do.'

'Thanks for the sunflowers. They're very cheering.' I turn the computer screen so she can see the bunch that she ordered, stems cut as she taught me to, in a large glass jar full of water. 'I'm sorry we're not there with you now.'

'It's not your fault, love. And September's not too far away.'

We fall silent, perhaps both thinking about how much can change in three months. About how much has already changed.

'I want to be better,' I tell him as we brush our teeth together before bed.

'You're definitely getting better,' he says. 'You've got more colour.'

I look in the mirror, determining if he's right. I see my mother's expression. Her worried eyes. I think he is right. I want him to be right.

It is another night of feverish dreaming. A mare reversing with such abruptness that the piece of twine her lead rope is tied to snaps. The horse stands there for a moment, rope and twine dangling from the halter below her chin, measuring her freedom. She spins on her hind hooves, ready to bolt, only to find that she's been tied up in a yard. She assesses the gate's strength, makes a run-up as abruptly powerful as her earlier reversal, and pushes the hinges right off the post with her chest. She finds herself in a paddock. This might suffice as freedom, the mare thinks – I think. I could stop and graze. Or I could gallop to the fence and take off at just the right stride, knees high enough to clear it. But the dangling lead rope could catch on the fence, pulling the halter. My hindlegs could drop. I could fall, lacerated limbs tangled in wire, and wait helpless for my owner to cut me free and call the vet. I could spend the rest of my life limping stiffly around that paddock, wounds white with disinfectant powder and always raw.

To Drive

Some drugs fill in the ruts that routine digs into your neural networks, Michael Pollan tells an interviewer as I drive to school. I picture snow, thick and soft, covering my tracks, getting me lost and forcing me to take a new way home, or find a new home. The paths I travel are narrow: home to daycare to school to daycare to home. Back and forth along the route. Deepening the ruts.

There are folders of writing on my desk, ready to be marked, to let me see where my students are up to. The teachers who covered my classes when I was absent are kind and organised for the most part. I sit with them and scroll through rolls, asking if this student's grandfather is out of hospital or not. If this student has spoken much. If this one is eating enough, whether these two are still in love. I know the students will be in my dreams this week, as I add to the mental catalogue of data about all the daughters of all the parents who are deeply invested in their children excelling.

'Do you have to remember all their names?' Ana had asked when I told her I had a hundred and twenty-five students. We were each sitting on our couch with a gin and tonic, staring at our screen. Lockdown cocktails, we called it; then it became just cocktails.

'Yes,' I said. 'At a minimum.'

By the end of the day I am rasping and wheezing. The staff meeting is via Zoom, so I listen through my phone as I drive to the supermarket to buy dinner supplies. We are reminded not to come to work if we're feeling unwell, and to remind students not to attend if they're feeling unwell. We are not to provide 'hybrid' lessons, meaning teaching in a classroom and online at the same time.

I think of my Year 9s who turned a laptop into an avatar of their missing friend, dressing the chair behind it in a blazer and resting the blazer's handless sleeves on the desk, either side of the screen holding the Zoom of the girl's face.

Outside daycare Aster comes running to me with her bag and jacket dragging behind her, then drops her burden completely and launches herself at my arms, wanting to be swept up. The pain under my ribs makes me gasp. I kneel and hold her instead, hoping she doesn't notice.

'I will be five in five hundred and fifty-five days,' she says.

'Sooner than that.' I hold her hand and hurry her out of the rain, into the car.

'How soon?'

'About thirty-five days.'

'Soon!'

There was a primary school in Wellington I'd walk past on the way to the shops when I was pregnant. I'd watch the kids playing on the tyre swing and in the cubby house and imagine my child joining them in five years. But, realistically, the school closest to our house here looks good. I should enrol her soon.

Everything takes longer than it ought to this evening. Putting away the groceries, making her a snack, chopping the onion, boiling the water, hanging up the washing, emptying the dishwasher; I go through all the motions slowly, with a lack of energy or love.

'Dinnertime,' I call. No one responds. 'Dinner now, darling.' Aster is drawing at the end of the table and ignoring me, so I serve three plates of pasta, sit at my place, and start eating alone. When she's done her picture she joins me.

'Tuna pasta again?'

'Yep.'

'Good. I like tuna pasta.' She senses it isn't the time to complain. Or she's being nice. I've almost finished by the time he comes to the table. His plate has stopped steaming.

'This smells delicious!' He sits and begins shovelling spirals into his mouth.

'It is delicious,' Aster says, avoiding the capers.

'How was your day?' I ask.

'Pretty good.' He seems buoyant. 'I'm on a roll now, I think. I have a title.'

'Go on.'

'*Love in the Time of Covid.*' He finishes his mouthful and smiles at me.

'Seriously?'

'What? You don't like it?'

'It isn't a bit – gimmicky?'

'It's supposed to be engaging for the layperson. Not just academic, but with commercial potential.'

'Well, in that case.'

He wipes his mouth on the back of his hand and stands up. 'Like I said, I'm on a roll and better get back to it.'

I look at his plate on the table, an olive and some diced onion lying in oil. 'Hey,' I say. 'Will you do stories tonight?'

He holds himself up in the doorway, as if I've thrown something at him. A wet tea towel perhaps. 'Did you not hear me? I need to get back to it.'

'I heard you. That's why I'm asking. It's your turn to do stories and I was just checking that that was still the plan.'

'My turn?'

'Yes.'

'Since when have there been turns?'

'Since I got sick, and you finally started to put our daughter to bed.' I stand up and stack the plates.

'Finally?'

'Yes, finally.'

He suddenly kicks at the doorframe. Aster gets down from her chair and crawls under the table. 'What is your problem?' he asks.

I pause, wondering where to start.

'If you haven't noticed, I am trying to write a book that is due next month and would've been finished if—'

'If what? If I hadn't got pneumonia and you hadn't had to do a bit of housework?'

'When did you get so bitter?'

Drunk on the adrenalin of the argument, I find words coming unusually easily. 'When you decided to move us to Melbourne without asking me.' I feel something at my ankle. Aster is hugging my calves.

'For fucksake. I didn't ask you because I assumed you'd be happy!'

'Can we save this for later? I need to put her to bed, and you need to write.'

He shakes his head and clenches his fists then strides down the hallway. The study door rattles in its frame.

I pick her up and hold her tight against me, to stop my trembling. 'Time for teeth and a shower,' I say as calmly as I can.

Even though I'm exhausted, I don't fall asleep while reading to her tonight. My heart is still fast. Aster is warm and her damp hair smells sweet. She sucks her thumb and holds her bear, which was once my bear, under one arm. I close the door softly and look down the hall. There's a yellow line under the study door. I can hear his fingers attacking the keyboard. God knows what he's writing at such pace. Maybe a masterpiece. He is many things but he isn't stupid.

I shower, trying to rinse off the argument, and take myself to bed. My body lies still, obedient with fatigue. I need to read something to reset my mind, but nothing is right. It's a terrible feeling, not having an appetite for a book. And at the other extreme, it's a brilliant feeling knowing that however bad the lesson, or the dinner or the loneliness or your health, there's a book on the bedside table that will hold you still, suspend you for a time from your own life and let you inhabit the lives of others. Perhaps it's not pneumonia but excessive solipsism that's left me wondering which corner of my life is the consolation, turning and turning like a dog making its bed, failing to find comfort. All I really want to do is stay in bed. Or, having forced myself out of bed, stay in the warmth of the shower. Or, once caught in the groove of the day and having driven to school, stay in the driver's seat of the parked car. I just keep stalling when I know I ought to be moving. I must drive myself somehow.

I am awake and lying still with my eyes closed when he tucks himself into his side of the bed. We're straight as knives and don't touch.

In the morning I am out of the house, delivering Aster to daycare, before he rises. In the evening we speak to our daughter but not to each other. It is evident in both of our voices that there is still tension, but it's lessened. When she's out of the shower, dry and pyjamaed, he comes in and tells her, 'Daddy stories tonight.'

Once she's in bed, he comes to the kitchen, where I'm cleaning up.

'Want a cup of tea?' I ask.

'Thanks,' he says.

I boil the kettle and find the mugs we like, put a peppermint bag in each.

'Thank you for putting her to bed,' I say stiffly. 'What did you read?'

'That godawful little sister one.'

'I loved that when I was a kid.' I put his mug on the table. When he comes to get it he touches my arm. I lean into him and let my hand find his waist, then slide it up to his shoulder until we're hugging. We hold each other for a long time. I start to cry.

'I'm sorry you're not happy,' he says.

'So am I.'

'What do you need?'

'I think,' I say, 'I need to write.'

'Okay,' he says. 'Then write! I want you to write too.'

If he weren't stroking my arms, I would pull away and wipe the bench, angry all over again. But he is trying, and I recognise this. It isn't that he's wilfully ignorant; he thinks he sees.

'To write,' I say, 'I need time.'

'Of course. Writing must be prioritised. It's the same for me.' He sits at the table now, apparently more comfortable, and I sit too, not wanting to feel like I've been called into his office for a chat.

It isn't the same for you at all, I think but do not say. Instead: 'There are other priorities too – teaching takes infinite time and energy. As does mothering.'

He sips his tea. There's a long pause, which anyone else might interpret as him not having heard what I said, or ignoring me, but I know he's considering what to say. I let him. In pedagogical speak, this is called thinking time.

'I believe,' he says eventually, 'that you've been giving an unsustainable amount of yourself to both of these things.'

Again, I rein in my initial reaction, collect myself before replying. All the indoor plants, I notice, need water. There are crumbs on the table. 'Yeah, you're probably right.' I think I'm being magnanimous, but as I say it I realise his comment is true.

'I see this at uni all time,' he goes on. 'Sessionals working themselves into the ground trying to prove they're amazing teachers and leaping through hoops for any measly researcher role, all for what? Twelve-week contracts. They're complicit in their own oppression.'

There aren't just crumbs on the table, there's flour and water, old dough from homemade bread, dried in the cracks of the wood. I pick at it with my fingernail, make a small pile of scrapings, brush it into my palm. The way he says it, and his timing, are tone-deaf, but, again, his words are well intentioned and at least partly accurate. I think of the files in my laptop I avoid opening. There's one called Selection Criteria that contains a hundred and nineteen documents. The number of times in my life I've applied for university positions.

'What do you suggest these oppressed casual academics – and I – should do?' My voice doesn't sound as injured as I expected it would. I even look him in the eye.

'Demand more for yourself. Set boundaries. It's your life.'

'Demand more from who? From you?'

'I guess so. Yes. From me.' He's looking earnestly into his mug. I can't tell if his eyes are just tired from staring at the screen all day or if he's about to cry.

'So, if I said that we had to start alternating nights of doing shower, teeth and bedtime, you'd say yes.'

'Okay.'

'I hate the word okay.' I manage to say this neutrally, without hatred.

'Why?' He sounds curious rather than defensive.

'Because to me it has a grudging tone.'

'To me it's just what I say for yes. Would you like me to say yes instead?' There's no sarcasm in his voice.

'You can say okay sometimes, but in this context I'd prefer yes.' I sound like a schoolteacher. A nagging schoolteacher.

'Okay.'

I laugh. And feel a bit lighter. Something settles.

'What else do you demand?'

'I demand time to swim on the weekends.'

'Fair enough.'

'I demand that we share pick-ups and drop-offs as much as possible.'

'Oka— I mean, yes.'

'Good, yes.'

'What else?'

I think about suggesting we go home. But this is home to him. He's happy we're here. And besides, the borders are closed. 'That's enough for now.'

To Ride

I think back to when I was writing most – articles, reviews, poems, my thesis. The only international conference I ever presented at was in Orléans. That was before I met him, in the final year of my doctoral study. It was held in early December, and when I walked by the Loire, a curl of hair not tucked under my beanie froze. I wanted to spend Christmas in Berlin but couldn't afford to stay in a hostel for a fortnight and didn't want to impose on friends for that length of time, so I applied to work at a farm that bred endurance horses. I worked there for two weeks in exchange for food and a bed.

On the day I was to start, I woke early, dressed in clothes I deemed more suitable for farm work than conferring with academics, packed my bag and checked out of the hotel. I'd shared a room with a German doctoral student I'd never met before and haven't seen since. I took the train to Nevers, where a friend of the farmer's collected me and drove us down narrow, snowy roads with tall conifers on either side.

At the farm the horses were awaiting their evening feed. Seventy horses in all. I have been fond of and comfortable with large animals since I can remember, but en masse and hungry the horses intimidated me. Turning in their stables, stamping their forehooves, snorting, tossing their haughty, dish-nosed faces. Caring for that quantity of beings is a type of work I hadn't attempted before; nor have I done since, unless you count teaching.

'You are intellect, not manual,' the farmer told me on the first day, frowning at the way I carried two buckets of water, sloshing the contents into borrowed gumboots. She was impatient and irritable and disappointed with me. I was less competent at speaking French and being a farmhand than my application had made me appear. But I was all she had; winter had landed heavily, and so she trained me as if I were one of her least promising animals. I fantasised about escaping, finding my way to the train station, and somehow travelling to Montpellier to couchsurf for the remainder of the fundless fortnight. Still, I worked diligently if incompetently and gradually became less disappointing. I could muck out twenty stables in an hour, mix seventy buckets of feed, carry a hundred bales of hay from tractor to shed. But no sooner had I achieved a level that satisfied the farmer than it was time to return to Paris. There I booked myself into a hotel room with a bathtub and consumed my dinner of baguette, brie, and a half-bottle of red wine while wallowing in the warm water and reading *Crime and Punishment*.

I begin by making a list. The first item on it is to clear my desk of schoolwork. The next is to plan. The next is to write. I have a lined book, an online document, and notes in my phone. The words go everywhere.

To Perform

Spring. Everyone's front garden along our street has the decadent scent of jonquils. The dregs of strange neighbourly behaviours from the past year of lockdowns remain. The teddy bears strapped to letterboxes are now bedraggled and cobwebbed. There are fresh chalk rainbows on the footpaths and weird congregations of spoons with hand-drawn faces arranged on the verge under the jacaranda. Instead of meeting with each other, this is what people did to cheer up the children.

It is Aster's birthday. The three of us walk to the playground. I carry a plate of cupcakes, a candle in the shape of a 5, and a lighter; he pushes the back of her new bike, keeping her steady as she pedals. At the playground I put the plate on a picnic table. No one is allowed on the equipment, but Aster's best friends from kinder have, coincidentally, come for their one-hour quota of exercise. One of them has a new puppy and the children chase it around the footy field. We adults stand a couple of metres apart, masked, watching the happy energy.

'Is this her second birthday in lockdown?' one of the mothers, Liv, asks.

'Yeah, second birthday Zooming her relatives in Perth and New Zealand.'

'That sucks.'

'Yeah. At least the weather's nice.'

'That's the spirit.'

I like Liv. She's someone I can imagine befriending. I decide to add another demand when we get home. Time to go out for drinks with friends, when we're allowed to go out for drinks again.

I sanitise my hands before spreading out the cupcakes and then call the children over to help themselves. In Aster's I put the candle shaped like a 5. He holds his large palms around the wick as I try to light the flame. When it catches I smile at him.

'Quick, before it blows out!' We sing 'Happy Birthday', swift and tuneless, and our daughter blows with gusto. The children swallow the sugar, run around some more with pink icing and brown crumbs on their faces, then return to their respective lockdowns.

Tired from the illicit socialising, Aster pulls a blanket around herself on the couch and gazes wistfully at the TV. 'I wish,' she says, 'that I could have a movie.'

While something involving a girl and a dragon plays behind me, I sit at my desk and open the document that is not a student's essay or a lesson plan or a slideshow. I have been writing in bursts of about a thousand words, without fear or hope or a sense of judgement. It is a little like swimming twenty-five lengths of the outdoor pool at the Brunswick baths – pleasurably onerous. Pleasing solely to myself.

I have been swimming twice a week again. The strokes of my stretched arms still cause an abrasive sensation under my ribcage, but the pain isn't bad; it feels controlled if it occurs while I'm doing something I've chosen to do. I am not helping anyone but myself as I swim, and I'm feeling less guilty about the fact. My view of pleasure is gradually less placental. If I'm too unhappy then I won't serve Aster well.

'When can I read it?' he asks a little later, putting a cup of coffee on the coaster next to my laptop.

'Do you want to?' I feel a flutter of something I'd almost forgotten – similar to being flirted with or flattered. A ripple of energy. I fascinate him again, I think; for years I've just been feeding him, but now he seems enchanted once more.

'Of course I want to.'

'Can I read yours?'

'Do you want to?'

I used to read everything he wrote before it was presented or submitted. That tailed off after Aster was born. I do want to, I tell him.

'I just didn't want to give you extra work to do. I know you're busy.'

I'd rather be busy reading his draft than folding washing or vacuuming or building Lego castles. But I'd also prefer to be busy doing my own writing than reading his. I should probably just tell him this, but I don't want to sound bitter.

'Let's swap tonight, when she's in bed.'

When the film finishes Aster announces she would like a haircut. 'Like the girl in the movie.'

'Are you sure?' The girl in the movie has a jaw-length bob and short fringe, pumpkin-coloured, as cartoon red hair often is. Aster's hair is down past her shoulders and, until now apparently, a source of vanity.

'Yes.'

'I don't know if I can make it look exactly like hers. She's a cartoon character.'

'Just try your best,' she says, sounding like me.

I save the document, close the laptop and take her to the bathroom. She sits primly on the stool she uses to reach the taps and lets me clip a towel around her shoulders and spray her hair with water and leave-in conditioner. She doesn't even wince as I comb it. I try the kitchen scissors but they are awkwardly large and threaten her ears, so I use nail scissors, slightly curved. I begin cautiously, taking off one inch, then another, until the floor is decorated with copper-coloured Cs. When her hair is up to her chin she shakes her head vigorously, like wet dog.

'Is this okay?'

'I love it!'

'Do you still want me to do the fringe, or is this enough?'

'Fringe!'

I rotate her stool and ask her to close her eyes. I comb a section over her forehead then pin back the top half, as a hairdresser instructed me to do with my own fringe. I pull the hair straight down over her nose, then watch it ping back up to mid-forehead when it's snipped. Her curls are not going to resemble the cartoon character's painted block of hair but they will hide the crooked lines of my work.

'Done,' I say. 'You can open your eyes.'

Her head is still tilted down slightly, so what she first sees is everything that she's lost. Bright curls piled on the white tiles. 'Oh,' she says, lip trembling. 'So much is gone.'

'But look in the mirror,' I say, hoping this will be a consolation rather than another injury.

She studies herself, looking oddly like my mother as she does so.

'What do you think?'

'Good! Very good.' She runs to show him. The study door is open these days.

'Look, Daddy! I'm a girl in a movie!'

'Very chic,' I hear him say as I sweep up the damp hair and put it in the bin.

'What's chic?'

'Elegant.'

'Thank you.'

To Balance

He cooks homemade vegie burgers for her birthday dinner, Aster's request. I do the dishes. He supervises the brushing of her teeth and showering; I read her stories. Then he and I sit together on the couch and swap laptops. Usually, sitting here on our usual sides, with our usual cushions, we're watching an old sitcom or a detective show, something distracting that relieves us from having to communicate. But now the TV is off as we read each other's words.

He writes well. Precisely analytical without being dense or pretentious. I've missed hearing this thoughtful persona; since becoming a teacher, I haven't read a single paper of his. The chapter he's given me, which he's been working on today, is titled 'Encounterless Love'. He is applying Badiou's philosophy of love to the socially distanced conditions in which we're all currently living and considering the ramifications of limited physical proximity and intimacy.

'I like this quote: "love is the dour desire to endure",' I say. 'Which poet are you referring to?'

'Paul Éluard. It's good, isn't it?'

'Very nice translation.'

We sink back into silent reading. Instead of talking to each other, we type comments in the margins. As if he were a student, I correct typos, ask questions where I'm unsure what he means, praise the wording I most enjoy. I finish his chapter before he finishes mine. I try not to look at where he's up to and what he's writing. I like it when he smirks. It's supposed to be funny.

'Well,' he says, eventually. 'Shall I go first?'

'Please.'

'I want to keep reading. That's the main thing, isn't it? I like listening to her voice and I'm interested in what will happen to her.'

'Good. I'm glad.'

'I've made a couple of notes where it gets a bit clunky, to my ear – a little too baroque, maybe? But you must keep writing it. It's working.'

I tell myself that I do not need his approval, but it's buoying all the same.

'Thank you. I'll try to finish it. My turn?'

'Be gentle.'

'I'm always gentle.' I tell him that I've missed hearing this internal version of his voice. It's been too long. 'I thought,' I say before I can consider stopping myself, 'that once I became a teacher you wouldn't see me as a colleague anymore, as someone capable of interpreting your work.'

'I never said that, did I?'

'No, but I inferred it. Or projected my own insecurity onto you. Do you remember those faculty drinks you took me along to at the start of last year? Whenever someone asked what I was doing and I told them that I couldn't find non-sessional academic work so had decided to become a schoolteacher, they were so full of pity and condescension. "Good for you," or "That's such a good thing to do," they said before moving across the room to speak to a real peer.'

'Maybe they really meant it? It *is* good that you're a teacher.'

'Not you too.'

'I'm serious!'

'It's not great for my publication record.'

'There's more to life than publications.'

'I'm going to get that put on a T-shirt for you.' My toes have crept under his thighs. Not just to keep them warm.

'Alright, teacher, what mark do you give this chapter?'

'Strong A-minus.'

'Why not A-plus?'

I tell him my thoughts and he listens without interrupting.

'Can I ask one more favour?' he says when I run out of feedback.

'What?'

'Cut my hair?'

I set him up in the bathroom, just as I did with Aster.

'What can I do for you today, sir?'

'Short back and sides, I think.'

'Seriously?'

'Something like that – pretty short, anyway. Definitely short enough that I can't be tempted to have a ponytail. I don't want to be a ponytailed philosopher.'

'Alright, but remember you asked for it. I don't want any tears at the end.'

'Promise.'

His hair is thicker than hers but almost as soft. I stroke the back of his neck as I gather up the lengths and pin half out of the way. I comb my fingers through, using them as a ruler and snipping along their lines. Luckily his hair is wavy like our daughter's; the jagged edges will be hidden. Soon the back of his neck is bare.

'I'd forgotten this,' I say, touching the burgundy birthmark that emerges from his hairline at the nape.

I move around to his ears next and then to his face, leaving something akin to the forelock he had when I first saw him sitting on the lawn reading Ted Hughes.

'How's that feeling?'

He rubs his palms around the back of his scalp.

I hold up the camera on my phone so he can use it as a mirror.

'Not bad,' he says. 'Much lighter.'

'You look younger.'

'I'm thinking of losing this too.' He strokes his beard. 'You don't love it, do you?'

'I've gotten used to it.'

'Right, it's going.'

A different person to the one I've been living with for the past five years joins me in bed. 'May I?' I ask, reaching for his cheek. So smooth and exposed.

He kisses me. We kiss each other. Equally soft. Equally rough. I roll him over and hold his wrists against the pillow. He submits for a bit before flipping me onto my back. We play clumsily, out of practice at pulling off garments, getting happily tangled and untangled, destroying the once-made bed, ignoring which is foot and which is head.

'Is that good?' he asks gently.

'Yes,' I say, meaning it.

The next day, Sunday, I sleep in longer than I have since I was in my twenties. It's eight when I go to the kitchen and find them sitting at the table eating breakfast.

'French toast!' Aster says, holding up a yellow square sticky with honey.

'Lucky us!'

After we've eaten, he writes and I take her to the playground again. We've planned to meet Liv and her daughter. As the girls play under the oak trees, Liv and I drink coffee from our keep cups and talk.

'How's it going for you, working from home?' I ask. Liv is something in IT, I'm not sure exactly what.

'If my partner and I weren't in love it'd be fucking dreadful,' she says. 'But there's that to be grateful for. The kids give me the screaming shits a lot of the time, and I'm sick to death of my furniture, and I miss my parents and I'm worried about my sister, but all things considered, we're lucky.'

'Why are you worried about your sister?'

'She's got MS and needs to be especially careful not to get sick. But then she also has to go into hospital regularly, which is full of the virus.'

'That's very hard. I'm sorry.'

'All we can do is leave stuff on her doorstep and wave through the window. But at least we're within five kay of each other. Where are your family?'

'New Zealand.'

'Oh god. That's shit.'

'Yeah.' I pause to think, then let myself keep going. I tell her more than I've told anyone other than Ana via Zoom.

'Do you reckon you'll go back when this has blown over? When the borders are back open?'

'It depends on his job. I'd like to, but I don't know if it'll be feasible.' I know it won't be feasible.

'Well,' Liv says, looking at the kids. My daughter is trying to hoist her daughter up onto the lowest branch of a tree. 'We'll miss you if you move back.'

To Plant

Once more I have had to cancel our flights to see my mother. To cheer myself up these holidays, I've decided to do something with our courtyard garden, even though we're only renting. Even though I still think I would like to move back to Wellington. My mother is a gardener and when I call to apologise again for not coming, I ask her what I should plant. Without the distraction of looking at each other on the screen, without Aster's bellowing interjections, the conversation is longer and easier than any we've had since I moved to Australia.

'Silverbeet and rhubarb are easy, and herbs of course. Tarragon has pretty yellow flowers and the scent is lovely. Native flowers are good for attracting birds, and bees and butterflies too.' I can tell she's paused to search online for Australian natives. I could do this myself, but it's better coming from her.

'Kangaroo paws look very striking. Why don't you have a border of those and —'

'Mum, the courtyard is very small.'

'Okay, well how about a balance of herbs and vegie seedlings and some small natives?'

At the garden centre I let Aster choose two of the native tubestock. One for each small hand. She opts for a chocolate lily and a westringia. We pinch the leaves and smell them. I add parsley, sage, rosemary, thyme and everlasting daisies to my basket. At the counter, I imagine how satisfying it would be to never waste food again and decide to buy a bokashi bucket. Aster holds a small blue trowel and looks at me longingly. When we eventually drive home, the boot is full: a bale of pea straw mulch, a watering can, gloves, trowels, a fork. It's an investment, I tell myself.

While I tear out weeds and turn over the turf, Aster speaks quietly to the plants. When the earth is ready, we follow the instructions on each punnet meticulously, spacing them as recommended, pressing them gently into place, pulling mulch around them like a blanket. We work without pausing until it's all done. My hands are stiff with encrusted dirt, my lower back wet with sweat. I wipe my hands on my jeans, find my phone and photograph Aster watering the little bed. I send it to Mum.

I fall asleep that night thinking of the delicate hairs of roots reaching down into the earth as the sprouting leaves reach for the moon.

To Learn

The zoo has been closed for seventy-seven days. On the day it reopens Aster and I are among the few early visitors to see the animals being fed their breakfast. Cloud is hanging low over the enclosures, the air heavy with moisture. We watch the baby baboons scamper to the glass and peer through the condensation at the human young, who are about the same size. Comparable hands pressed on either side of the glass. Similar faces cocked and listening.

'Look at the monkeys!' a mother tells her toddler.

'They're not monkeys,' Aster says quietly. 'They are baboons.'

Have the baboons, watching us with interest, perhaps even pity, missed our presence these past few months? Have they wondered: Where are those poor creatures who used to be animals? Are they okay in their softly furnished cages?

Watching Aster swinging on the ropes in the play area that resembles a small version of the orangutans', I imagine the future zoo will contain more humane animal enclosures, more animatronic displays of extinct species, and more gift shops selling plastic approximations of life. Perhaps the snow leopard cage will remain, like that of the zoo's first orangutan, Mollie. A low-profile reminder of historical and ongoing cruelty.

Mollie was just a few months old when she arrived at the zoo in 1901, the same year *My Brilliant Career* was first published. She lived in her small enclosure for twenty-two years, the bars just the right width apart for the passing of cigarettes and bottles of beer. Several times she set her bedding on fire, having learnt to operate a lighter. One fire damaged her wooden cage to such an extent that a concrete replacement had to be made. When Mollie died in 1923, she was stuffed and displayed, an honour reserved for only the best-loved inhabitants.

Her cage has remained as an acknowledgement of the zoo's 'changing face', my philosophy students were told on an ethics tour. When Aster and I pass it, all she notices is the meat on a spit outside and the ice cream trolley and the queue of people lining up for lunch. All we feel is hunger.

When I get home I vacuum the whole house, raking at the carpet in vicious time with Berlin techno. Even in the shower I keep moving. I think about shaving my armpits and legs but don't. I am feeling more animal. At my feet are a plastic orca and a shark, and a pink plastic crab in an old plastic bowl for a pool – with a single rock, a squash ball. The detritus of end days capitalism or Aster's treasures? Morning Star, Evening Star, Venus. When I was pregnant, I thought I'd buy only wooden toys and not litter our home with cheap, colourful rubbish. And yet here we are.

We finish the day by playing zoos, of course. Aster is a siamang. To make the enclosure we heap all her soft toys on the floor. She waves like a person. I'm instructed to film it, as I would an animal at a zoo. She passes a toy through invisible bars and gives me orders: Pretend you understand what I need. Pretend this squeak means that's for your child. Pretend he wants to get out but can't. Pretend that's glass. Pretend the keeper said if I go over here it means I want you to come in the enclosure. Pretend you do! Pretend I can talk, pretend I'm the only animal in the world that can talk.

The trip to the zoo has made me think of Ana, who's fond of sending me links to stories about sperm whales. She's fascinated by their communication, so sophisticated that it allowed them to adjust their collective behaviour and protect themselves from whaling boats. Until the surge of human predation, the primary threat to sperm whales was orca attacks. The best way to fend off orcas, if you're a pod of sperm whales, is to form a ring with your tails facing out and keep young guarded in the middle, a formation that rendered them easy targets for whalers. Those that survived the early slaughter learned from it, and this learning was passed along by matriarchs throughout their pods. Within only a few years, the rate of successful harpoon strikes plummeted.

Now it's noise pollution, from military sonar exercises and other sources, that's threatening whales. Last September, three hundred and eighty pilot whales died on the west coast of Tasmania, the worst mass stranding in Australia's history. Two months later came an inventory of the three billion animals killed, injured or robbed of their habitat during Black Summer. One hundred and eighty-one million birds. Fifty-one million frogs. One million wombats. Sixty-one thousand koalas …

Aster has a pop-up book about rabbits and the Fibonacci sequence. The final page is an explosion of bunnies out of the snow, too many to count.

To Sustain

'What does "sustained" mean?' Aster asks while we are baking a black forest cake for his birthday. I have read her a story about a witch who feels that way after eating burnt cakes.

'It means filled up,' I say inaccurately.

Cherries are not in season yet and the expensive ones I found at the supermarket taste watery. They look fine, though, glossy and purple, and we later eat the whole cake between the three of us. I tell myself this is good for my body, which has lost too much weight during the months of antibiotics and coughing. Now my waistband is getting tight again. I don't mind feeling more substantial.

'How many words are you up to?' he asks that evening as I type. The days are lengthening and there's still light outside, despite Aster having gone to bed an hour ago.

'Nearly twenty thousand.'

'Great. Keep going.'

I grab his hand and kiss it in a way I used to. The habit of affection is re-forming, is no longer a motion to be gone through, but a natural inclination. He leans into my chair for a moment, not rushing back to his study as usual.

'Are you nearly done?' I ask. We plan to drink some of his birthday bottle of whisky when he's finished his urgent work.

'Meet you on the couch in half an hour?'

'Perfect.'

While I wait, I write about Linda losing weight and hope. I write about her being propelled north in a train carriage to a place she has no interest in. I write about her baby son and moustachioed husband and absent sister. The woman whose voice I imagine is not

Linda (because there was a real Linda and that presses upon me), and is not me, and is not Gertie (Miles Franklin's fictional sister), but a sort of ghostly overlapped self who is with me all the time now. She is there as I teach and cook and drive and do all the many other verbs of each day.

To Absorb

Priya emails a video she's made for her chemistry class, which over a Friday afternoon beer she promised to share with me. Before it starts, all I can see is the caption *Add a catalyst and things move quickly*. Maybe that's the way to teach etymology, I think; to show the word in action. This, I imagine saying to an English class, is a catalyst. From the Greek *katalusis*, meaning to dissolve. Watch the dissolution of the chemical and see how it precipitates the event that is the water changing from clear to blue. Now choose something that could be compared with this chemical. Illness, weather, a word, whatever. Consider what that thing precipitates.

Or I'd use the word 'absorb'. I wouldn't need a video for that, just a sponge and water, which are not dangerous props. It means, I would say unnecessarily, to suck in.

When I say the word 'homesick' it sounds to Australians like 'homesuck'. This is strangely apt; it's as if the very feeling is sucking me back to Wellington, and it makes me picture Aster with a strand of spaghetti disappearing into her pursed lips, a stain of sauce around her mouth.

He and I exchange all sorts of things now, not least of all more words. I try harder to absorb what he's saying. Now, he hears when I speak. And if he doesn't hear the first time, I raise my voice, not in anger but in the knowledge that he wants to receive what I say. For years I felt as if I were talking under water while he was above the surface, with nothing but a muffled bubbling getting through.

It's nearly summer. We have an afternoon together, when neither of us needs to be at our laptops and Aster is at kinder. We go to the baths. The slow and fast lanes are both full, so we share the medium lane. He moves smoothly through the water, a glistening layer sliding off his shoulders as he hoists himself out to rest. Yet to finish my twenty-five laps, I tumble-turn and keep swimming. There's no longer a pain in my side. I've a head full of words. Thinking and thinking about sisters.

To Sister

It's unlikely but not impossible that I once had a sister. A twin reabsorbed in utero, who in a way still sustains me. I regress thirty-seven years and imagine this twin growing next to me but not surviving to birth. Odd to think of myself as the stronger of the two, not a position I'm used to holding. But what if she had lived? And maybe been a star? A firebrand. An art monster.

I'm startled by how easy it is to imagine this. There's already a flickering of grief at my loss, like the beginning of a fire.

But, if you were whole, a whole sister – who sucked her left thumb and had eyebrows that curled up at the ends and a pigeon-toed gait – what would you have done with your life?

You might've had an odd voice. This might've led to your being bullied by other children. I, your only friend, might've recognised the social risk of being affiliated with the pariah and been cruel. I might've said, 'It's time we made our own friends,' and proceeded to do all I could to fit in. This might've involved ridiculing you for mishearing the teacher's instruction and writing your own story on the blank piece of paper you thought you'd been given, not realising that on the other side was a fill-the-gaps exercise in which you were expected not to create whole sentences, let alone paragraphs, but to choose only adjectives. I can imagine being unkind, spurred only by the desire to win acceptance. But it's also likely that your aloofness – an apparent imperviousness to the attacks of jealous and confused children – won you admirers eventually. Perhaps one of the boys I liked was more interested in you, given that you were more interesting. But you didn't bother to attend our school balls, finding the tradition boringly gendered. Maybe you and a friend sneaked a bottle of vodka and lay on the roof of the packing shed in her dad's orchard and drank it, watching for shooting stars and wondering, when there was a shallow earthquake, whether you were just drunk or the plates really were shifting.

I expect you drank too much. Even more than I used to. And then stopped altogether. At the age I am now, I imagine you would drink no caffeine, no alcohol. Nor would you take drugs of any sort. You would have an elegant ceramic mug made by a friend/lover and sip herbal tea from it during our Zoom conversations, which we would both enjoy but which would be infrequent. You'd ask after your niece and I'd ask after your music. These would be our contributions to the world, and we'd possess a complicated respect for each other. During the conversation, I'd try to focus on your half of the screen, but my eyes would keep flicking back, comparing your face with mine, checking my expression. This is something you'd notice, and not do yourself. If I were to call you right now, I'd see you with the familiar wooden panels of the bach, which used to belong in part to our parents, at your back. You'd be renting it for the year, living there alone, supposedly composing a new album and going for walks along Ocean Beach and waiting for the world to open and allow you to tour again. I'd say, 'Hopefully late May! Or if not May, then June. Or maybe July? August? I can't wait to see you.'

'I'm going to gobble that child up, you know.'

'We'll see you soon, Stella.'

'Yes, I hope soon.'

And your eyes would mirror mine.

Two

STILLWATER

Will it always be this ghastly aloneness? Why am I not good and pretty and simple like other girls?

MILES FRANKLIN, *MY BRILLIANT CAREER*

I Remember, I Remember

You always said to fire straight into the story. Stop fretting about quality of penmanship & poor expression; for the love of life just write! I haven't a pen this time, but that's no excuse not to start. Sister, here is a novel in thoughts.

There's plenty of time to think in transit, as you'd know by now. Though I'm certain your journeys by sea afforded more glamorous distractions than this second-class sleeper on the standard gauge to Dalveen. Ted is dead to the world at last – a warm weight breathing wetly through my blouse – & Charles has escaped to the parlour carriage (a blessed relief). I'm as free as I'll ever be to attempt what you said I never could – to give you what you gave me. How? Via – what's it called? – telepathy? Sisterly telepathy. It doesn't matter how.

Of course, I've no brilliant career to speak of, but I'm nonetheless harbouring an egotistical wish to share with you a story all about myself, which in turn must be a story about you, dearest (most costly), for I believe we're parts of each other. Substantially distant now. What do I remember? Difficult to think, let alone say. I'll lean my lit-up cheek against the night window & let my eyes close; when Charlie returns, he'll assume I'm only sleeping, not gathering up our lives.

This is my last journey. Charles is taking us to Queensland, to start a new life, and I have no doubt that it is there I will die.

So I might as well begin with my first journey, from Brindabella – the Arcadia I don't fully recall – to Stillwater. *Stillwater:* I believe you viewed Mother's lyrical name for the place as a kind of denial. I can smell the dams and see the slime, the same green as the horses' lips in Brindabella where clover grew lush.

You've always splashed about & I, not two years behind, have bounced in your wake. The day before I left Brindabella for Grannie's (at Talbingo, to be out of harm's way for the move), you puckered your small mouth and kissed Zephyr next to the snaffle, a green streak left on your cheek. I did the same, of course, & the horse's head flicked – and I lost a tiny triangle of tooth to the bit. I held my face the whole walk back to the house, eyes welling hot with the sick sense a smack to the nose gives. When Ma saw us she thought I was kicking up a row about leaving.

'Not you too, Linda.' Wide as a ten-gallon drum with Talmage, she'd no time for whining.

I shook my aching face. 'No, Ma, Zeph whacked me.'

'Let me see.' Broad, warm palm on each cheek. Kind, rough. I wrapped my arms round her stretched waist & pressed my chin against it, feeling for our brother.

'At least it's a milk tooth; you haven't ruined that smile. Sweet child, you can still marry well one day.' Smoothing my white-blond hair. No kiss.

Married & tall as Zephyr, strong enough to hold children – to grow folk! I would've given a chipped grin, running my pink tongue over the sharp new ridge of tooth. Eight years old, I was then. You, nearly ten and naughty, kicked Zephyr's dried droppings, letting them rush through the dust towards the chooks. Our mother's dark stare followed the scattering hens, then returned to you.

'Not going to marry well with that demeanour, no, no, no!' Contrary contralto, which you've never lost, a turn on the heels, which I'd wager you still perform, & a dash into the packed-up house, muslin shirt stuck grey with sweat to your back. Mother's laugh, deep and rich, was a great relief. That's the last time I remember hearing her make such a sound.

She's a quiet woman, isn't she? Our mother seldom makes a noise. Instead, she causes them to be made. Wet cotton against board, hot iron on wet cotton, broom across tiled floor, mats thumping the door, water pounding into the tub, into the bucket, water up from the well, bacon into the pan, dough on the bench, lamb in the oven, apples rolling out of aprons. Even her scolding was quiet, though the outcomes were loud; you, bad goat, would bleat & rage against the injustice of her rule. I would simply melt into tearful remorse. Imagine if we'd all been loud as you? Unbearable.

But I meander already, which I haven't the luxury to do. There're many things I wish you knew, Stella, indeed, that I wish to know myself.

When I first arrived at Stillwater, you were sitting on the veranda steps, face in the hammock of dirty skirt between your knees, sobbing.

'Child, what have you done?' Grannie asked, using your head to steady herself as she climbed the steps. I sat next to you, patted your back and examined the aspect – shallow hills like a green unmade bed slipping into scrubby valley, splattered with lagoons reflecting sky. You squirmed away.

'I missed you, Stella,' I tried.

'Nobody missed you, mouse!' With a sniff you pulled yourself up, galloped into the house and disappeared down a dark corridor. Grannie shook her head. 'Froward-hearted. No resemblance to you, Linda. Let's find your parents.'

We discovered Father & the boys feeding calves in the new front paddock. Well, Mervyn had a bottle & teat; Norman, the youngest, a mouthful of grass. I called him, and when he heard me he toddled on fast, fat legs, chin shining with saliva & green with blades. I, seven-year-old mother, hoisted him onto my hip, kissing his hair.

'The pleasant sister is home. How nice.' Father climbed the fence to greet us. 'Welcome to Thornford, Linda and Mrs Lampe. What do you think?'

'A much less perturbing distance from civilisation,' Grannie said. 'Especially with Susannah so near term. How is she?'

'Resting, I think. If that hellish child isn't tormenting her.'

'Stella isn't hellish,' I lied.

I would've been keen to see that the horses had settled into their new paddock, but Father and Grannie declared it teatime, so to the kitchen we went, where Mother wasn't resting. She looked strained, standing at the stove stirring something savoury, so instead of saying anything I just hugged her, smelling her & stew on her pinny.

'Hello Linda. Not now, dear.' She flinched away from me. I understood I'd been spurned again. The feeling was familiar from three years earlier when Norman arrived, and you informed me that when Mervyn came I'd tried to scratch his eyes out – an accusation I cannot endorse, having been two at the time. I know you claim to have crystalline memories of infancy, but this, Stella, this first day at Stillwater, and the chipped tooth from Zephyr before it – these are my earliest.

'Linda dear, go and find Stella, would you? Tell her it'll be teatime soon and she's promised to set the table.'

I doubted this promise but agreed to find you.

They're faded and foxed around the edges, these recollections. On my first exploration of the house the woodwork smelt like a chapel; that polished sweetness, and the tall doorways, unfamiliar rooms, made me walk primly. I felt I was in a place of veneration, a sense we evidently didn't share. You'd calmed, at least, when I found you in what I presumed would be our room, sitting on the sill exactly as Mother always told us not to, the sash window up & ready to guillotine in a gust.

'Stella!'

'It won't do it,' you said, not looking up from your scrapbook. 'I know what you're thinking, and you're wrong.'

'What am I thinking?'

'I've taken the precaution of checking. It isn't like the windows at Brindabella. I'm quite safe.'

I let out my breath.

'Sweet child, you really were worried, weren't you?' You looked at me, for the first time in a month, grinning, eyes black as berries in a face puffed with recent frustration, no longer a dropped pie.

'Of course.' Have you ever known how I adore you? I was still standing in the doorway, waiting for an invitation to enter. You offered none, but instead removed your straw hat and let your coiled plait fall like Rapunzel's.

'Look.' You nodded downwards.

'It reaches the floor!'

This was the first time I doused personal disappointment with shared pride. I wished for my own blond wisps to grow long, but they refused. So instead I decided to try to share in your success, a part owner of that ropy braid.

'Mother wants you to set the table.' I'd hoped that, in this moment of triumph, you'd take the message well.

'And so we shall.' You grabbed my elbow and cantered me to the dining room. 'But first, a tour. That was our room, of course. Mine's the bed by the window, but if you want to share, I don't object. The desk is mine too. And here is Norman and Mervyn's little sty. Mother and Father's is behind the door that must not be opened without permission. And this corner will be for the baby.'

You whisked me so fast up & down the corridor that I barely saw anything. We've never moved at the same pace. You disliked the house, but enjoyed knowing it before I did.

'And the cherry on top – look!' We'd finished in the parlour, with a vista over the valley, but you cared nought for the view. It was the piano in the opposite corner that caused delight. You sat side-saddle on the stool, ignoring the pedals & thumping out a double-quick rendition of 'Cherry Ripe'.

'Stella, we should set the table.' This was the beginning of subsuming myself into your responsibilities as well as your successes. A busy day of firsts; or had every day been rich with such character conditioning? It's important for me to trace these origins as it may help me understand where our paths started to diverge. I expect I'll find it was at birth – my brain's simply not like yours. But possibly there was a time when we were equal. Equally what? you might ask. Virtuous, valuable, clever, right?

'Stella Franklin, that is not setting the table.'

I was afraid of Grannie at that age; it was before I realised that her sternness was cultivated to restrain her amusement at your antics.

'I tried to tell her, Grannie.'

You slammed the lid down over the keys. 'Holding with the hare and running with the hound, again!'

I couldn't comprehend the expression's meaning back then, beyond a vague sense that eventually I was going to be eaten.

'Linda dear, would you like to come back to Talbingo with me in a few days? Your sister isn't being kind, is she? It may be best if we keep you apart a stretch longer.'

At this you leapt up, plait swishing behind you like a provoked cat's tail. 'That would be an injustice! Grannie, if you must separate us, then at least take me with you. Linda has already had her holiday from this godforsaken swamp.'

'Language, child.' Grannie roosted in our father's armchair next to the piano, facing the view. She appeared to be readying herself for a prolonged battle.

'Look at it!' You hopped onto the window seat and gestured to the valley, glowing coolly with the last of the afternoon's light. 'See, there's the neighbour's house. They are called the Baxters but we haven't met them yet. It's insupportable to be so near other people.

I feel cramped. And listen. Really listen! You can hear the train howling on the hour.'

I'm certain our grandmother was biting the inside of her lip, but she nevertheless bellowed, 'Insolent child – why would I invite a wretch, who tramples over clean cushions in her boots, to stay at my home?' Grannie was not quiet like Mother.

You'd wrapped yourself in the curtain during this admonishment. All we could see were the offending boots, two stout, stockinged legs & the hem of a faded navy skirt. The curtain started twitching & emitting a snivelling sound. I went to it, cautiously pulled aside a corner, & tried to share your shelter.

'Linda, don't encourage her. Please show your sister what a good girl is like and help me begin setting the table. You do a better job of it than Stella in any case.'

I was torn, as I've always been, between seeking praise from two opposing forces. Your praise required deviation from rule and order – relighting the candle after being put to bed; jumping the full-wire fence. My fingers burrowed into your tight fist and you gripped me suddenly with your nails.

'They love you more than me, Linda,' you hissed.

'No.'

'Yes.'

'I love you best of all.' My hand was stinging as if caught between Zephyr's teeth, but I didn't make a sound. The jaw of your own hand relaxed, releasing mine. And then there was a groan from the kitchen. The only time our mother is loud: when a new sibling arrives.

Nobody set the table that evening. Grannie and Mother disappeared behind our parents' bedroom door. Father permitted you, Mervyn, Norman and me to eat stew from the pot on the kitchen table, with hunks of day-old bread. I dripped gravy on my white collar but it did not matter, for the only people who cared about such things were otherwise engaged.

'Do you think Mother would like some music?' you asked after tea, when we were left to our own devices in the living room & were trying not to listen to the ordeal. Norman, who'd never witnessed it before, was most upset.

'I don't know about Mother, but Norman might enjoy a song. He may like to play with us?'

I sat on the stool next to you, hoisted our small brother onto my lap, & held my hands over the keys, ready to contribute when you nudged my arm. I never learnt to play properly myself & I regret it. Mervyn decided 'The Bluebells of Scotland' needed a percussive accompaniment, so fetched a spoon and *Mrs Beeton's Cookery Book*.

Our father arrived with the doctor during our song. Neither was impressed with the performance.

'Have a heart for your poor mother or I'll switch the lot of you.' Father's eyes were bloodshot & vague, his breath rank with vinegar; he'd been a long time finding the doctor.

So we put our brothers to bed soon after, then clung to each other in our new room. The first night I spent at Stillwater was, I think, one of the only nights you fell asleep before me.

A Lifeless Life

Do you remember you had your way? Despite those florid claims that Grannie loved me better than you, it was you rather than me whom she bundled into the buggy when she left the following week. I stayed to help Mother with our third brother, the new mewling boy they named Hume Talmage.

We'd only been together six nights before they separated us again. I couldn't explore the new run or enjoy our new room (which felt like yours) without you there too. Yet you were thrilled at the prospect of a journey. I had to balance our moods, though I felt like the left stirrup of a loose-girthed saddle – the great boot of your leaving pulling me down at the same time it hoisted you up. I willed the world to slide a foot into the right stirrup and straighten the saddle. I wanted Father to pull the girth tight, to dodge Mischief's nips. As I always have – and still do – I wanted to feel exactly like you.

But it wasn't to be. So I pretended. By seven I'd gained control of my tears. By fourteen I was such an accomplished shapeshifter that I began to forget which bits of my person were true and which devised; perhaps that's a sign of womanhood. *No*, I can hear you protest. *I've always known who I was and have stayed true to those instincts*. Yes, sister – you are exceptional.

When Talmage was grown enough to pull himself around the wooden floors on his rear in hot pursuit of Shadow, you returned to Stillwater at last. I had asked after each of Grannie's letters when we would be reunited and the answer was most often 'not yet'. I'd grown taller than you, but the months that had passed since we'd last met made me shy. You seemed sophisticated after your stay at Talbingo. Had I? I doubt it.

The day you came back, Mother freed me from bringing in the washing – it was a perfect drying day; hot, gentle wind, no smoke and little dust – so that I could greet you & Aunt Lena. You had a new pair of gloves that I liked very much & were in an especially chipper mood. Remember Shadow pawing at us as we embraced? Or was that during another reunion? We've parted and reunited more times than most sisters, I'd wage.

'This is a lifeless life,' you whispered with theatrical ennui when we were supposed to be asleep. I kissed your forehead, as if you were the younger sister – or my daughter – and told you not to be silly. 'Lifeless life' didn't make sense, just as a plotless plot, or characterless character, was nonsensical. How could that be? My silent workings led me to understand what you meant, but you began berating nevertheless, although unusually gently due to drowsiness.

'You wouldn't understand, you're too loving and happy a creature. Give you a dress, a pony and a new pair of gloves, and your life is full.'

These were undeniably good things that you listed; I was only eight, remember. It would've been dishonest to say these weren't treats.

'But you love your new gloves. Aren't you happy?'

'No, child! I'm not. This place is suffocating.'

I turned away from you, facing the wall. The word 'suffocating' was new, but the feeling that I was to blame for your frustration was not. I put my thumb in my mouth & gave two careful, silent sucks (if you'd heard what I was doing, there would've been trouble). The thumb helped my eyes close, & my breath come evenly, slowly. It's tempting to try the trick now. Imagine Charlie returning to find Teddy and me both babies. That's likely what he sees anyway. I may as well remove these gloves, which our younger selves would have thought fearfully elegant, & relax. There's no point in pretence now.

In the morning you'd extracted yourself from that mood, so we swapped back to our usual roles.

'Darling Linda, it's time to rise and shine. We've cows to milk.' I was already awake and making my way out of bed; we'd both heard Father's call. 'How many do you think you'll manage this morning?' you asked.

'Ten?' My hands immediately felt feeble.

You raised your dark eyebrows at me. 'I'll do fifteen then.' Grabbing my elbow with your strong little fingers you said, 'Up, up, up, lazybones.'

'I'm not lazy.' Although it was late summer the floorboards were cold. The wallaby skin was out of my reach, under your feet.

'No, you're *delicate*, aren't you? *I'm* lazy and you're *delicate*. That's what Mother says.'

'I'm neither of those.' I was the one making our bed while you pulled on your stockings & teased.

Milking was not my favourite of our chores because I was obviously worse at it than you. Inside the house, despite being younger, I triumphed. The beds I made had smoother sheets with tighter corners. I was allowed to cook scones on the griddle unattended.

My mending was almost as neat as Mother's, though much slower. And I didn't frighten our younger brothers as you did. But in that shed, which we would walk to together while the day's light still clung – lazily, delicately – to the eastern hills, you reigned.

'Watch your sister, Linda,' Father said, again. 'See the rhythm of her hands – that's good work, Stell.'

'I know, and I'm trying, but I can't.' I lost control of my voice as I'd lost control of my tired hands; both were trembling.

Father ordered me back to the stool. He knelt behind me. 'Try again.'

'I think she's sick – got the blight.' I was trying to save face. 'The milk won't come. Only watery stuff and flakes.'

'Sit, Linda.'

I gripped the teats, hard as I could with my thumb and fore-finger & looser with the rest of my hand, as he'd taught me. I pulled & squeezed, nodding in time to the rhythm I knew he wanted. The milk dribbled rather than squirted. The cow tried to stamp her bound hind hoof, couldn't, so resorted to flicking her tail instead. Father's hands hid mine now. I felt like part of the cow as he squeezed us both, my skin a flimsy layer between him and her. The milk, it seemed, was now jetting straight from my fingertips.

'No trouble with this girl,' Father said, meaning the cow, not me. 'You need to build up strength. The only way is to practise.'

I milked not ten, but one-and-a-half cows that morning. You milked fifteen, just as you said you would. We, & the boys, had fresh milk & porridge dosed with sugar for breakfast before riding to school. I remember it being in the old church hall next to St. Saviours, but perhaps I'm wrong. What I'm certain of is that it was your first day being taught by Mae Gillespie & you resented the fact that I rode in the lead on Mischief, with Mervyn's arms hugging my waist, while you & Zephyr followed. Naturally, that arrangement only lasted until we were out of sight of Mother on the veranda. Once we were on Thornford Road, I heard you click your tongue – you would've cracked the whip if Father had let you carry his – & Zephyr's hoofbeats change from the four falls of walking to the three-beat drum of a canter. As you passed us, Mervyn chuckled at the hand that ruffled his white hair & whacked me on the back of the neck. Mischief shied towards the ditch at the sudden race.

Without Mother to disapprove, I hitched up my skirt & threw my right leg over the pony, to keep her from stumbling and me from slipping. Although it wasn't a long way to the ground, the dry summer had made the turf forgiving as granite. And Mischief, true to her name, had a wilful streak.

'Hold tight, Merv.'

He whooped as I let Mischief chase you & Zeph, now dust & black rump in the distance. Our pony couldn't catch your horse, as you knew. By the time we'd reached the crossroad, you'd chosen the wrong route, but Mischief refused to stop pursuing her paddock mate. I pulled the blowing pony in a circle until she'd slowed to a jog, then called for you to turn back.

'Wrong way, Stella,' Mervyn echoed my yell.

I dropped the reins on the mane, stuck both fingers in my mouth & whistled. The dust cloud cleared. Taking your sweet time now, you walked the horse back to us. Mischief whinnied, relieved.

'School is actually this way.' I took pleasure in the correction.

'Maybe I'm not aiming for school. Perhaps I was going to the station?' Your cheeks were red & powdered with dust.

'Why would you go to the station?'

'Are you leaving us again?' Mervyn asked, with some anticipation.

'She's just being silly.' I reached behind & gave him a squeeze under the ribs.

'I do not care for this Thornford Public School,' you said. 'All these people. It is suffocating.' Did you prefer to be tutored by our sweet Aunt Lena in Talbingo?

'Remember Mr Blythe said it'd be good for you to show off your intelligence.' It stung that he'd not seen me as a fit rival for you.

'Besides, the other people are nice. I've made a friend called Edie Paton.'

'A friend?'

We were walking two abreast now, nearing the school (it must have been at the church, then). I remember the Paton children cantering to meet us – Edie in the lead on fat Porridge. Your morose tune changed when Edie asked, 'Is she your big sister?'

It was obvious in that moment – Edie, Eric & George sizing you up; a small, hard, pale thing with a black plait that brushed the black back of the proper-sized horse on which you sat – that I, whom they seemed to have liked and admired, was fading into dim familiarity. You were novel, bright & would stay that way forever. So I did what I could; I agreed with breathless pride. 'Yes, this is Stella.'

'It's more comfortable if you have a leg on each side,' you said to Edie. 'I can ride both ways, of course.' You threw your right leg over Zephyr's withers, suddenly elegant. I wondered whether I should do the same.

'I don't have to wear a dress,' Mervyn contributed to the conversation.

'Only when I tell you to,' you said, making the Patons laugh. It wasn't a kind thing to say, for Mervyn was just as keen to impress Eric & George as I was Edie. He kicked Mischief's sides behind the numnah. 'We're going to be late for school. We're going to be late.'

'He's right,' Edie said, turning Porridge & kicking him towards what I remember as a woody rosemary bush, & Miss Gillespie with her bell. I was pleased Edie had not heeded your advice; she still had her skirt neatly arranged & both legs on the left side of her pony.

By the end of your first day at school, I understood your complaint of a 'lifeless life'. It seemed that the nearly nine years I'd lived were not really mine, but yours. Edie still sat next to me in class, but you, seated directly in front of her, swishing your plait from side to side as you raised your hand to answer Miss Gillespie's every question, were the main attraction. At lunchtime, Edie offered the Cox's Orange

Pippin she'd picked that morning to you instead of me. You let me have two bites of the apple, & then fed the core to Zephyr.

'I'll bet you've read a lot of books,' Edie said, having already complimented you on the length of your hair, the quality of your gloves & the height of your horse.

'A fair few, but my real passion is music,' you said, lying back in the grass & pulling your bonnet over your pale face.

'Stella can play anything on the piano,' I said, settling for glory by association over no glory at all. 'And she sings beautifully too.'

'I'm learning to play the piano! It must be a sign from heaven that we're destined to be friends.'

Without removing your hat from your face, you started laughing. Edie looked at me, unsure of her mistake. I laid my finger on your skirt, letting a ladybird crawl onto it, & wearing this tiny red jewel, I said solemnly, 'Stella's stopped believing in God.'

Edie blinked.

You emerged from under the bonnet to correct me. 'No, Linda, you've got it wrong. It's not that I don't believe, so much as that I do not like His style. Why should we revere someone who was so cruel to His son?'

Edie frowned for a time. Without considering her action, she picked a stalk of soursob and chewed at it. 'Aren't God and Jesus the same person?' she ventured finally. I admired her courage, crossing you like that. 'Was it not a personal sacrifice?'

You sighed. 'Edie, Edie, Edie, it's a lucky thing that I've come to Thornford, I think.' You didn't elaborate upon the nature of the luck.

Edie was dissatisfied. 'I'm going to ask Miss Gillespie.' She picked herself up, brushed the dried grass from her skirt and left us; we were alone for the first time since leaving our bedroom.

'Miss Gillespie will not agree with you about Jesus and God,' I said in a small voice.

'Do you agree with me, Linda?'

I couldn't gauge the question's sincerity; I wanted to believe that you sought my opinion and were not, as usual, testing my resolve, so I answered carefully. 'No, I do not think so.'

'Why not?'

'Because, because Jesus had to be sacrificed – that is the nature of His existence, to be sacrificed. That's simply how it is.'

Your eyes closed as if I had shamed myself terribly & it was too much for you to witness.

'What, Stella?' I chased you back to the schoolroom. 'What's wrong with that?'

Miss Gillespie was as kind as ever in the afternoon, and complimentary of my reading aloud, but it was you to whom she gave her personal copy of *Jane Eyre*.

'You girls must read it together,' she said hastily, noticing my expression.

'Oh yes, I'll read it to her,' you said, as if I were Mervyn's age, as if I needed you to help me.

Your Career

'I am writing a novel. On no account wake Mother and Father.'

I'd believed you were Bertha come to set fire to my bed, and almost screamed. My next care was for the extravagant use of our candle & the trouble I assumed would follow. Then, at last, the word 'novel' sunk through the waking layers of thought. That burning compound of pride & envy lit me up, sat me up.

'Go back to sleep,' you hissed, but I didn't. I wanted to watch, to keep watch: a silent vigil of my novelist sister. Your hair was loose, I remember; when you sat on its ends you didn't immediately notice. Your pen scratched at an alarming pace over the page of the red-bound notebook Grannie had given you that Christmas. I wanted to ask what you were writing but knew it would be futile. So instead, I imagined your story myself. Eyes shut, and my fingernail scratching on the underside of the bedsheet as if it were pen across paper, I traced a tale about two sisters.

The older sister was bold and wise, the younger beautiful and kind. Their father was an out-of-work drunk – no, an invalid (I felt this was less vulgar) – and their mother had died during the birth of their younger brother. The sisters, Sybil and Isolde (I gave lengthy consideration to their names), took great care of their brother, Rupert, but, but … I knew something must go wrong, yet feared the upset to our doubles' calm lives.

One afternoon, when Isolde was washing the family's clothes (a task I felt confident I could describe accurately, though it occurs to me now that she would not have been washing in the afternoon in winter), Sybil took Rupert for a long walk across the run to find their father, who hadn't come home for lunch.

I'd stopped scratching the words onto the bedsheet by now, for my fingernail could not keep up with my mind. And frankly, what was the point of miming?

The lunch, a good mutton pie made by Isolde's own fair hand, is sitting half eaten on top of the oven. The siblings, one with a long, dark plait and broad-brimmed hat, the other a blond-haired sprite prone to rushing at the cattle like a failed working dog, trudge together across the paddock. Isolde, like the miller's daughter spinning straw into gold for Rumpelstiltskin, turns the pile of dry, dirty shirts, hose, petticoats, singlets and drawers into flat, wet, empty skins hanging clean on the line. When the last sock is pegged, Isolde hears her brother's wail. She takes her bonnet from the hook, ties a bow at her chin, & follows the path her siblings took. Whistling, she summons the dog, Shadow – no, Lightning – to her side; he will be a help if protection is required. The white dog streaks ahead of his mistress, nose to the ground, seeking out her frightened brother.

It was very late by now and you, having blown out the candle at last, returned to the bed and rapidly began a satisfied snore that lasted until morning. I, however, eyes tight shut and body still as a waiting snake's, kept telling my story.

'Where is Sybil?' Isolde asks when she finds her brother sobbing under a willow near the dam.

The dog licks the boy's face, cheering him enough for speech to overcome the crying. 'Syb was taken.'

'Taken?' Isolde kneels next to him and pulls him close to her apron that still smells of pie – reviving.

'Yes, there was a man under this tree with a tall grey horse, at least sixteen hands.' Rupert looks up into the branches. 'He met us as we were passing.' He sniffs. 'I was afraid, but Syb was brave. She asked the man what his business was on our land, and if he knew our father.'

'What did this man look like?'

'Like a jackaroo. Broad, with a red shirt.'

'Did you see his face?'

'No, it was dark under his hat.'

'And how did he sound?'

'Rough and good-tempered.' Rupert is no longer afraid. This man is manageable now that he has been described.

Isolde sits the boy on her lap and looks him sternly in the eye. 'Brother, what became of our sister?'

Rupert says what Isolde fears. 'She went on the horse with the man.'

It is a winter's afternoon that feels ready to freeze over once the sun slides behind the western side of the run. Rupert's hands and cheeks are cold; Isolde can see his breath thicken as he speaks, so she takes him back to the house. There, she lights the fire, feeds the dog, gives the boy a second piece of pie and forbids him from leaving the warm living room. 'I will be back soon, and I will have Sybil and Father too.' Rupert nods, trusting her.

As night fell in my fairy tale, morning broke in our bedroom. Mother noticed my fatigue at breakfast.

'How many did she milk, Father?'

'None. I have her cleaning the teats now instead, until her hands grow a bit.'

'They won't get strong unless she practises,' you said. You'd noticed my weariness too, and it made you scowl & pinch the underside of my arm.

'Why are you so tired, Linda?' Mother asked. Another scowl from you; another threat of a pinch.

'I don't know,' I lied.

'Perhaps you're ailing again. A day at home in bed instead of school, I think.'

'No, I'm quite well.' While I wanted to sleep, I dreaded leaving you & Edie Paton alone together for a whole day; I knew that when I returned to class, my chair beside Edie would be full of you.

'I'm glad you enjoy school, but you're delicate and must take care of yourself.'

You would've rolled your eyes at this. 'She's not delicate, she's a whingeing work-avoider and, as she tells you, actually quite all right.'

'If I say I'm quite all right, then how am I also a whinger?' I asked.

'Is that a whinge? Yes, I believe it is.'

'Out of my kitchen now and off to school. But Linda, put your scarf on.' I remember seeing Mother, her belly distended again, this time with Laurel, lift Talmage up and rest him high on her hip, his plump legs spread wide around her girth, like Edie's around Porridge's.

On the way to school, we rode side by side, a reward for my secrecy.

'You see, Linda, a career isn't something you're born with. A career isn't being female, or beautiful, or having very long hair – actually, perhaps that is a career of sorts.' You stroked your plait. 'A career requires toil, good honest toil. And unlike you, I relish work. I wrote a good bit last night.'

'I wish you'd let me read it.' If I responded to your every needle, I'd not have had time for a word of my own.

'You will, of course, dear Linda. You shall be my first reader.'

'What will she read?' Mervyn asked.

'Nothing, Merv, just keep counting the trees. I want a definite total by the time we're at school.'

It was a fascinating feeling, riding with you that morning through the light, which faded Thornford Road in stripes, and holding not only your secret but also mine. I simultaneously wanted to tell you about my story & to keep it safe; both paths seemed equally satisfying.

'Stell, I ...' I would begin, & then falter. Frequently I wouldn't have to invent a different topic of conversation, as you'd fail to hear my soft voice at all. It occurs to me now how often it is that only I catch my words.

What is a *career*? Something that propels you forward, that makes time move fast, that eats up the path of your life. The dusty trail, as you once called it. Aged nine & eleven we were both careering happily on, oblivious to obstacles. Following your lead out riding, I would aim Mischief at the gate rather than the half-spar, and, a leg securely on each side – sometimes with stirrups, sometimes without – I'd feel the pony move under me at my command. That heady mix of control & abandon resembled what, in you, seemed utter fearlessness. I kept the fear down deep in my gut, under bunches of skirt, while you didn't appear to know any such thing.

'Linda, how many shillings would I have remaining in my purse?'

I was mid-yawn, tears leaking from the corners of my eyes. 'I'm sorry, Miss Gillespie. I don't know.'

'That is because you were not attending, Linda. Are you feeling well? It is unlike you to be so insipid.' Miss Gillespie had paused next to my desk. She was holding her ruler, but not in a threatening manner, yet.

'My sister is delicate, Miss Gillespie. The delicacy interfered with her sleep last night.' You were sitting diagonally in front of me, beyond the reach of my right boot that was now itching to kick you. The class, including traitorous Edie, laughed.

I squinted at the scratchings on the blackboard. 'You'd have three shillings remaining in your purse, Miss Gillespie.' I didn't know what she'd bought to leave that vast sum.

'Good girl.'

For the rest of the arithmetic lesson, until lunch, I stared at the board blankly & let my story unfurl further. I wanted to write it in my primer, but there was the risk that you, or Merv or Mother, or Miss Gillespie would find it. And, then my story would lose the gloss of secrecy. At nearly ten years old, I owned something that didn't have to be shared with anyone – not even you.

Isolde catches and saddles the horse she shares with Sybil, a chestnut mare called Goldie, with a mane the same colour as Isolde's hair. Kicking the horse from walk to canter, she makes for the only road the man and Sybil could have taken. Cold stings her nose and eyes, reminding her of their missing father. She feels that if she finds her sister, then her father will turn up too. Sybil's whip is coiled like a snake in her right hand, the stock thudding against her thigh. If she needs to use it she will, but never at Goldie's expense. The mare, confused by the late hour of the outing, obeys nonetheless, at a gallop now that they've reached flat paddock. Smoke hangs white in a clear night sky and the scent travels far across winter air, so Isolde knows there's a fire long before she sees it. Just as she reaches it, the figures huddled around it notice the drum of hooves on freezing ground, approaching fast.

'Syb!' Isolde calls, seeing her sister, standing now, behind the long plume of smoke. She seems unhurt but is unusually quiet.

'You shouldn't have come, Isolde. Who's minding Rupert?' Her voice is higher than normal.

'Who are you?' Isolde demands, with her sister's sass, of the man who's moved from shadow to firelight and put his arm around Sybil's shoulder.

'He is not your business,' Sybil replies. The man's expression is indecipherable, only briefly illuminated. It is an attractive face that stares at Isolde with unattractive amusement.

'I want you to come home now.' Isolde speaks only to Sybil.

'Give Goldie a rest and warm yourself.'

Goldie's sides are damp and steaming with sweat; finally halted, she will soon begin to shiver. Isolde removes her shawl and drapes it over the mare's flanks, behind the saddle. Now she shivers herself. 'I want to go home.'

'Linda, what's the matter?' Miss Gillespie was standing by my desk again, no ruler this time. You'd turned around in your chair to examine me, not yet sure whether the matter called for teasing or sympathy.

'Nothing. I'm sorry, Miss Gillespie.' The heat of the blush was leaking up my neck & behind my ears; I knew there would be a scarlet rash at my collar.

'Are you sure, child? You were muttering.'

Involuntary muttering. Was there anything more humiliating?

You, loyal sister, understood then which response was called for. You raised your hand and explained to our teacher that I was unwell, that our mother had tried to keep me at home today but I would not stay for I loved school so dearly.

'I see,' Miss Gillespie said. 'It's nearly lunchtime, so may I ask you, Stella, to accompany Linda home. She appears febrile.'

I did feel sick. And would continue to be unwell – defined as an invalid – throughout the rest of my life.

When you led me into the kitchen and presented me as a specimen 'mad with fever and *muttering* in class during an arithmetic lesson!', Mother marched me upstairs and knelt on the wallaby skin next to our bed and tucked me tight, ordering complete repose – no reading, no drawing, no embroidery; just rest. Back where my story had first started only hours before, in the dark of the early morning, I feigned sleep again & continued to narrate. Mother could not confiscate my thoughts, much as she might've liked to.

Disjointed Sketches

The truth is, I didn't know what Sybil was doing with the stranger, sitting by a fire a short ride from home. I didn't know where the girls' ill father had disappeared to & of course had no notion of how these two mysteries related to each other. But none of this uncertainty concerned me. Perhaps I was feverish? The story gained momentum as it grew, pulling me along. Without calculation, just for pleasure, I let it coil like the wool Grannie spun.

Isolde does not recognise Sybil's tone; it is hard and distant. In the past, Syb's voice has been at turns cruel, callous, teasing and condescending, but never so secretive. Why would she lock the meaning of her words away from her only sister?

Isolde speaks to the man now. 'What have you done to Sybil? She sounds odd.'

In answer, he squats and rearranges the smouldering branches on the fire, pushing the unburnt ends into the glowing centre. When his eyes rise to Isolde's, they reflect the flames. His lips stretch into a smile and his wet teeth shine.

'Sybil, come on now. Rupert will be wondering where we are.'

'Don't worry about Rupert. Father should be with him now. They'll be finishing the stew by the fire, oblivious to our absence, mark my words.'

'How do you know about Father?' Isolde gathers her reins and rides Goldie out of the path of the smoke, closer to her sister.

The man stands. 'You've joined us at last.' He reaches for Isolde's stockinged leg, poking out from her bunched-up dress.

'Stay back!' Letting the stockwhip slither from her fist, she flicks her wrist and the warning crack splits the night in two. Goldie shies back from the man and the sound; Isolde's calming palm strokes the mare's neck until the muscles under the chestnut coat relax. 'Don't touch me or my sister again, or I will use the whip on you, sir.'

Should Isolde call him 'sir'? My own wrist flicked under the sheet, imagining gumption I would never have exhibited. Eyes and curtains shut against the afternoon light, I eventually slept, and my story continued beyond my control.

'I have to take one pretty girl,' the man says. Isolde is off Goldie now, and lying close to the fire, which gives off no heat. Sybil's feet are a pillow that makes the back of Isolde's scalp ache.

'Then take me,' Isolde says, voice cold as the air and faint.

Sybil stands, letting Isolde's head hit the turf. She whistles and the mare Goldie trots through the dark to her. 'I'll return for you, Isolde,' she says. 'But now I must help Father and Rupert.' She puts her left boot in the dangling stirrup and starts to jump into the saddle, when the man's voice tugs her back to earth.

'Wait – I haven't chosen which girlie I want yet. And what's more …' He pauses. 'What's more,' in a muffled tone, 'I'm not sure this one wants to come with me.'

'Where would we go?' Isolde asks.

The stranger stares at Sybil as if to say, 'She doesn't even know, poor mite.' Sybil returns her foot from stirrup to earth and says, 'You're right. Isolde, go home this instant, while you may.'

'I won't leave you.' Isolde tries to sit up, but can't.

'Child, one way or another, we must part.' Sybil kneels and kisses her sister's forehead, drags her to her feet, dusts off her skirt and pushes her towards the patient mare. 'Put on your shawl now, and gallop home. Give Goldie a large feed and kiss Rupert from me.'

'I don't understand.'

'What do you not understand?'

There was a beloved face above mine. 'Sybil!'

'Who's Sybil?' You were sitting next to me on the bed with a plate of bread and jam and a cup of tea. 'I've brought you sustenance.'

'I dreamt you were called Sybil.'

You looked impressed – an expression I seldom received from you. 'Linda, that's rather good. I like that. If you've no objection, which I'm sure you don't, I'll steal Sybil for my –' and here she dropped to a conspiratorial whisper – '*novel*.'

'I don't mind,' I said. Drowsy, beginning to feel like an invalid simply from having slept in the middle of the day, I let my eyelids shut again.

'Oh Linda, I know what would cheer you.' You left my plate & cup beside the bed & went to find your red notebook. 'I'll read something special to you.' As you read, you changed the heroine's name to Sybil; only a few Mauds slipped through. Your story, of course, was far superior to my own silly tale. I thought it so sophisticated how you'd managed to sketch London with such detail; the governesses, gruel & chimney sweeps were familiar from *Jane Eyre*. Your Sybil was the ward of a rich gentleman, Lord Dunleve, and at fourteen had two sinister suitors. This, I realised as I listened, was what my story would have been if I'd possessed your imagination and industry rather than just weak fancy.

On creation, Isolde and Sybil (my Sybil, not yours) were substantially, incomprehensibly (how did I know what would come?) older than us. But gradually, as the years passed, we caught up. The nonchalant venture of Isolde into the winter night to save her sister, & Sybil's coquettish encouragement of the strange man's attentions, eventually seemed dull. I, at twelve, had been sent on solo rides to rescue mislaid brothers, and you, at fourteen, were receiving notes of admiration. I remember you reading aloud, with cruel glee, the message in a card signed: 'from a boy you do not know, whose heart beats true for you'. Even Mother smiled, though she scolded you for unkindness. It was Christmas after all, and we were supposed to be exhibiting goodwill.

'Consider the poor boy's feelings,' Mother said before letting you stir the mincemeat. 'It must have taken some pluck to deliver such a – a heartfelt missive.'

'Yes, he must admire you greatly, whoever he is,' I said. 'Do you have an inkling?'

Our fingers, buttery and sweet from pressing shortcrust into the small tins, turned the letter over again & again, looking for clues in the ungainly looping cursive and sombre blue stationery. Another hint came in the form of a pressed flower, which Mother was concerned would be baked into one of the pies if we weren't careful.

'What are they, Mother? I can't tell, they're so squashed.'

'They aren't squashed; someone has pressed them. I believe they are forget-me-nots.'

I burst out laughing. 'Oh, that poor boy.'

You confected outrage, but I knew this hid great pleasure at the compliment. 'What a dodo! How can I forget him not if he's too lily-livered to sign his name? What a sap!'

When Merv and Norman returned from feeding the calves, we put them to work studying the handwriting.

'I've narrowed the suspects down to Bill Baxter, Russell Smith and George Paton,' Mervyn said.

'They aren't criminals,' I said.

'No?' you asked. 'I find the sentimentality *quite* criminal.'

'George is too young,' Norman pointed out. He's only a year older than me and I couldn't write like that.'

'Oh, Lord.' You collapsed your face into your hands and for a moment I thought you were about to cry. 'That means it must be that drip Bill Baxter.'

'Don't be unkind about the Baxter boy,' Mother said. 'And both of you are overlooking a flaw in your deduction.'

'What flaw?'

'The possibility that this admirer could have asked somebody else – a parent, or sibling – to write on his behalf.' Mother wiped her hands on her apron, untied it at the back and went to feed the hens.

We never did solve that 'crime', but fate, or rather a black stallion called Lord Clive, soon led you closer to the Baxters. Sent to the post office to collect our parcels, you'd persuaded Father to let you drive the buggy unattended. Your dramatic account of the morning is all I have to go by, as I was helping Mother with the laundry.

According to yourself, you set a cracking pace in the buggy, taking the corners like a Roman charioteer, & pulling up to a trot only a half-mile short of Thornford so as not to startle any passer-by on foot.

You were tethering the pony when you noticed a distraught beast tied to the post a few yards down. The stallion had taken it into his head to loose himself and was pulling back. Noticing the reins were simply buckled to the post, not knotted securely, & predicting the animal's next move, you tied up Mischief's lead rope quick smart & approached the fractious horse. As you got a hold of his reins, the buckle snapped & the horse careered backwards into the road, dragging you along. 'Steady, sir!' you called, trying to calm the animal by bringing a palm to his shoulder while keeping your feet clear of his freshly shod hooves.

'What are you doing frightening my animal?' A voice & a hand over yours on the reins appeared all at once.

You were briefly silenced by this insolence, but only briefly. 'Your horse would be fifty miles to Goulburn by now, or more likely tangled in a fence, if it weren't for my catching him.' Freed from the animal, you removed a glove & sucked the cut finger. 'You should learn to tie your horse securely,' you added, noting that the young man was of an agreeable build & in possession of surprisingly thick eyelashes.

'I should thank you then.' He held out a hand. 'Jim Baxter.'

'Stella Franklin.' You wished you'd not been sucking your finger, but held out the moist right hand nonetheless. He took it, unfazed, & examined the small injury.

'Lord Clive,' he said, still holding your hand but addressing the horse now, 'you brute, look what you've done. You've wounded our new friend Stella.'

'And then,' you said, having spoken of little else all evening, 'he returned to the post office and assisted me with loading our parcels into the buggy. And then —'

'Then he rode with you all the way back to the gates of Stillwater.'

'So as to ascertain my usual habitat! And do you know what he said before he left?'

'He said he'd return and take you for a ride on Lord Clive at your convenience.'

You looked injured by my tone. 'But, honestly, have you heard a better story lately? What a dream! Jim Baxter. Nothing like his baby brother.'

'It was a good story the first time ...'

So, the year that women got the vote in New Zealand was the year of your first admirers and crushes. The year that you famously called across the school pony paddock to Russell Smith, 'You may send your love to my father, who will bottle it and give it to the Goulburn Science Museum!' The year Miss Gillespie called you a little shrew, and the year our poor darling sister was born. It was the year I stopped writing my story about Isolde. I think, from this calm distance (as the train hurtles on towards Dalveen and wee Ted eats an apple on my knee), it was the last year we were true conspirators, rather than rivals. Perhaps it's simply the fate of people whose adolescent girlhoods coincide under the same roof to loathe each other for a time, or perhaps it's just that we were cut from very different materials. My muted off-white muslin, starchy from helping Mother with a multitude of chores, unable to hang in the same wardrobe as your showy black velvet, or the cracked black leather of the stockwhip Father gave you for your fourteenth birthday, which Mother deemed an unseemly present for a girl. Sister, I miss when we were twelve and fourteen.

Revolt

Your fifteenth year began with a fight – started as it meant to go on, you might say.

'Ida.' You only used my given name when intimacy was absent. 'You swear to being with the hare, but really you run with the hound, do you not?'

The hound was Mother. 'I will not talk to you when you are in such a mood.' I resolved not to answer to 'Ida' in future.

'Then leave me be!'

I wanted to remind you that this was my room too, but timidity intruded, as usual. I grabbed my hat & shawl and made for the plum tree at the bottom of the orchard, which I saw as my territory. I cried on the hot, jammy grass because I knew you were right. I agreed with and wanted to be the hare, who, in your exquisite confirmation gown that morning, had declared to the whole family that God was not worth following until he made a world in which it was recognised that women suffer the cold on winter mornings before the fires are lit every bit as much as men. Yet it was safer & easier for me to follow the scent of the hounds – who apart from Mother were Father, Grannie, Aunt Lena, even Miss Gillespie, even the Queen! There were certain ways one had to behave to keep the peace and I, as you said with a sneer, was a 'peacemaker'.

What's wrong with peace?

Your punishment for the morning's declaration was finely judged. You accused our mother of not knowing you, but really, in this she read your desires well.

'No piano.'

At this you had replied, 'We'll see about that.' You turned on the heel of your pearly confirmation slipper (which I inherited the next year) and strode to our room.

'I'm serious, Stella. No piano.' Mother stood in the hallway, hands on hips.

'Preposterous!' you bellowed. 'Have you forgotten my Trinity exam in three months? What a waste of money that will be if I haven't practised.'

'You can be withdrawn from the exam. It is easily done.'

I had trailed you halfway down the hall, between your nemesis outside her bedroom door and you outside ours: a perilous position. Unable to step forward towards you or back to Mother, I stood staring at the daguerrotype of Grannie on the wall. In the dim light it occurred to me for the first time that she may once have been like you. I had teased that you would grow up to be her – a short, round woman, yards of fine hair pinned tight to her skull and covered with a yellowing lace cap. But it suddenly seemed possible that these women who made us, carved us into acceptable shapes with instruments of punishment & praise, may have once been screaming, froward girls themselves.

'I hate you, witch! You're ruining my life, wasting my potential!' Our bedroom door slammed. I looked back at Mother.

'Oh, Linda. Yes, go to her – see if she'll let you in.'

I tapped on our door, knuckles a chick's beak, & whispered, 'It's only me.' I was admitted and covered in your tears and wrath. I tried to stroke your sobbing back. 'There, there.'

'Dear simple sister,' you recovered enough to say. 'Don't become one of those narrow-minded harridans.'

'I do think it was unfair of Mother to forbid your playing.' But, I thought, but you shouldn't call her a harridan.

You brightened faintly. 'Linda, you're such a pet that she might listen to your side. You will go and tell her what you just told me. Persuade her she's been wrong.' Your piano-playing, whip-cracking, cow-milking grip insistent around my wrists, pleading.

I agreed that I'd try. With the exhaustion that comes only from a fight with one's mother, you flopped onto your bed to wait for good news.

Mother was now in the kitchen, preparing what had been intended as a celebratory dinner. Laurel was growling at the cockatoos, and at intervals eating a raw bean. The argument had marked Mother in a subtler way.

'Why are you loitering there, Linda?'

'I want to talk to you about Stella.'

'Very well. Top and tail these beans while you talk, please.'

Deft with years of practice, I snapped each end of the beans that the boys had been charged with picking before we left for church. They'd done a good job, a large pudding bowlful.

'Go on, then.'

I threw the juicy green ends into the chicken-feed bin. 'It seems a little unfair that Stella be forbidden to sit her exam.' Blood thudded in my temples & heated the skin of my neck.

'Oh yes? Why is that?' She continued to stuff the chicken.

Why? Because she wanted it so much – the piano wasn't just a hobby, it was a new career path in Stella's mind, and the withdrawal of this privilege was hurting her. Would this seem reasonable to Mother? I tried out my rationale.

'Linda, you do understand why Stella is being punished? That what she did was sinful?'

'Yes.' Top, tail, ends in bin, next bean; top tail, ends in bin, next bean.

'If Stella doesn't start facing the consequences of her misdemeanours, she will turn into a very wayward woman indeed. More so than she is now.'

'I agree that punishment is necessary,' said the hound. 'But depriving her of the exam seems too severe,' said the hare. 'Perhaps,' said the hound in hare's clothing, 'she could be forbidden from playing the piano at home and allowed to practise at church.'

'Using the organ, at St. Saviours?' Mother raised an eyebrow. 'Honestly, after today's performance?'

I was halfway through my beans and badly wishing to leave the kitchen. Then an idea alighted as if from heaven. 'The first is only a theoretical exam, isn't it?'

'I believe so.' Mother consulted *Mrs Beeton's* then stuffed more bread & sage into the bird.

'In that case, Stella doesn't need to play the piano to study for the exam. Let her sit the exam, Mother dear!'

Was there a small smile on her tired face? An acknowledgement that I'd argued well? 'Thank you for helping with the beans, Linda. You may go to your sister and explain the new terms of her penance.'

My satisfaction was squashed immediately on sharing the news with you.

'Hound!' you yelled. 'Get out, hound! Go and catch some defenceless, noble creature and tear its head off. You're all ruining my life!'

'But you still get to sit the exam.' It was feeble consolation to you, who at that time desired little more than three hours after tea every evening to practise your scales.

And so I found myself under the plum tree, crying for you and against you, for and against myself. It was an unsettling experience, lying back with tree roots for a martyr's pillow and sun-soaked plum leaves in my eyes, wondering for the first but certainly not last time who I was – whether I was good or evil. Was the real me the one who sided with you or the Linda who reasoned with Mother? Shifting & rippling like the surface of the dams in a storm, I lost hold of myself.

It was the beginning of a fever that never quite left me. The boys were somehow more resilient. Sad little sacks of rash & heat while ill, they returned abruptly to their regular boisterous shape apparently at will within a fortnight. Two weeks doesn't seem a long time when, say, one is at Talbingo and enjoying evening parties with Aunt Lena and Grannie's guests & anticipating an impending return trip to Thornford. It isn't even an especially long time when febrile dreams blend one's days & nights into a mass of fantasies. However, I imagine it must be an age when for fourteen days you're charged with caring for six ill family members, not to mention a farm of cows & chickens, unassisted. This, sister, was your rough lot. It seems, in your ability to repel the measles germ, you were indeed less delicate than I. Had you been just as susceptible, your irritation at us all may have lingered, fanned by gusts of fever. Instead, the gravity of the situation turned you into a competent nurse.

To avoid contagion, you made yourself a bed on the sofa beside the living-room fire. When our parents' bell was rung during the night, or a cry slipped under our brothers' bedroom door, you would rise without pause and go to the source of the sound, ready to provide water, fresh laundry, or a steady arm as the invalid tottered to the lavatory. By the time Henry the cockerel had started his dawn solo, you were in your boots and coat, trudging down to milk the cows. I gathered our Uncle George sent one of his and Aunt Margaret's boys from Oakvale to help eventually, but two mornings at least you were responsible for a solid two hours' work with the animals. It must have been a respite of sorts from camphor, calamine & steam. An efficient nurse you were, but never solicitous.

On about the fourth morning of my sickness, I recall realising your position of helpless servitude and feeling guilty for not assisting. Without bothering to dress or find slippers or dressing gown, I made my way to the kitchen, holding doorframes and furniture as I went, weakened by the long rest. I found you scowling at the oven, a lump of wet brown dough on the table behind you & your hands sticky with the same substance.

'What are you making?' I asked.

'Lord, Linda, I thought you were a ghost.' The hand you'd brought to your mouth to cover a gasp left flour on your cheek. 'Look at you; so ghastly. But the rash is fading – that's something.'

'Is it bread?'

'It is supposed to be loaves of bread,' you said. 'I dislike this stove.'

More versed in the oven's temperament than you, I wanted to offer suggestions, but even in my compromised state of health I understood that nothing I said would be taken with gratitude. So I stood watching until my legs felt weak, then I perched on a kitchen stool. At length you asked, 'Well, how do I know if it's hot enough? Or too hot? Confounding apparatus!'

I approached the oven and peered into the door you were holding open. 'I'd put two loaves on the top shelf and two on the bottom,' I said, 'and rotate them every quarter-hour until they seem cooked. And add a dish of water.' In truth, I wasn't sure either; the inside of the oven was Mother's business. Father and I, and occasionally you, were permitted to use the stovetop for boiling, toasting, and scone-making with the griddle pan.

Astonishing me, you took my advice without argument, washed your bready hands & escorted me back to bed.

'You're still not well,' you said, holding the back of your palm against my forehead in the way Mother did. It struck me then how large a part of the task of mothering is interpreting and gauging temperatures so that plants, animals, bread, children and husbands thrive. At that moment you were cool but not cold, calm but not quite kind. This lack of heat made you almost unrecognisable.

Steely, quiet Stella remained, even once the rest of the house had returned to its usual duties and appearances. Having noticed your eccentric evening occupation of sitting at the desk in our room and running your fingers across its edge as if it were piano keys, Mother invited you to play on the real instrument.

'Stella, it's so long since we've had a song in the house and Laurel adores it when you play. Would you entertain us after tea?'

Your fingers finished the imaginary bar before you looked up.

'No thank you, Mother. I have become accustomed to practising at my desk, which will serve adequately until my exam.'

'So stubborn,' Mother complained when she was back in the kitchen, where the rest of the family were having an evening milk or tea around the table. 'I don't know what to do with her.'

'Do with her?' Father asked. 'Nought needs to be done with her. Stella will always do for herself, I feel. That's why I'll not worry about her.'

'That is precisely why I *will* worry,' Mother replied. 'She needs to learn to compromise and to forgive – how on earth will she survive a marriage without such qualities?'

Father reached across the table, picked up Mother's hand and gave it a quick kiss, to our brothers' alarm. We were not accustomed to seeing affection displayed between our parents.

'There's no need to look so concerned, Linda,' Mother said, barely acknowledging Father's gesture. 'You are not like your sister. You will endure marriage beautifully.'

'Will I endure marriage?' Mervyn asked. 'Beautifully?'

Father laughed, and Mother called Mervyn a silly sausage. Why? I wondered. Why was it so silly a question to ask? Because, the hare in me answered, because, silly sausage, for men marriage is not a state of endurance. If it were, they would not sign up for it.

I excused myself and went to our room, wanting to share with you my epiphany, of which I felt sure you'd approve. But when I found you scribbling at great pace in your notebook, I knew it best not to disturb you with my ideas. It turned out that I was right to let you study in peace; the next month you sat your piano theory exam & achieved ninety-five per cent. Miss Gillespie referred to you as Thornford's virtuoso.

A Rose Without Its Thorns

I never healed from the measles. The following year was like a small, tightly folded map, my movements never venturing far from the grid of Stillwater's hallways & gardens. I didn't even attend school, in large part due to our boarder, Miss Gillespie. It was the Franklins' turn to host the teacher in Thornford, so she took the room in which Grannie usually slept when she visited. Monday to Friday our instructress belonged to us entirely; only on Saturday and Sunday was she free to escape to her own home in Goulburn.

Sensitive to how demanding we could be, Mother established on the evening before our visitor's arrival that we mustn't intrude on Miss Gillespie's personal time or area; after school hours, she would be our guest, not our teacher. However, it was Mother herself who flouted this rule. Concerned that my fever would return, but anxious that my education at least appear to continue, Mother arranged for Miss Gillespie to assign me tasks to complete at home each day, and in the afternoons to 'very briefly' correct my work and answer my questions.

'Only if it is convenient to you,' Mother said. She had broached the idea while showing Miss Gillespie her freshly made-up room, a jar of sweet peas on the chiffonier; you and I had left our bedroom door open and listened to the quiet but firm words travel across the floorboards.

'But of course, Susannah. It is the least I can do.'

We knew our teacher's voice better than our mother did; we were accustomed to its different tones – irritation, disappointment, glee. Miss Gillespie's response was superficially calm yet lacked warmth.

'You're going to have a governess,' you teased.

'Don't let her hear that,' I whispered. 'She'll escape in the night.'

'Not to worry. If she does a runner, I shall teach you myself. It's no trouble.'

I didn't know whether I wanted to learn from you or not; or, rather, I doubted whether I could. Learning from you, I assumed, meant emulating you, turning myself into you, and I was past the days of mimicking your phrases, intonation, gait & habits.

If you were the loud one who argued with our mother, I was the demure and agreeable girl. If you scored ninety-five per cent in your piano theory exam, I shrugged amiably; in the place of talent, I cultivated humility. If you rose after dark, relit the candle & wrote your novel until three, I'd roll over and squeeze my mind shut & determine never to try to write more than a letter.

What did I have instead of stories? Beauty, praise, ailments & sympathy; these were sufficiently consoling when I was fourteen. In contrast, you were a stout young woman of robust health, with a round, rather oily face & obstreperous nature. However, in Miss Gillespie we had a buffer. The teacher was sweet-tempered & docile, attractive to look at & listen to, yet in her lessons there rose an eccentric ambition, a set of rigid opinions for which she alone was responsible. Of course, opinions don't flourish without sustenance; Miss Gillespie's were fed not by local gossip or family mores, but by a carefully selected diet of books & periodicals. It was in Miss Gillespie's reflection that we were able to reconcile our seemingly irreconcilable symmetry; that is, our intimate opposition.

'Linda, you are not as ordinary and sickly as you're told,' she said one afternoon when her returning my homework had turned into an impromptu lesson. We were sitting on her bed with a copy of Christina Rossetti's *Goblin Market* between us on the coverlet's faded roses. 'And nor is Stella as outrageous as the world deems her to be.' This sermon followed my response to the question of which sister I believed myself most like in *Goblin Market*, the ailing Laura or Lizzie. The question & the text in question were particular to our private lessons; neither would've been appropriate in the school.

'If you had a sister like Lizzie, what would she bring to make you well?' Miss Gillespie asked.

Did you mind when I mentioned that we were reading Christina Rossetti's illicit poem? If so, you pretended not to care, revealing your disappointment only in an implausible lack of interest. It hadn't been chosen for you, so you ignored it. Why, I wonder now, did Mae Gillespie deem it suitable for me?

If I did have a Lizzie, what would she bring to make me well? I'm struggling to recall how I answered. I will try to give my answer now, gazing up at blurred constellations out the window, with *My Brilliant Career* on my lap instead of *Goblin Market* and my child sitting wedged between my hip and the train's side. Charlie is fast asleep, so I've opened the blind. Teddy should be sleeping too, I tell him, but I'm setting a poor example. I close my eyes and yawn theatrically. *Night, night, Ted.* The boy grins and murmurs and snuggles against my thin frame, so I set your novel on the seat beside me and replace it with my child; I hold him close and soon his eyes shut.

If I had a Lizzie, she would bring back Isolde and Sybil. She would give me a little of the story to sustain me, not so much that I refuse to sleep and begin muttering during arithmetic. This wise older sister would show me how to be at once in the world & out of it, above it, observing. Laura was never the same after her rendezvous with the goblins, but it occurs to me now that perhaps she was better.

Do you remember what Miss Gillespie taught us both during her stay at Stillwater? Of course you must remember – you took to the game of draughts swifter than any of us and seemed almost your old self again when you played, not the martyred artist forced into servitude, waiting upon her ailing family.

Mother seldom had time to play, so never had the opportunity to learn a strategy, but I, often bedridden as I was, got in plenty of practice and became a crafty opponent for you. I was never quite devious enough, but our games were more even than those you played against Father, who was a surprisingly enthusiastic contestant in the evenings. The discomfort this enthusiasm appeared to cause Miss Gillespie, I later understood, had to do with the real source of Father's enjoyment, which was also responsible for his bloodshot gaze. Of course, it was easy for us to beat him when he was drunk.

That year – the Year of Miss Gillespie (though she did not stay the full year, more's the pity) and the Separator, as I remember it – resulted in a deterioration of his faculties. Drinking was the toasting of a new chance at success; our father had ordered a milk & cream separator, an American model. 'Turn the smallholding around' was the phrase bandied about, for we could supply a new product without employing any extra staff or breaking our backs.

Mervyn and Norman liked the sound of the separator, for they enjoyed contraptions, and Talmage & Laurel – still greedy dumplings – were delighted by the notion of plentiful home-churned cream & butter. But, perhaps influenced by the quiet scepticism of our mother, mirrored faintly in Miss Gillespie, you and I were not easily impressed. We knew the machine had cost a pretty penny and that our family no longer had pretty pennies; this inconsistency appeared to be shortening our mother's temper. That was, in hindsight, likely why she didn't indulge in draughts. To enjoy a game, one needs to feel a certain freedom from reality. Perhaps that's why you excelled? I know you adore the actual and should really have been a journalist, but what I mean is that you're fanciful in the way a novelist must be. In the way I'm not but would like to be. This, I see now, is what I would have wanted Lizzie to bring me if I were an ailing Laura: a draught of fancy.

Stillwater Left Behind

My memory skims like a stone, hitting the surface of what happened at its worst moments and gliding above the months that must've been tolerable. When one's father stops talking to one's family, when bailiffs threaten to hold an auction in one's yard and sell off not just the separator, but furniture as mundanely familiar as one's mother, along with the farm itself, and when one's sister is whisked away from the tumult to spend the year with one's beloved grandmother, a lack of fancy is an advantage.

I could've railed against Father with all your gusto, I could've thrown the milk pail back at him when he hurled it at the two of us & called him a drunken incompetent, as you did – then I might've been sent to Talbingo too. But instead I gripped your arm & shook my head. No. No, we must behave well. For Mother, for Uncle George, even for our disappointing father. So, to quieten the house & prevent a scene at the auction, Grannie's carriage arrived for you. I stroked her horses' noses as you threw your bag in shortly before yourself; despite the premature anger at the prospect of Mother & me forgetting to write to you, you left in high spirits, barely looking back at the farm our family was losing.

On the morning of the auction, Mother had planned to take us for a picnic under the blue gums next to the lower corner dam. As I took my place next to her at the kitchen table and began slicing and buttering bread, I noticed she'd dressed carefully, her hair in neat waves as if for a photograph. I wanted to ask her if I should change my dress, but didn't know what tone the question would come out in. So, without any words but the ceaseless prattle of four-year-old Laurel, who was permitted to arrange pickled cucumber on the sandwich bread, we made our lunch.

'Lovely weather for it,' I finally said, having run out of loaf to work with.

Mother's back was to me as she took a batch of scones from the oven. When she turned, her spectacles were steaming, so I couldn't tell if there were tears in her eyes.

'Fetch the boys, please,' she said, when there was no more kitchen labour to be done. I wondered, but knew better than to ask, whether our father would be invited to join the picnic.

Merv & Norman were hauling out the saddlery, which they'd been instructed to clean yesterday.

'Mother says it's lunchtime,' I said. 'Where's Tal?'

Merv waved at Mischief's yard. They seemed ashamed. I'd hoped to avoid the horses, especially the elderly pony that had carried us to and from school. I was afraid I'd resort to what Tal was doing.

His face was so stuck against the stout chestnut neck that his sobs were inaudible, evident only by the jerks of his back.

'Tally, it's picnic time.'

He wiped his face before turning, but still had a beard of chestnut hairs on his damp cheeks.

'Poor, Mischief – you've left a wet patch on her neck, see?'

Tal stroked the tear marks and patted the mare bravely, as if they'd just finished a long ride together.

'Ready to come inside?'

He nodded. I put my arm around him once he was out of the yard and wished he were the pony, wished fervently for a moment that I'd said goodbye too.

Tal had just about composed himself when we reached the veranda. Uncle George was hugging Mother. He grinned at us over her shoulder & waved a piece of paper, before letting our mother go.

'Is it good news?' I asked, turning over the many conversations I'd eavesdropped upon during the previous nights. Bitter whispers of argument and optimism. Our Uncle had the monopoly on the latter; the phrase I'd heard repeated was 'certificate of release'. 'Is it a certificate of release?'

Mother glanced at me vaguely, somewhere between admiration and censure. 'How do you know about that?'

'I overheard Uncle George mention it.'

'Well, then, yes – that's exactly what it is. Do you know what it means?'

I didn't know, but I did hope. 'Are we released from the auction?'

'We are, Linda. We are.' Behind her spectacles, Mother's eyes shone again. She approached slowly and did something she'd not done in several years – embraced me.

'Tal, did you hear? Mischief won't be auctioned.'

He just nodded, seeming not to trust himself to speak.

'Do we put the tack away now?' Norman asked. 'It's beautifully clean.'

'Wait.' Our uncle raised his calloused palms. 'There won't be an auction today, which is indeed good news, but there will be changes.'

'What changes?' I asked, before Mother scolded me for interrupting.

'Let's go on that picnic, and Uncle can explain the situation thoroughly,' she said.

None of us enquired as to Father's whereabouts – not even Laurel, who didn't know enough to blame him in the way we older children did. We simply lay back on the blankets and enjoyed a decadent lunch of fresh-bread sandwiches, thick slices of egg pie, and scones with butter & blackberry jam. When Laurel and Tal wandered down to play at the edge of the dam, our mother and uncle explained to the older boys & me how life would be different henceforth.

'You'll be allowed to stay in the house, of course,' Uncle George began, not a promising opening as far as I was concerned. 'And from the vegetable garden to the driveway and front gate will still belong to you. But all the land beyond – the farm itself – will belong to the bank. I've taken over the lease and will make sure you're well kept.'

I looked at Mother to guide my own reaction. She brushed a fly off her finger-waved hair and replaced the jam jar in the hamper.

'Why,' I began, recognising your own tone in my voice, 'why does Father not take over the farm's lease?'

Mother gave me her look that usually accompanied 'Really, Stella.'

'Your father is seeking employment elsewhere at present,' Uncle George said carefully. A scone crumb fell from his beard as he scratched his chin. 'I think the Baxters need a man to do their fences. It's convenient, as he wouldn't have to travel far.'

I looked to Mother again. She was staring at the picnic blanket and shaking her head, as if denying the plates and knives something they'd demanded.

'It's a good thing Stella's gone to Talbingo,' I said quietly. 'She wouldn't be coping with these changes with equanimity.'

Uncle George laughed. 'No, indeed. You're a sensible creature, though, aren't you, Linda? We don't have to worry about you flying off the handle.'

Was I close to flying anywhere, in any direction? I assessed my state and found it difficult to read. I was quiet, dependable, strong but never wilful. I seemed to also have adopted even the physical appearance expected of me – slim, willowy, fair, clean. Within these acceptable edges, what did I find? A stark tidiness; nothing recognisable or comfortable – no belongings of my own at all. I couldn't believe that after fourteen years alive I'd be so empty. The most personal parts of myself – silent desires, resentments, fears & needs – had been folded up tightly and boxed away. Ready to auction off? Surely, without weighty possessions, there would be a degree of floating off the handle, if not flying off. I was not a skittish girl, so assumed that somewhere inside there must be some substance keeping me in place.

Mother rolled the stones off each corner of the picnic blanket & stood to shake the grass from it. As she did, a gust of warm wind picked up the blanket and wriggled underneath it, sending dead grass flying and the tartan rippling against the burnt sky. A dreadful thought occurred: external forces were weighing me down like stones, keeping my acceptable edges smooth & straight, while Stella was bulging with air, held only by Mother's strong fingers. No one would sit on her to eat luncheon, or spill jam on her fringing.

'Help me with folding,' Mother instructed, so I grabbed the two loose corners and felt strangely traitorous as together we halved, quartered & then rolled the blanket up tight.

'Just think,' Mother said with some levity as we began walking back to the house. 'They would've been sending up clouds of dust down there,' she pointed to the Thornford Road, 'galloping to get a bargain and a nosy at our expense.'

'Who's they?' Mervyn asked, alarmed.

'Oh, everyone in Thornford, I assume. The Baxters, the Grahams,' Norman said, sounding just like Mother.

'Wouldn't it have been just awful if another boy had started riding Mischief to school?' Tal said.

Mother caught his shoulder and halted him for a moment. 'Talmage, while it's very good news that we'll be staying in our house, we'll no longer have the farm. We will have to consider the matter of the horses seriously.'

Our little brother scowled and jerked his shoulder from her grasp. He ran the rest of the way to the house, so fast Shadow thought it was a game and set off in pursuit.

'No easy way to do it,' Uncle George said to no one in particular.

'It would be easier for him if his pony had died,' Mother said. 'He's right; another child may well be riding Mischief to school, and that will humiliate him as much as becoming a day labourer will humiliate John.'

Hearing her refer to our father by his name revealed a piece of Mother I hadn't previously considered. She was talking to our uncle, of course, not to me, but I was walking alongside her, with the adults, while the boys raced ahead and Laurel slept on Uncle George's back.

I ventured a suggestion. 'Would it be at all feasible to send the horses to Talbingo? Grannie could use them, perhaps? And it would save the boys some shame.'

Mother nodded. 'It's not a silly thought, Linda. I'll speak to Mother.'

At home, we found the tack packed away, the bobby calves fed, the cows milked. Father was drying his hands as he greeted us. At his voice Laurel woke and slithered off Uncle's back. Our father hoisted her up and kissed her forehead – affection none of us had received from him in weeks.

'Thank you, George,' he said, and in a strangely formal gesture held out his free hand to shake his eldest brother's.

'Happy to help.'

'Linda, will you take your sister. She needs to use the lavatory,' Mother said.

With some difficulty I extracted the reluctant Laurel from Father and left the adults to talk. A recent initiate, I realised when I was no longer welcome.

Once Laurel was helped, I went to the living room and opened the French doors, hoping the voices would travel around the veranda. I expected to hear Mother's scolding whisper and Father's deep, vague explanations, but not even phrases or single words were audible; instead, the only voice that reached me was Uncle George's. To my surprise he was laughing.

'Can we play the kitten game now?' Laurel asked, pawing at my sleeve. I would rather have pretended to read the gazette and continue eavesdropping, but my little sister had on her imploring eyes. I could see she was making a concession, asking me – an almost grown-up – to join her game. She would've preferred Talmage, but the boys had made themselves scarce & left her behind again.

'Will you be the mother cat or the kitten?' I asked, knowing her answer already.

'Kitten,' she said.

'All right, then.' I got down on all fours and started prowling about the living room. 'Follow me, baby cat.'

'Not with words,' she whispered, disappointed. 'Miaow!'

I tried not to laugh, for I knew that mother cats didn't do such a thing. 'Miaow,' I replied, butting my head into her shoulder gently as if to say, Stay in line, kitten, and everything will be all right.

Mother's Recipe

Benevolent Soup began as a joke at our own expense, but soon it was a staple, served every week from April to September. The soup came about after I found Mother crouched inside the chicken coop stroking our oldest hen, Eunice. It was an unfamiliar position to find her in. I watched from the vegetable patch for a few moments before gathering the courage to approach.

'There are no eggs again,' she explained when I asked if Eunice was well. I wanted to ask when you would come home from Talbingo but feared it would seem impertinent. Or I feared the answer would be that you would never return. It seemed that Grannie was alternately adopting one then the other of us, to prevent us from ever living more than a few months together at a stretch. I wanted Mother to tell me you'd be home soon, but instead I asked about the hens.

'Do we need new pullets?'

She shook her head. 'I've been too profligate in the past; you children have developed a taste for fried breakfasts.'

'The new diet is fine,' I said. 'We like porridge and soup.' I tried to sound bright. 'We won't have to eat Eunice yet.'

Mother stared at me as if I had the axe in hand. Maybe she didn't expect such wryness from me. Perhaps we have, at intervals, been shocking each other ever since that moment.

'Who said a word about slaughtering our hens?'

'I only thought because she's in your lap that —'

'Her end is nigh?'

'Yes.'

'No, there's a beef cheek for supper this evening. Eunice is safe. I was just attempting to coax an egg out of her.'

I could never predict Mother's reactions. I couldn't tell whether the stress of our straitened circumstances had softened her mind or if she was joking now too. A small smile seemed the safest response.

As usual, Mrs Beeton told us how the beef cheek might be persuaded to feed seven people. When I showed Mother the recipe titled 'A Useful Soup for Benevolent Purposes' she was scornful.

'Benevolent?'

'Yes, for serving out charitably to those who need it.' I refrained from saying 'the poor'.

'We will be eating it ourselves.'

And we are now poor, I thought. 'There's celery, carrots and turnips in the garden. That's why the recipe caught my eye.'

It was my job, later, to ladle the portions into bowls and distribute them to our family, the smallest for Laurel and the largest for Father. My own bowl I filled last. Generosity was becoming a habit, I thought to myself as I swirled the ladle through the broth and found it hit very few solid items; the chunks of beef and vegetable had been doled out, leaving a thin substance of stock and pearl barley with the odd floating bone: my share.

Joining the table, I lowered my head but didn't close my eyes at the saying of grace; I wanted to check that Mother was not scrutinising the portion sizes.

'Bread, Linda,' she offered, after the prayer. I hadn't asked for it.

'Thank you.' I accepted a half-slice and gradually, during the dinner, let its airy white interior fill with broth. Slowly, deliberately, I chewed the crusts. I do not remember the taste of Benevolent Soup, only the smell of boiled cartilage, & that this odour seemed to emanate from every savoury meal thereafter. Even now, from time to time, I still smell it when I try to eat.

We were heartened to hear that you were feeding well at Talbingo. I remember reading aloud to the family excerpts from one of your rare letters, in the evening after the first Benevolent Soup, I think – but, really, it could've been any evening that dreary, dry autumn. They clump together like a sod of earth, those days after I finished my schooling and stayed at home with Mother. You requested me to write more frequently – cheek, considering I sent a message weekly, faithfully, and received only a few in return – and sent your love to all. You described in succulent detail the Granny Smith cobbler and clotted cream served for afters by a real maid called Mary. You yarned, as you do, with lengthy vigour & few pauses, telling us all about Aunt Lena's puppies, the quality of the piano, the vivid red of the rhododendrons in Grannie's garden.

'"And, that is that, except for all my love to Father, Mother, boys and little Laurel, God bless & goodnight. Yours in exile, Stella."'

Mother's eyes rolled at your sign-off. I folded the letter, returned it to its envelope, & slid it into my apron pocket. When the oil lamps were extinguished, the fire shrunk to glowing coals, I assisted Laurel with her toothbrushing and then excused myself.

In our room, which was now just mine, I felt more inclined to kneel beside the bed and pray; you'd have scorned me if I'd behaved as such in front of you, so I took advantage of your absence to be pious. After thanking our Lord for keeping our family in soup & bread for another evening, & for sending news from our dear, entertaining sister (The postman is to thank for that, not God, I can hear you say), I settled in bed & unfolded your letter again.

> Linda, you have strayed into private territory now, so if you are reading this missive to the whole family, I would ask you to skip to my gracious sign-off and keep the next paragraphs between the two of us.
>
> It will not surprise you that I was responsible for picking the Granny Smiths that went into Mary's cobbler. The best of the fruit – is it not always so? – was in the uppermost bowers, so I was forced to tuck my skirts into my knickers and scurry up the tree like a koala bear. Those old brown lace-ups performed admirably as hind claws. Once I had both feet on the bottom branch and a hand on the next, it was a simple matter, like climbing a ladder. It was only when I reached the fruits themselves that I – poor fool – realised my predicament. If I filled my apron, which was my intention, I would have to descend the tree one-handed. Unless, I thought, unless there is some hope of fashioning a sort of bag, by knotting the apron up. As I chose the ripest specimens and considered my options, a rather luscious tenor voice called up at me and said, 'Hello, my beauty, are you new here? I don't recognise that long plait.'
>
> I can tell you, the long plait twitched at the presumptuousness of such a remark. I turned more swiftly than I ought to have and

a cascade of my best pickings plummeted from my apron, bruising their sunny green skin against the tree trunk before bouncing on the turf around the man's boots.

'No need for an assault,' he protested with great joviality, realising the precarity of my situation and the safeness of his own. 'I say, do you need some assistance? Shall I fetch you a ladder? Or I could catch you if you jump – you do seem a featherweight sort of creature.'

It was that laddish smirk that let me finally place the face. Everything about it had grown – the neck, the ears, the beard, the voice – but something in the eyes resembled our old friend Charles Graham. He evidently did not recognise me, disguised as I was among the apple bowers. I decided to give him a fright.

'No, Charlie Graham, I require none of your assistance. But I would thank you to leave me in solitude to harvest this tree. I shall descend in my own good time.'

Well, that was a fine joke. You should have seen his sunburnt skin lose its colour and the smirk collapse. He'd clearly taken me for a servant girl, not the lady of the house (don't tell Grannie I referred to myself as such). What a good wheeze it would have been had I played along and pretended to be Mary. If the opportunity ever arises again, I shall. Instead, there was much hasty rein-backing on his part – like Mischief when you try to make her ford the stream. Many *Oh, dear, Stella*s and *You must forgive me for my impertinence*s, though I suspect my memory has improved Charlie Graham's vocabulary. As it was, I felt suddenly sorry for the boy – although he must be ten years my senior, he seemed only boyish then – so I made it up to him by requiring his strong arms after all. I chose another six decent apples, removed my apron & knotted the bundle, which I threw down to him, on the condition that he promised not to drop it. I then requested that he turn his back while I emerged from the leafy upper boughs, as I'd just recalled my compromising state of dress.

He complied, at least until I was two yards from the ground and my blasted boot slipped. The situation was decidedly undignified. I was hanging from a branch by one hand and trying to extract my skirts from my knickers with the other. I must have yelped when my foot slipped, for Charlie neglected his duty of discretion. Two enormous warm hands were around my waist and there was that voice again, not teasing now, but telling me firm as Father to let go of the branch – he had me.

'Featherweight – I knew it,' he said to me, when my feet were safely on earth once more. Although it's clear to me now that his making light was an attempt to water down the awkwardness of the interaction, it can't have been obvious to me then, for, I'm somewhat ashamed to say, my instinct was to slap him across the cheek. As you know, when I have an instinct, I struggle not to follow it.

I paused in reading to touch my own cheek and then cover my mouth to keep in my laughter. What a fiend you could be!

I dare say he shan't be putting his great bear-paws around my little waist again in the near future. It occurred to me that he might tell Grannie, and I could be sent away from this Garden of Eden to earn my keep as a governess, so as a peace offering I apologised for my hasty violence and gave him his pick of my apples.

Talk about the tree of knowledge – such a lot I have learnt about the thicker sex. Since our encounter, Charlie and I have met twice more. Once, he visited for dinner – in fact, he partook of the apple cobbler, though neither of us mentioned our previous experience with the fruit to my family – and once he invited me to dinner with his great-aunt, who lives

> near. She's a queer old soul with a weakness for pet parrots and a quaint belief that her great-nephew is some sort of gift to the world. I must say he's proving more fun than on first inspection, but still, only a man.
>
> With that lengthy anecdote out of the way, I have other news. It is not good. For me it was rather the opposite. But I have regained my strength of resolve sufficiently to confess it to you, sister. Remember my novel, 'Lord Dunleve's Ward'? Well, I was foolhardy enough to finish the wretched thing, and not just that, but to send it out into the world, in all its misshapen glory.

You had never referred to it as such before; glorious, certainly, but flawed, no. I was shocked at your sudden disloyalty to the work.

> The publishers, Messrs Angus and Robertson, were good enough to give a little advice. Apparently, as a young hayseed from New South Wales, I haven't the credentials to write about London. They went so far as to explain that it was patently obvious I'd never set foot in the city and that this lack of realism would be a problem. There was some consolation in the fact that they praised my style and voice. If I applied these talents to writing on a subject with which I was familiar, they suggested, I might have better luck. So, Linda, it's back to the drawing board. I must examine more closely the things that are at hand, to learn the secrets of their soul and meaning.

Again, I had to let your letter fall upon the sheet. You see, Sybil and Isolde had returned – my friends from childhood. Only a matter of a year had passed since I'd last thought of them, yet it seemed much longer. *I* had tried to write – or, at least, think, which of course doesn't count at all – about the *things at hand*. I had done what your publisher requested without any guidance or prompting.

This realisation urged me to write – to find any scrawlable instrument & begin telling my own story in the margins of your letter, however badly it came from my head in the moment. It felt, then, as though I might birth a whole novel at once.

If you birth too swiftly, I know now but had no notion of then, there's a greater risk of injury to you & to the baby. Sometimes it seems as if an idea is growing inside me and pushing against my lungs, shortening my breath. Do you know this feeling? It gives me the sort of excitement that comes at the expense of self-preservation – the thrill of shrinking oneself to make room for something new.

Charlie Graham

I would return to your letter so often that lines of it were memorised. As I stirred boiling laundry and steam curled the fine hairs around my temples, I saw those 'two enormous warm hands' around your waist. For I'd examined those hands and heard that voice myself, heard it say my own name. Charlie Graham had returned to his family farm in Thornford and, no doubt out of courtesy to you, visited your mother & siblings.

'Good day, Mrs Franklin,' he called from the back of Red Rum, the gelding Laurel and I enjoyed talking to while Charles paid his regards to our father.

Mother removed her apron elegantly and invited Charles in for a cup of tea. I was unsure whether to play with Laurel outside or serve the tea, or sit at the table, but then Mother summoned me to the kitchen & instructed me to find jam for the scones.

'Do we use the good cups?' I asked.

'Would you like to use the good cups?'

'I've no opinion on the matter, but I thought you would.'

'Are you well, Linda? You are snappish all of a sudden, like your sister.'

I apologised and chose our everyday cups & saucers in bluish green, though I was careful to keep the chipped one for myself.

It eludes me how you could have seen him as boyish. From the girth of his forearms to the dark coat of hair escaping from his collar, I saw only a man. A youngish one, true, but still a man. Perhaps it was because I could not remember the boy, who you recalled playing with at Talbingo while his parents visited Grannie. Later he claimed that he remembered playing with us both, but I'm sceptical. You are more memorable than I.

The cup shuddered and jingled against the saucer as I passed his tea to him. 'Thank you, Linda.'

When he drank, his Adam's apple rose and fell, rolling under the skin of his throat like a trapped swallow's egg.

'Have another scone, please. They'll go stale.'

'I'm sure they'll not. You have three growing boys out there to feed.' We were sitting at the living-room window and looking out at the yard that no longer belonged to us. Norman was leading Red Rum in circles and Tal & Mervyn were on each side, stroking the handsome creature's shoulders.

'They ought not be meddling with your horse,' Mother apologised.

'Rum won't mind. They're doing no harm. How's school, Linda?'

I was startled to be addressed directly. When I looked him in the face, I saw he was only taking a polite interest. 'I have finished my schooling.'

'Congratulations. And do you have plans for your future?'

The future – *my* future – as I saw it then, honestly, involved our grimly narrowed home for the next year, where I would assist our mother with the mindless and tiring chores I'd perfected since the age of ten. Then, perhaps, I'd be fortunate and win myself a stay at Talbingo with Grannie & Aunt Lena, as you'd done. Or I'd be unfortunate & find myself exiled to a wealthy house in Sydney, where I'd perform similar chores but this time for a wage, and without the rights afforded to the eldest daughter in residence. I believed I might make a fair teacher; I could imagine leading a life like Mae Gillespie's, but did not know how to arrange such a thing. And then, of course, after my years of work, there would be the inevitable wedding. I would become like Mother, though with less to lose.

'Heavens, Linda, it's not a difficult question,' said Mother.

'I was just considering.'

'She's a great help to me at present,' Mother told Charles, 'but in good time I expect she might take a paid position – a governess, perhaps. She's intelligent. Unless, of course, someone worthy deems her to be a suitable bride.'

'Mother.' I hadn't heard her so animated since we lost the farm. She seemed to grow as I withered.

'Yes, I'm sure you're greatly appreciated at home at present,' he said kindly. 'You are …' He paused, looking at me more closely, causing me to tuck a strand of hair behind my ear in the way Mother told me not to, as my ears weren't my best feature.

'You are not like your sister, are you?' It seemed neither a compliment nor an insult, merely an observation.

'We're similar in some ways, I suppose. But,' I said, and let myself smile, fearing I was seeming dim & humourless, 'our temperaments and appearances are rather different, yes.'

'Linda is our fair weather to Stella's tempest,' Mother said, indulging in a rare lyricism.

'She is a very fine girl, Stella,' Charles said. He perhaps read my disappointment because he added, 'But tempestuous seems to about sum it up.'

'I hope she hasn't been insolent towards you,' Mother said.

He laughed. 'Not at all – at least, not more than I deserve.'

Do you remember I wrote you a letter about this conversation? It's possible I failed to send it. The missive would have explicitly flattered you, suggesting that Charlie Graham cared not for our company, but simply wanted to see where you'd grown up, to ingratiate himself with your mother & sister. The implicit meaning would have been quite contrary, hinting at his attention to my appearance and to my graduation to the adults' table. What the letter would have neither mentioned nor hinted at was the worry which germinated that afternoon without any coaxing at all, like a blackberry plant. Charlie Graham's question was the seed, that question I should have had a better answer to, should have at least considered: the 'what will become of me?' question.

'Do you think I could become a governess?' I asked Mother when we were washing the green cups & beginning to prepare the next meal.

'I do.' There was some hesitation before her answer, I thought. It seemed to be a moment in which I might tell Mother what I wanted to do with the rest of my life, and to ask her what she had wanted to do with hers. Naturally we were both taciturn, reluctant to stray beyond the everyday niceties and necessaries: chickens, the garden, the children, cookery, laundry, relatives, you.

'I believe Charles Graham was quite taken with Stella.' I used you as a means of steering the discussion back towards him.

Mother dried her hands with the kitchen towel and said nothing for a time. 'If Stella impressed him, then he is a foolish young man. Did you think him foolish?'

'No.'

It's difficult to write about Charles as he was then, a surface yet to be fleshed out with flaws and whims, the intimate distinctions to which the past ten years have made me privy. Perhaps you're aware of them too, but I suspect not, unless I described them well in my letters. His hatred of ants, for example; his irritability at toast crumbs in the butter; his lower back pain – all foibles invisible before marriage. But, let me try to remember.

After his first visit – I'm not sure how long after – we met on Thornford Road. I was walking to the post office & had old Shadow as my companion. Charles's dog, Kip, that red and white beast with one blue eye & one brown, rushed at poor blind, deaf Shadow, who cowered and curved himself around my legs. I bellowed at Kip to get away and was about to give him a kick in the side with Mother's boots, which I'd recently inherited, when that low, dusty voice interrupted.

'He's all right, he won't do any harm.'

'Shadow's too old for hijinks.' I'd squatted down to comfort our dog. Kip had returned to his master, wagging his tail in a witless manner.

'He means no ill. Just playing.'

My skirt was reddening at the hem with road dirt, so I stood. I noticed as I did that I wasn't much shorter than Charles Graham, and I remember thinking his face was gentle & strangely younger with a day's stubble.

'Are you going to Thornford now?' I asked.

'I am. You?'

'Yes. I have letters to send.'

'I have a filly to collect.' A reminder that our family's circumstances would not allow for such arrivals in the foreseeable future – nothing on the scale of a horse. Unable to reply sensibly, I just nodded & we began walking side by side. I watched Mother's old boots walk in time with his new black ones.

'I'd offer you a ride home,' he said, 'but she's young and unreliable yet. Wouldn't want you getting thrown.'

'Thank you, but I like walking.' It was true. I could relate to little of the lives of heroines in the books I read, but trudging for miles was a familiar pastime.

I must have been a rotten conversationalist, for that's about all of the exchange, on that walk, I recall. Instead, I'll imagine the things I considered but was too timid to say – minor points about the green parrots pecking at the verge & the sweet weight of wattle in the air. I knew that if I let myself start rabbiting about insignificances like that I'd be liable to lose my head & talk apace about any old thing, as if Charles Graham were one of our brothers, or even you. That wouldn't do. Obviously, I felt it important that I seem grown-up to him. Proper grown-up women, I believed, said little. Their language was one of eyes & smiles, baked goods on good china plates, pitchers of chilled drink or pots of tea.

As we approached the main road, I hoped it would be bustling with acquaintances – if not Edie Paton, then at least one of her siblings or parents would have been ideal. In fact, as I imagine it, there was almost no one about, only short-sighted Mrs Beveridge sitting outside the pharmacy, organising her lists. Had she bothered to look up from the papers in her lap, she would've seen no more than Charles Graham giving me a brief nod before setting off briskly towards the horse yards near the station.

After posting our letters and examining what I had no money to buy, I whistled Shadow and returned home, retracing our footsteps. Ordinarily, to avoid boredom, I'd cut through the paddocks rather than taking the road, but that wouldn't have afforded a view of Charles Graham on his new filly. When we reached Stillwater's gate and had still not been overtaken, I stopped to retie a bootlace.

As in dreams, in memories I feel no cold or heat; I must deduce from other details what the day would have been. While the boots were heavy – by necessity, being the last pair at home that fit me at the time – the skirt was light grey & white gingham and must have belonged to my only summer dress of this description. I recall it fluttering against the sagging gate as I undid the latch. Shadow slid through – as usual, since his jumping days were behind him – before the gate was properly open, and I followed in a similar style, practising taking up as little width as possible, the world my corset. It was only then, with the gate latched behind us and Shadow padding back to the cool of the veranda, that I heard hooves, dull and unshod, beating a rapid two-three rhythm against the dirt. I turned, shading my eyes with the brim of my bonnet, to see Charles Graham canter by on a red bay, her hindquarters swinging out sideways in disagreement with her rider's commands. Despite the animal's apparent agitation, Charles lifted his hat to me as he passed, one hand holding the reins short & severe, the filly's muscles under her ewe-neck bulging in protest.

I'd not ridden in months at that point. There was no call for it, no time for recreational outings, even if there had been Mischief or Zephyr to ride. Watching the filly's black tail fountaining behind her as Charles rode over the hill and out of sight, I wished with startling force to be invited to ride that horse one day.

Yah!

The house still stunk of Benevolent Soup when I left the letters I'd collected from the post office on the hallway stand. No one was in and there was still an hour until lunch, so I went to our room and let myself lie down. I took the small muslin parcel of dried lavender from my clothes chest and balanced it on my upper lip, inhaling deeply. I felt as if I were a proper invalid, which made me feel better; the heat of the walk left my legs and feet. Very light and fresh I felt then, in the unusual quiet of the empty house. I let my eyes close and slept as is only possible in daylight – purely, without the force or fear of fatigue, without the threat of midnight thoughts. What seemed a few minutes later, I woke at the sound of the front door opening, a refreshed individual. Even the stale scent of bone & carrot no longer nauseated me, but instead roused some forgotten appetite from a time when I let myself eat without worry.

'Susannah?' It was my father calling up the stairs.

I took one more inhalation of the lavender bag before swinging my feet to the floor and straightening my dress & hair. Father would want his lunch. Indeed, I found him sitting at the table, reading the Bible and waiting placidly to be fed.

'Good morning at the Baxters'?' I asked.

'Not bad. Where's your mother?'

'I don't know. Not in the garden?'

'Not that I saw.'

'Was she expecting you home for lunch?' It was just as common for Father to take with him to work a parcel of bread and cheese or cold mutton.

Father didn't reply immediately, his face angled towards the fine print of the book. It was a habit I noticed Norman and Mervyn were acquiring – that delay between a question from their mother or sister or wife and their reply, during which I'd wonder whether they'd heard or not, whether our voices sometimes came out at a frequency beyond the ears of men and boys.

'Father?'

'I don't know if she was expecting me. I'm usually to be expected.'

It didn't feel usual at all – Father sitting alone at the table, reading silently, and me the only one there to look after him.

'What are you reading?' It looked to be a Bible.

His eyes were still following the text. 'While I was working a line came to mind, and I want to find it – to be sure I'm not misremembering.'

He said no more and continued reading silently to himself, his bottom lip trembling as if it wanted the words to emerge aloud. I took this as a sign to go to the kitchen & prepare lunch. When I returned I heard him muttering.

'"What profit hath a man of all his labour which he taketh under the sun? The wind goeth toward the south, and turneth about unto the north; it whirleth about continually, and the wind returneth again according to his circuits."'

I asked if he'd remembered all that, and if he would like a cup of tea. He replied with a nod, so I put leaves in the pot.

No more was said about the quotation, for my father had put the Bible aside and was now scanning the previous month's *Thornford Chronicle*. I sensed my questions would embarrass him, or embarrass me, and so to avoid any awkwardness besides silence I kept my mouth shut.

It hadn't always been like this, you may remember, between Father & me. When I was smaller, I'd prattle sweetly about our ponies, the weather, Miss Gillespie – anything that came to mind, really, and he'd encourage the conversation with soft chuckles, the odd question. But now, the conversation I wanted to have was, I knew, likely to annoy him; I wanted to know how much money my parents had left in the bank, how much he earned each week from fencing at the Baxters', why he seldom spoke to Mother, whether he worried about us. None of my questions were easily answered, so they remained unasked.

It was a relief when Laurel's voice tumbled into the hallway. Mother had taken her to pick blackberries down the bottom end of what used to be our land. Uncle George was pulling the weed out that afternoon and Mother hated to see the fruit go to waste, and so, with Uncle's permission, a small picking party was enlisted. Laurel had returned with red-stained fingers and lips.

'Best be back to work, then.' Father nodded to his wife & little daughter as if they were Mrs Beveridge outside the pharmacy. Mother didn't bother asking when he'd be home – it wouldn't affect our schedule – she simply went to the table and collected the crumbed plate and the cup with tea leaves stuck to its inside.

'Shall I top up the pot with more boiling water?' I asked.

'Please,' Mother said. 'I'm parched. Must have some tea before making the jam.'

'The boys will be sore at missing the blackberrying,' I said.

'Jam and scones after school should soothe them,' Mother said. 'I had a good helper, didn't I, Laurel? We didn't need those boys.'

'I scratched myself twice.' Laurel showed me her hands. 'But I found a good many fruits.'

'Well done, little thing,' I said, giving her fingers a quick kiss. 'It's lucky the blackberry plant wasn't cursed by a witch; otherwise you might have turned into Sleeping Beauty. Remember she pricked her finger on a cursed spinning wheel?'

Laurel nodded, pupils shining and dark as berries, like yours. 'She was well in the end. When the prince kissed her.'

'That's right, my dear. Now, you need to eat some bread and mutton.'

When the boys and men weren't home, we tended to eat as we worked in the kitchen, instead of sitting with any formality at the dining table. Sitting at that table was for people who had others to serve them. For some reason, perhaps the slick of cold mutton fat on the roof of my mouth, the thought of my father quietly waiting at the table with nothing but the Bible and the expectation of a meal had the same effect on me as the smell of Benevolent Soup. The sensation sat heavily on my forehead and tugged at whatever morsels I'd allowed into my stomach. How quickly my appetite had vanished.

'You should sleep if you aren't well enough to help with the jam.' Mother was watching me.

'I'm sorry. I don't know why I feel like this.'

'You've lost your colour. Go and lie down until it returns.'

'You don't need help?'

'I'm quite capable of making jam.' Mother, I thought, never had time to lose colour or lie down.

But at her insistence I retreated to my bed, still creased from my lavender nap. But this time the rest was not pleasant or rejuvenating; it resembled my midnight waking, the only difference being that the curtains glowed like marmalade, the room was warm & I was fully dressed. All these comforts made the unrest of my thoughts more distressing.

'Thoughts' is too grand a term for what it was that occupied me – I seemed to be overflowing not with ideas, but with wants. I wanted to be back in Miss Gillespie's schoolroom, reading aloud & being praised for my intonation. I wanted to, with a too-long leg on either side, gallop Mischief over the far hills and let her hop across the drainage ditch, then over the fallen log. I wanted to write my Isolde & Sybil story and send it to you, fully formed, finished. I wanted to hear you say, with a touch of regretful envy, 'It is good; you should publish.' I wanted to say to you, all magnanimity in my success, '*We* shall publish; we shall be like the Brontë sisters and publish together. Little Laurel can be Anne, and you can be Charlotte and I'll be Emily.' I wanted to eat something that I felt I'd earned – to use my body & mind in a way that required refuelling. I wanted, I realised then, a single fresh blackberry to bite down on, to let the tart juice sting the cankers on my tongue. This desire could be fulfilled if I hurried, if Mother hadn't already tipped all the fruit into the pot.

'Did you sleep?' Mother asked without turning away from the stove, where the jam was already beginning to steam.

'No, but I feel better.'

'Good. You can wash the dishes.'

'Have all the berries gone into the jam?'

'Yes, it'll be a sharp brew because we're low on sugar, but I thought it best not to waste any.'

The disappointment was oddly strong, similar to the feeling that had surprised me while watching Charlie Graham canter past the gate on his bright bay filly. A spoonful of jam would have to do.

About an hour later, the boys' voices sharpened from gusty murmurs to cackles of laughter & lines of poetry as they approached the house, still full of the schoolroom's energy.

'"He was hard and tough and wiry – just the sort that won't say die – /There was courage in his quick impatient tread; /And he bore the badge of gameness in his bright and fiery eye, /And the proud and lofty carriage of his head,"' Mervyn recited to the others' amusement.

'Mother, I've learnt it! Do I get a treat?'

'There will be fresh blackberry jam for boys with good memories,' Mother said.

'That's very good, Merv, did Miss Gillespie teach it to you?'

'I taught it to her!' he said with an arrogance, which, honestly, reminded me of you, but became him very ill, as if he'd borrowed your bonnet.

'He did.' Talmage backed up his older brother, clearly proud.

'So, where did you learn this poem, then?' I asked.

'Stella sent it to me and ordered me to have it memorised by the time she comes home. It's very long.'

'When's she coming home?' I asked Mother. I hadn't been told of your return. You hadn't mentioned it in a letter.

'Not for some time yet,' Mother said. 'I'm sure you'll have it learnt, Mervyn, even if it's very long.'

'I like that bit of it,' Merv went on, enjoying being the expert in your absence. 'It makes me wish we had horses.'

'Can we get another pony, Ma?' Talmage asked. 'It's a long, long walk to school.'

'Long walks are good for noisy boys,' Mother said.

'I saw Charlie Graham with a new filly today,' I said without thinking. Mother scowled at me.

'What was she like?' Norman asked. 'Fast?'

'Very. Proud and lofty carriage to her head too.'

Mervyn smiled at this.

'Did you speak to Charles Graham?' Mother asked.

'Yes, briefly. He walked me into town when I went to post the letters.'

'I hope you were polite.'

'Yes, Mother.'

The boys saw no significance in this story besides the bright bay filly. As they ate their afternoon-tea treat, I answered a succession of questions about her size, proportions, colour, breed, speed & temperament. Sometimes, talking about the things you cannot have is sufficient; it's merely the idea you crave. However, on this occasion, as my description gained detail, I could see Mervyn growing frustrated with the futility of his want. He wouldn't have a horse again until he finished school and got work of his own.

I felt sorry for him then and forgave him for memorising a poem that you'd sent. It's easy to be jealous when you have many siblings, I think, but easy too for the jealousy to evaporate with a hotter emotion. Pity and love overpowered the feelings that made me want to yell *Yah!*

Grand Passions

My first year at home without you may have been the longest of my life, full of the pretence of occupation without real direction. I began to question the value of repeatedly dusting cobwebs from the corners of the bedrooms; if we were to let the daddy-long-legs be, they'd deter other pests. That belief was missing the principle of the thing, according to Mother; slovenliness led to ill-disciplined children & ungodly behaviour. Why live if you would not live tidily? She didn't say this, of course – we wouldn't speak so deeply to one another – but in my silent, imagined conversations with her, such opinions were shared.

Outdoors, the jobs I was assigned made more sense to me. If you dead-head the lavender and roses, there's room for more flowers; if you prune the lower & crossing branches of the apricot & quince, green growth will be the reward. I wished I could trim off parts of myself and have fresh, waxy limbs. The best approximation I could devise involved culling my small collection of belongings. So, after the children had gone to bed & our parents were reading or sewing in the living room – after the mindless tasks of the day were done – I pulled old petticoats & dresses, knitted cardigans & hats out of my clothes chest. They smelt less of the muslin lavender bag than of stale soap. Most still fitted to a degree, due to my shrinking figure. I was growing up but not outward, which tended to necessitate letting down a hem rather than making a whole new outfit.

The clothes were faded from repeated washing; faint stains of butter from baking, and the russet blush of old dirt around the edge of a skirt were permanent features now. Several buttons had the tight, jaunty appearance of being sewn on hurriedly by my own hand rather than with Mother's precise stitches. Thinning material over my sharp elbows had been darned in a similar lumpy fashion. All of these old branches of myself were still wearable & so, in their way, necessary, due to our reduced circumstances. I couldn't prune any of it.

A slightly different problem arose with my childhood toys. The cloth doll I kept sitting on the window ledge, where you'd once sat, was not worth culling; she took up so little space. I had named her Maria and she was not wanted by Laurel or the boys, who'd inherited our other outgrown toys – the bear called Whisky, the homemade hobby horse with a quizzical expression painted onto his chaff-sack head. Maria was doing no harm, so it seemed malicious to remove her. But perhaps that was the trick to gardening; although the dried lavender spears and unruly fruit branches appeared innocent, they prevented something better from taking their place. What might sit on that window ledge if Maria were gone? I decided to find out.

The doll, with her blond woollen hair and blackberry-coloured skirt, was lighter than I remembered. A mauve layer of dust had gathered in the creases of her white collar (Mother wouldn't have approved), and her squinty, stitched expression was not kindly, as I'd once thought. I put her in my clothes chest, underneath the disappointing garments, and resolved to give her away to another child if the opportunity arose. I was too young at that stage to consider my own children – to foresee Teddy.

I wondered then what you'd done with your doll, Delia, with the exquisite china head. Surely you hadn't taken her with you to Talbingo. Without prying, you understand, merely out of a specific curiosity regarding her fate, I knelt & looked under your bed. Your section of the room often appeared neat as a pin, but I knew you took shortcuts by stuffing possessions without order or ceremony into baskets hidden behind the dusty cream valance. There were two square baskets, each containing a miscellany of papers, clothing, gifts, & objects presumably deemed treasures once. In the toe of a small black house slipper with an unfixable hole in the sole was a perfect cicada skin, translucent and golden as burnt sugar. Its feet clung to my finger as I held it, a strange appearance of residual life in a clearly vacant shell. Under the slipper were loose sheets of paper, perhaps torn from your scrapbook, revealing your lack of talent for drawing. The fact that you'd kept these attempts at portraits of myself & our parents, of Zephyr & Shadow, the quince tree, despite dismissing them as failures (a frustrated line through each image, sometimes so violent that the page was torn), was curious. It's possible that you were simply hoarding paper, planning to use the blank corners for recording your thoughts, but I don't believe it was that. As others rest on their laurels, you'd sleep on your disappointments, a sort of heathen penance for not practising sufficiently, or not seeing clearly or working dextrously enough.

Underneath the discarded drawings, swaddled carefully in the square of pale blue muslin you used to insist on holding and sucking to help you sleep – a remnant of one of mother's dresses, I think – was Delia. At first I assumed you had done this to keep your doll safe, but then it struck me as just as plausible that you were keeping yourself safe from her, stowing her where there was no risk of seeing her again. I fetched Maria from my clothes chest and placed her top-and-tail with Delia in the centre of the muslin square, then wrapped them up together, so tightly that it might have been only one doll inside.

I did feel freer. The windowsill was empty, ready to hold books, or a jar of flowers, or nothing at all – to simply let me look out at the world, however small it was. Beyond the garden, round to the right, we used to enjoy watching the horses amble up to the home fence for evening feeds or treats. Around to the left was the milking shed, & next to it the smaller paddock for the bobby calves we would mother until they were big enough for veal, which we ate on special occasions – Mother's veal-and-egg pot pie for Father's birthday. Aloud, we would thank the Lord for what we were about to receive, but silently I'd give my gratitude, and guilt, to our treacle-eyed babies.

Because we no longer owned these things in the view's periphery, I stopped seeing them. The quince was still ours, so I watched that instead. When I read *Jane Eyre* and imagined her walking through Mr Rochester's orchard and finding the lightning-struck chestnut tree, split down the middle and blackened, I pictured our quince. That's how fiction works, isn't it? Jane was a mongrel of you and me – with your hair & small stature, and my frailty and pallor. Her employer and husband I couldn't picture; he was someone I believed I was yet to meet. Her cousin and potential husband, St John, was a clean-shaven Charles Graham.

I sat, doll-like, in Maria's corner of the sill and read when nothing else was required of me. The position numbed the small of my back but provided the best light & I believed I would've looked appealing had someone coming up the driveway glanced at my window. Jane replaced you as a companion, I suppose, her grand passions – like yours – dwarfing mine entirely. I was – am – not a passionate creature; passivity isn't a passionate quality. Instead of being passionate, I *wanted* to be passionate; instead of being a writer, like you, I *wanted* to be a writer; instead of earning my own income, I was vaguely wistful about what a job might entail; instead of falling in love, I came to realise that I wanted to be in love with Charles Graham for it was expected of me, it was right, and I'd assumed – mistakenly – it was what you yourself had done. If I'd felt more strongly about any of these aspects of life, would I be in this carriage now, watching my husband sleep, missing you deeply? Perhaps this trait explains why I took so much pleasure, if not passion, in riding; the decisions I made on horseback were often partial, influenced by the animal's own desires and based on a faith in something more than myself.

This realisation was yet to come. At fifteen, as I recall, I didn't understand my inertia. I thought it was ladylike and Christian to wait to be asked, rather than to perform – as you always managed to – without invitation.

'Linda, I need you.'

'Linda, help.'

'Where is Linda?'

Without Mother, Laurel, & the boys, I may have perched on that windowsill until I was numb from shoulderblade to heel, imagining how life might be rather than living it; that is to say, reading.

No wonder my replies to your letters became shorter and shorter; what supreme eventlessness. Yours continued to be long & vivacious. You'd had an article accepted by the *Thornfield Chronicle*. You were considering an acting career in Sydney. You were writing a new novel. You were riding the neighbour's horses. You were corresponding with Charles Graham and had learnt that the name of his new bay mare was Star. 'Not,' you wrote, 'dissimilar to *Stella*, it must be observed.'

Yes, I'd observed the similarity and felt what I'd thought was passion but now recognise as simple envy. With delicacy, I read this portion of your letter aloud only to Mother, skimming over the announcement in the reading to our siblings and Father.

'What an opinion of herself she has developed,' Mother said, shaking her head but not expressing the level of disapproval I'd anticipated. There was amusement in her voice. 'What a lofty daughter and sister we have, Linda.'

'Lofty' didn't seem to me severe enough. I punished you in my own way, by mentioning Star's bulging ewe-neck in my reply. 'Charlie wanted to give me a ride home from the post office but was concerned that the ill-broken animal might throw us both and didn't want to risk my safety.' You neglected to respond to this jibe, rightly so, I suppose. It's easy to be censorious of this pettiness, but I must remember that I was only fifteen – it was ten whole years ago.

I was a different person then, and so were you. Charles, too, was a different person, perhaps worthy of such competition.

He

What was and is he really like? The charmingly insolent boy-Charlie of your letters; the smooth-faced Charles who drank from Mother's best teacup on subsequent visits; the stubbled Charlie who spoke continually of you but tried, and eventually managed, to kiss me; the moustachioed Charles of that hot sombre day spent ruining white silk shoes; bearded Charlie who passes me our crying son.

There are as many Charlies as there have been Fathers, though I suspect your memory is less kaleidoscopic than mine. There was strong, kind Father who let me ride on his back and galloped like a horse as I kicked his ribs. There was taciturn Father, distant with worries to which only Mother was privy. This Father became irritable and erratic – a Father who would throw a stirrup iron at his daughter for messing the stable floor with spilt grain – then increasingly silent. In the year of leaving Stillwater and living with a husband, I found this Father shrunken & paler, both more good-natured & disappointing than I'd noticed before. Mother seemed to flourish beside him, like a plant whose preferred season had arrived.

There are of course several versions of our brothers, too. The puppyish kids, smelling of sour milk and stained with berry juice. The loud boys seldom scolded for voices that Mother wouldn't have tolerated from our throats. The serious youths who found their eldest sister an eccentric and their next a bore, but who never failed to spoil their youngest. They turned into the men who left, who wished to outdo our father, and upon whom Mother still dotes.

Oh, to be 'he'. Do you remember what Mother said when she caught you wearing Mervyn's trousers in the cowshed? *'Never, ever let me see you baring your form like that again.'* A tone of voice that made even you pause before offering a rejoinder. I believe that was the time you claimed to be rehearsing a Shakespearean play (I forget which, perhaps *Twelfth Night*) and thus required a doublet and hose. Mother didn't smile at this reply. A daughter of hers play-acting, with delusions of Shakespeare no less, on a stage stained with dung? What had she done to deserve such a farcical family? Where was our father?

Later, Mother spoke more gently to us both. It is only rational, natural, she'd said, to want to be born a boy – every girl goes through such a phase. Luckily, my phase had passed; I was behaving beautifully as a little girl ought. But you, stubborn Stella, persisted in veering off the correct course of femininity, whether by refusing to use the side-saddle or stealing your brother's clothes.

That may be why I felt relief when Teddy was born. I'd been afraid for the whole pregnancy that I was carrying a blighted person, who would turn into me and would turn me into Mother.

You succeeded in turning yourself into a he, albeit briefly, did you not, Miles? Mr Lawson wasn't fooled by the pseudonym. However masculine your temperament appeared, your experience was surely feminine. This was palpable even in ink, from the uncharacteristically neat, small copperplate – you wanted to make the most of the expensive white paper your indulgent father had sourced – to the intimate understanding of disappointment, of the pain that our fellow young Australian women related to all too easily, & which I congratulated myself for killing with deliberate routine. What I didn't realise was that below the numb skin was a feeling that wouldn't die, that would outlast the smothering effects of habit, exhaustion and hunger.

If I'd been a he, I like to think I wouldn't have gone horse-mad like our brothers and pursued the farming life that we witnessed devour our parents' pleasure. Instead, I might've conducted some sort of investigative expedition, like Charles Darwin's. You, who know how to capitalise on the dreariest situation, would probably say – were you were sitting in my seat now, the train window lightening, revealing a country I haven't seen before yet struggle to feel curious about – that this is just such an expedition, that Dalveen must be brimming with hidden creatures ready for my expert eye. Alas, I'm not an expert.

So, remove yourself from the clutches of pointless busy work, I can hear you chastising. *Get out; get out as I did. Bring the baby to Chicago & we shall care for him together while working as administrators for the feminist league.* If only I'd the energy & cunning & capital, Stella, to extricate myself from this train carriage. It seems that I'm running a fever – may the heat fuel my getaway.

Oh, it's too peculiar to cordon oneself off from the real morning & imagine talking to you, when I could in fact be writing. I shall find some paper and write you a real letter now, dear. Wait for me.

Letter

Dearest Sister,

I apologise for the state of my handwriting, but to fit on the back of a prescription forgotten in my bag it must be minute, as if penned by spiders. Not the enormous species that I'll doubtless soon discover at my new home, but the innocent jumping variety we played with at Stillwater.

How many apologies can I fit on this page? I'm sorry for being an envious creature, a dullard, Mother's puppet, a naysayer, a conventional disappointment. Do you think that's why they are called convents, the places where wayward girls are sent to learn to behave well, to come together with the exemplars of their sex & swear off all aspiration of which society refuses to approve? I would've liked, I think, to sing & brew beer. Perhaps I missed my calling. I'm sorry for lording – ladying? – my marriage over your singledom, when I knew that you wanted not what I had, but a different variety of companionship, & that you wished this for us both. Dear, clever Stella, I understood your perspicacity on my wedding night & my understanding improved tenfold over the following week, as I felt myself crawling along that path you wished the women of Australia would somehow fly above. Sadly, we aren't all like you.

I apologise, too, for being unwilling to roll off the path – which I picture as Thornford Road. Imagine if I had, instead, hidden in a ditch until that nightfall &, when my new husband had given up searching for me, got myself to the station somehow, boarded the train alone, in my own name, and taken it all the way to Sydney.

Yr loving sister,
Linda

When the Heart is Young

I fold the prescription in half so that my apologies are contained. I fold it in half again, to prevent the words from springing open, exposed, and continue turning & folding. Ted has woken, & with his knack for understanding what I'm trying to achieve & instinctive desire to thwart it, he reaches for the paper. I open my hand and let his strong fingers take it. Staring at me with his blue mischief, he unfolds it, flaps it like a small flag & shows me his four milk teeth.

When my son is disobedient, when he subverts my intentions, when he puts me at risk, my first thought is not for my own loss but for what he has gained. I stare into his clear eyes with my own grey ones and feel an easy sort of satisfaction. This is time well spent, I tell myself.

Heaven sends us habits to take the place of happiness – one of Mother's adages, with a biblical tone, but I don't know where exactly it's from; you no doubt do. If a habit so closely resembles happiness that the two are interchangeable, then I see no practical problem with this exchange. Perhaps it's a benevolent sort of fraud, letting us weaker, less honest, more cowardly folk feel pleasure without the balance of desolation that people like you (who I firmly believe have never mistaken habit for happiness) suffer periodically, like a migraine.

Of the two of us, you'd be the authority on joy, but I shall claim contentment as my territory. Content, convent, contempt – my mind slips over the consonants as if I'm writing with tired eyes, one hand ready to reach out to my son at any moment. I have been, & may return to being, perfectly content & I realise that this state of being frustrates you. I've already mentioned numbness as one of my talents: I know you would never sacrifice your feelings – your outrage, disappointment, jealousy, loneliness – for anaesthesia. That is what I, the Australian womanhood that you dismissed with such (might I say smug) regret at the end of your novel, have mastered. But no, that is unfair, for I do feel. I feel many things, but ensure that certain sensations are controlled.

Behind the blind on the carriage window the sky is blossom-pink. Ted has begun chirping in his wordless way, so I decide to move myself for the first time in several hours. I tell my son we are going to find the best view of the sunrise. With him on my right hip and his bag of provisions in the crook of my arm, we make a wide load to manoeuvre through the narrow doorway to the corridor. Charles stirs when the bag hits the doorframe but does not open his eyes. I believe he's awake and trying not to be.

My son wants to walk himself down the corridor and kicks at my side to suggest the idea, but I'm concerned he'll bolt & meet some form of accident, so I distract him by pointing out the window to the east. In the distance, I know, there must be ocean, but all I can see is an expanse of what will shortly be green but is now pinkish grey; the jasmine beginnings of the day are reaching up under clouds as fast & long as our train.

'Beautiful, isn't it?' I tell Ted. He places his fingers on the window, seems to find it colder than expected – as if the sunrise should render it warm – so instead reaches for what is familiar, my cheeks and nose. He burrows his face in beneath my collarbone. I stifle a cough and decide not to let myself die yet.

I take him to the lavatory at the end of our carriage and lock us in the dark, pungent room. Unwieldily, I retrieve a blanket from the bag and spread it over the floor, coax Ted to lie still while his nappy is changed. He is understandably concerned by the rattling of the tracks that echoes up through the porcelain seat that I intend to use if my son agrees after his own toileting has been completed, so I sing to him quietly, flatly, in that inhibited way which so frustrated you.

'Tom, Tom the piper's son,' I sing & cough, 'stole a pig and away did run.' The soiled nappy is off and wrapped neatly into a tight rectangle. I have forgotten the next line but continue with what seems right for the rhythm. 'But all the tune that he could play was over the hills and far away.' Enjoying his partial freedom, Ted resists the fresh nappy's application. He twists his hips and tenses his face, ready to emit a cockatoo shriek. I pride myself on being quick, and have pinned the newly folded cloth before the cry starts. I stand & hoist my son in the air, surprising him, robbing his chest of the breath he's just taken.

My action leaves me momentarily blind, a white light replacing my sight. I sit and fortunately find the seat. When my head has cleared I produce Ted's rattle from the bag, in a bid to distract him while I relieve myself. The ruse works.

These are pleasures, I realise with clarity, uncoloured by any resentment. At this moment I have no complaints. Watching the sun at its youngest, pinkest best, making my son comfortable, making myself comfortable – these achievements are not novels or city dinners, they are not silk dresses, or thoroughbreds, or epiphanies, but they are satisfying all the same.

To you this may be a lame sort of thought. I would reply it is not a thought at all – it's simply clean skin, cold air, divine colours, the odour of milk, & silky curls. Perhaps this state of pleasant sensations is dangerous, as it allows for, indeed requires, so little reflection. I have been engaged in such activity for the better part of every day since Ted's birth fourteen months ago, and my characters Sybil & Isolde have become increasingly insignificant. When I tried to read a bit of *Goblin Market* last week, having rediscovered it while packing our belongings, I found myself moved only enough to consider the garden I'd be leaving behind and to wonder about the fruits of Queensland.

Sometimes, I believe, it's enough merely to live – to dig the vegetable bed, boil the sheets, feed the baby, stew the meat, take pleasure in ice-blue cotton for a summer dress. If I'm content with these activities, what need is there for writing, which stirs the clarity of my thoughts, making them troublingly cloudy? Why not keep the water still and let its silty bed settle? I suppose you'd say that knowing the murk is there and yet declaring the water clear is dishonest. Your approach would be to splash about barefoot until you caused its disturbance – your place, not mine.

How will this new place Charles & I are travelling to be? What a distance I will be (am already) from Mother. Though it's nothing to the miles you've travelled. There's a financial imperative to our move, my husband says. It might also improve my constitution, the doctor says. I have difficulty imagining that any of it really matters, though I do wish Teddy could remain closer to Mother. Not to be helped now. When could it have been helped? That is the best part of why I am writing this, Stella: to determine how or if I could have changed course.

I tiptoe into our compartment, shushing Ted to keep him from waking his father. We settle in our corner beside the blind, now glowing grey. In this low light, I find the bottle wrapped in cloth at the bottom of the bag. There's no need to unbutton my coat with one hand and begin on the tiny fastenings of my blouse. I've seen such undressing pique other babies' impatience. Molly Graham's Benjamin tries to burrow his head into her skin before the layers of wool & cotton have been peeled back, howling and too annoyed to suckle properly. I admire her agility – pulling at her clothes, her body, her son, guiding each into place. It was never like that for Teddy and me. Persistent blockages and fevers meant that I missed the dubious honour of feeling like one of the cows I failed to milk as a child, of feeling like a woman. The doctor told me it's natural to feed from the breast – a reason to be alive.

Now I understand that bottled milk can also soothe my child. Leaning back into the cold leather seat and feeling my son get heavier with each mouthful, wiping golden hair to the side of his forehead, watching his eyelids close while feeling my own fall: time well spent. You may shake your head at these admissions, say I'm full of the chemical that keeps Australian women shackled to such drudgery, but what if this perfect satisfaction, of feeding a beloved, is the same sensation you had on publishing? Did you in fact feel that heady hormone release itself and fill you with warm pride? Or did it ache & take you close to death? When the child's mouth is latched in place, all that's false or ugly in the world is drowned out. The moment is true and beautiful as the answer to a riddle.

Charles opens his eyes and the first thing he sees is his son drinking. If baring my breast were necessary, I might find this intimacy discomfiting. As it is, there's still a shade of shame at being incapable, but now – perhaps because you're with me, listening, making me consider the situation rather than simply enact it – I smile.

'Good morning,' I say to my husband.

'When he's done, let's find a cup of tea. You'll be needing your own breakfast.'

Charles stands and stretches, as much as he can in the cramped compartment. As he waits for his son to drain the bottle, he pulls up the blind and watches the country trundle by. With my husband's fingers on my shoulder, and my son's holding his bottle, I feel neat & contained. Here's the moment at which you'd remind me to question the shape of the container – comparing my husband's care of me to his care of his livestock, for instance; or my son's need of me to that of a calf & its mother. Instead I sit still, glassily watching the moving scene the train window affords: a flock of ibis landing in formation, a smear of cloud still rose-tinged, ewes with healthy winter lambs on a sage-green hill.

Sermons

Words can, as anyone knows, be a form of nourishment. The best, like breastmilk, inoculate against the myriad contractable ills of the world. They're a medicine as well as a source of comfort. You've fed thousands; I've fed only one, and not with my own milk at that. On the release of your book I saw the effect of your own words in the flush of your face, heard it in the tenor of your letter. She's a preposterous bore, I thought. I should have felt nothing but embarrassment for you, or pride in you, but instead there was a small, hard stone in my gullet. If this stone could be spoken of, it would sound like: *fuck*. Fuck her & what she's done. Her hideous stupidity – flapping with happiness at every gesture of acceptance from the industry, the public, the readers, the men she's so scorned, the women she's scorned even more. Her pathetic desperation to be loved by strangers, so painfully acute that she's prepared pay for it with the love of her family. Her hypocritical toughness & eccentricity, flakiness & insensitivity, which rely on the other women in her life being pliant & steady. Her monstrous desire to be known – not just her name, her *nom de plume*, I should say, but her insides, the pinkish wet parts of her mind, her stained petticoats. 'But it's not autobiography!' she cries. Fuck her naivety, or more accurately, disingenuity. Her selfishness. Fuck her for that condescending reinterpretation of the word. ('I am not self*ish*, Linda, I am *my*self in all my glory; there is no *ish* about it. If anything, you are self*ish*, wishy-washy and unsure.') Fuck her simultaneous knowingness and ignorance. Fuck her for being my brilliant sister.

Do you remember squeezing my thigh when Thornford's reverend used the word 'paps' in his sermon, knowing I was struggling not to laugh & that if I looked at you, saw the trembling corner of your mouth, we'd both collapse?

'"As newborn babes, desire the sincere milk of the word that ye may grow thereby",' said the reverend. You loved the phrase 'sincere milk of the word' but shunned the imperative. You could feed yourself, thank you very much, on more interesting solids – the Cox's Orange Pippin of Wordsworth, the roast pumpkin of Lawson, the lamb cutlet of Shakespeare.

And do you recall the conversation we had afterwards, while retrieving windfalls from Stillwater's pathetic little orchard? 'But mustn't we all start with the Bible, before we grow our teeth?' I recall asking you. 'Before we can read Shakespeare?'

'How literal you are, child,' you replied. 'What if Shakespeare were mashed into a liquid form – would it not be as sustaining as the Bible, as mother's milk?'

I paused. The analogy was galloping away from me. I could no longer see it clearly.

'Would mashed-up Shakespeare really be the same as the Bible?' Often I confused Shakespeare with the Old Testament; perhaps that was what you meant.

'Well, they have a lot of the same words, don't they? Like foods that contain the same vitamins. '"For if ye live after the flesh, ye shall die." "O, that this too too solid flesh would melt."'

We silently pondered the nutritional value of these lines. All I could think about was lamb, served only at Easter and in spring.

'They're not really the same, though, are they?' I ventured again. I imagine we'd now abandoned our aprons of pears and were sitting with our backs against the trunk, eating the overripe fruit. 'Other than saying "flesh"?'

You frowned. I couldn't tell if you were impatient with my lack of perspicacity or trying to order your own thoughts. 'There are more similarities. Paul is talking about living beyond bodily concerns, nourishing the spirit. Hamlet is wishing that his body were gone. He's on the brink of dying, as Paul said he would, having lived after the flesh.' Your voice took on a clipped pace, excited by the ideas it was forming. 'Do you follow?'

'Yes,' I said with dishonesty. It had become a habit, outwardly appearing to understand an idea while inwardly grasping little beyond the gist, like falling off Mischief and finding strands of russet mane in my fist. Perhaps this was to be the fate of your younger sibling, ever attempting to keep up or stay on?

It was not Laurel's fate, though. Indeed she, nearly twelve years younger, was telling me things I'd never considered. It's tempting to believe she was made from the better parts of each of us, and perhaps that's why she didn't survive – such a fine balance of contradictions couldn't be sustained.

Nonsense, I can hear you replying. *Sentimental nonsense. Laurel died because the pneumonia got her. It was simple, horrible luck.*

Is it possible that the condensed cow's milk I fed her when she was an infant and Mother was unwell could've been in part to blame for her illness? I loved playing at being the mother, just as we all enjoyed feeding orphan animals. I thought I was a good substitute, despite my ribby, chicken chest. I fed our sister through her mouth, and you fed her through her ears when you finally returned from Talbingo and realised the dark-eyed imp was more a little you than I'd ever been.

You fed her before that too: do you remember telling her stories about the koalas that lived in the windbreak behind the milking shed? I'd hold her, feed her, change her nappy & dress, while you soliloquised about the Koala family who hated going to church. Little Lollie Koala was our sister's favourite. When she was old enough to hold her bottle and make words, she'd ask after Lollie first. Then she wanted to know why Old Mother Koala insisted on the family going to church. 'Well,' you'd reply, 'because she was a very good and pious sort of a koala-lady, wasn't she, Lollie, I mean Laurel.'

There must've been a time when I repeatedly asked why too. Laurel never stopped asking, for she died so young, & you never stopped because you're unusually inquisitive. But I began to think it seemed impolite or inelegant, obstinate or undignified, to question, and I developed that habit for concealing my ignorance & feigning understanding. At the time I believed it a genteel talent. Now I feel it was simple foolishness, or cowardice – a fear of taking up too much of anyone's time.

Your endless questioning tended to incense Mother and amuse Father. 'For pity's sake, stop asking why,' Mother would plead. 'Some questions do not have an answer, and many others should not be asked. The remaining few could probably be answered with your own nous if you stopped and considered before badgering me.' She particularly disliked your theological enquiries, whereas Father, at least in the early days at Stillwater, seemed braced by them.

'Well, Jesus had to be sacrificed to die for our sins.'

'Why would God send his son? Why not sacrifice himself? You wouldn't sacrifice Merv or Norman or Tal, would you?'

'No, but I am not God, Stella.'

'You are a sight better than God, in that case.'

'Stella!' Mother would call from the kitchen.

'That's kind of you to say, but you must remember that Jesus was not just God's son, but part of the Almighty himself. It *was* a self-sacrifice.'

I nodded sagely, as if recognising a truth with which I was already familiar. But you were not satisfied with this answer.

'Why did he call Jesus his son, though, instead of just calling him his human form, or something?'

'You would have to ask him that, Stella. I cannot say for sure.'

'But what do you *think*?'

'Stella, stop interrogating your father. And Father, stop encouraging Stella. If you persist in answering her questions at home, she'll think it appropriate to ask them at school.'

'Is that such a bad thing, Mother? This questioning does not come from insolence, but from innocent curiosity. What better place to be innocently curious than at school?'

'I wouldn't be so quick to assume innocence.'

Even though you were being told off, I wished it were me Mother was speaking about; there was an element of awe in her scolding. Without the gumption to outwardly question our father about the morality of God, or to admit to uncertainty of any sort, I nevertheless maintained a secret streak of curiosity. As Mother had said, many of the questions you asked simply didn't have answers – these I could mull over privately. Those she claimed should not be asked I needn't bother myself with, and the answers to the rest I would discover independently. The last sort appealed most to me, for when I nodded blithely and concealed my ignorance from you or our parents, or our teachers, it was not always dishonest; what the nod often meant was that I would understand eventually, in my own time.

Offering to dust the shelves in the living room gave me a clandestine opportunity to refer to the household's various compendia – to look up a quote with which I was unfamiliar; to check in the encyclopaedia whether the capybara was the world's largest rodent, as you'd asserted; to remind myself of how to bake a Victoria sponge. Quiet independence was cultivated. *Why*, I can hear you asking, *did it need to be quiet?* Here are a few of the 'unnecessary' questions with which you plagued our parents & Grannie:

Why is marriage essential?

Why is it necessary to bear children?

Why not pursue an acting career?

Why do women not vote?

Why is God so unkind?

Each of these questions would cause Mother to close her eyes, reach under her spectacles and gently massage her eyelids with her fingertips. Most would make Father lick his sunburnt lower lip, glance at Mother and give a wink. All except the first question, which seemed to discomfit him. The imperative, of course, for us particular women to marry was financial. He couldn't provide for us indefinitely. Our marriages would give our whole family a better chance of comfort in later life.

There were occasions when I felt I could ask a question without fear of ridicule or exposure of ignorance – when I believed I had no means of understanding what you meant, or when I believed you were wrong. Do you recall the letter I sent while you were at Talbingo, asking why marriage was such anathema to you? And why a holy union with another person, provided you chose them well, must be incompatible with the life you wanted to lead? Would walking down the aisle arm in arm with Father, I asked, prevent you from continuing to write your novel, or from competing on horseback at the Tumut Show? Could it not perhaps even enable you to participate in these endeavours more easily than if you were still simply living off Father's meagre income?

This letter, along with many others I sent, went unanswered. At the time I believed I was being properly courteous (and that you were behaving otherwise). It is only now, as I follow my husband's broad shoulders & balding pate to the dining carriage for breakfast, that I see other reasons for your not replying.

My Ladylike Behaviour Again

Ted is perched in my lap, happy for now, sucking a crust of toast. Charles is reading the newspaper, and I'm sipping English breakfast tea. I would like to be opening a letter from you. Instead, I recall the contents of the adolescent letters I sent you, particularly one written in winter:

My dearest sister,

Please forgive the tightness of this script, but you see my hands are still numb, only just thawing after a morning spent filling the woodshed. I could barely hold my tea after lunch, let alone this pen.

I do hope your hands are warm in Talbingo. [I didn't hope any such thing. When I imagined your hands warm, I saw them enclosed in the hands of Charlie Graham.] How is the writing, playing & singing coming along? You're a bad girl for not sending more regular [any] updates, especially as you know how uneventful life can be in Thornford; I'm in great need of hearing about your adventures and triumphs in order to survive this drab season. If there were snow, it'd at least be beautiful – though the poor winter calves would not appreciate the beauty, would they? – but no, instead there's a wet haze hanging over the valley, which doesn't lift. Mother curses it for preventing the laundry from drying. All our linen is smoky from being hung so close to the fire.

I'm sure conditions are more comfortable at Grannie's house. If you'd write and tell me of the dinners you've enjoyed, the witticisms you've entertained guests with, the guests themselves – no doubt more letter-worthy people than the few families we associate with here – then I'm sure I'd warm up with laughter & pleasure at your good luck. [And, let us be clear, jealousy. A sense of injustice at being abandoned by you. Perhaps if written honestly, this letter would've provoked a reply.]

Yours,
Linda

A response arrived in the spring, not from you, but from Grannie. I was letting the living-room curtains billow in the warm wind like the throat of a frog when Mervyn tossed the envelope in through the window to me. I caught it in my skirt & instead of waiting until lunch, opened it then & there. It was rare to receive a letter in Grannie's script addressed solely to me.

Dear Linda,

We hear you have survived a bitter winter in Thornford and feel that a treat is in order for the summer, so please consider this an invitation to exchange places with your elder sister come Christmas and delight your Aunt Lena and me with your company.

All good wishes to your poor mother and to the boys and to dear little Laurel, and you may pass on that we are in fine enough health here in Talbingo and our stores have lasted the winter nicely. If you are in need of pumpkins, apples or a side of bacon, I can provide.

Yours,
Grannie Lampe

When Fortune Smiles

Perhaps with a sense of obligation after Grannie's letter, you wrote to us – not just me, but the whole family – the following month. Mother read it aloud from the rocking chair on the veranda. When I recall her voice reading your words, I smell jasmine, jonquils and wisteria.

'She says she will not be a burden to us.' Mother looked up over the rim of her spectacles at Father, who was polishing his boots and not noticeably listening.

'No, I expect not,' he replied. 'Not our Stella. How does she propose to not be burdensome?'

'Is she going to become a jillaroo?' Norman asked.

'Goodness.' Mother had paused her reading aloud to skip ahead in the letter.

'No, a nurse,' she said.

'A what?' I asked.

'Stella played doctors and nurses with me when I was littler, she was very good,' Laurel offered. She had been combing Shadow's coat with her fingers, pulling out the loose winter fur. Now, in the excitement of the news, she gathered up her skirts and threw one leg over his back, as if mounting a pony.

'Laurel, leave poor Shadow. You know he doesn't like being ridden.' Mother was briefly distracted from the letter.

'Why a nurse?' Merv asked.

'She doesn't explain. She only says that she has an intention to attend nursing school, and in the meantime she has arranged to – gracious, she seems to have turned into a practical creature.'

'What, Mother?' Her interjections were becoming irritating.

'She has arranged to cover for Miss Gillespie at the school for a fortnight. Miss Gillespie requires time to visit her parents.'

This news shocked me, not least because I didn't know how to react. On the one hand, there was a sense of relief at your appearing to pursue a humble, earthly rather than heavenly path at last – to aspire to the sorts of things I did. On the other, there was a pang of jealousy at not having been invited to cover for Mae Gillespie myself. That you were older, more intelligent, and most specifically that you would be in Thornford while I would be holidaying in Talbingo, were not immediately obvious to me.

'Not a burden at all, then. Well, well.' Father, having finished his boots & being satisfied that he had heard enough of your news, left the rest of us to speculate at your change in character.

'Does this mean Stella will be our teacher?' Norman asked with some trepidation.

'I suppose it does,' replied Mother. 'But then you are accustomed to that already, are you not? Was she not your teacher when she was at home?'

'I don't remember. And she was never everyone else's teacher too.'

'It sounds as though it will only be for a fortnight,' I said, trying to comfort my brothers. 'You can endure anything for a fortnight.'

'What does endure mean?' Laurel asked, dragging Shadow over to me so that she could wedge herself between us.

'It means to survive, to live through.'

Laurel nodded sagely, as was her way. I kissed her hair. 'Perhaps you're ready for school too?'

'It isn't such a foolish notion,' Mother said. She had returned the letter to its envelope, as if planning to move on to her next task, but this idea stalled her. 'Laurel, you're close to five, aren't you? Would you like to go to school, if you had your big sister there as your teacher? And your three big brothers too?'

'Yes.' There was no hesitation. 'Will you be there?' She pulled on my sleeve.

'No, darling. I'll be staying with Grannie and Aunt Lena in Talbingo then.'

The holiday, for which I'd longed since it had been awarded to you, was losing its appeal. Why, I wondered, was I never satisfied – perhaps I simply wanted to be in the same place as you.

Laurel scowled at my explanation, then began to chant, 'Talbingo, Talbingo – Mummy, if we get a new puppy can we call it Talbingo?'

'That's a good idea,' she said. The evidence of your finally settling down had honeyed her mood.

'It is just such a relief, Linda,' she continued the following day after lunch, as we took advantage of the clear weather to hang the laundry outside.

'Does the suddenness of this change in her not worry you?' I asked. The wooden pegs in my mouth muffled my speech & tasted of pencil.

'We do not know how sudden the change really is. I shall write to Mother and ask her opinion. It was her intention all along to break Stella in, and it seems she's succeeded.'

Whether it was horses, cattle, sheep, pigs, farmhands or granddaughters, Grannie had a way of exerting her control. Was I to be broken in too, I wondered? If so, what would be broken – what was there left of me to control? Perhaps, I considered with gratification, Mother had been concerned at my interest in Charles Graham. Really, I knew this to be implausible. What I regarded as a *rendezvous* was merely a crossing of paths; what I flattered myself was flirting was simply politeness.

'Why the sour face? And you should use your pocket for the pegs rather than putting them in your mouth. I scolded Shadow for chewing them, but it seems he was wrongly blamed.'

I used the pegs in my mouth to secure another two sheets but didn't apologise or reply. I felt that Mother's unusual sweetness might balance a little acidity on my side.

We learned a fortnight later that Grannie, just as she might use a rope to hobble a fractious filly while teaching her to wear a saddle, had used a threat to bring you to reason.

'She must have said it with more gravity than I could muster,' Mother said, 'for I'd mentioned this possibility to her more than once.'

The possibility was, in your view, ignominious servitude. Uncle George, whose generosity had rescued us the previous year, required a governess for his children. While our parents were no longer bordering on destitution, they could ill afford to repay this loan, so Uncle George had offered to write it off if one of the clever daughters be spared for a year to teach his children in Yass. Apparently, your reaction to this suggestion was violent, moving swiftly from anger to sorrow to pleading to bargaining. Anything but working for our own family, you said. Grannie accepted this on the condition that you devise an alternative, one by which you would earn your keep.

'She is a capable, resourceful young woman when it suits her to be, I must admit, for not a week passed before she'd arranged her work at the school in Thornford and settled on the idea of nursing school, which I approve of heartily and believe you will find congenial too,' Grannie wrote in her persistent style.

Father let out a sigh of pipe smoke. 'It's a shame – that deal as a governess would've been highly convenient. As it is, we cannot fault her on finding a sensible solution.'

'I could go to Yass,' I ventured.

'What was that?' Father asked.

'I said, I could go to Yass, to help settle the debt.'

Father looked at Mother and Mother shook her head.

'Why not?' I asked.

'You're too young to be sent out to work yet, Linda,' Mother said. 'And while I have no doubt you could teach every bit as well as your sister, you don't have her strength.'

'Strength of will?' I asked.

'Physical strength,' Father said. 'You're sickly, Linda. We are hoping that a spell in Talbingo with warm weather, good food and much rest will help you.'

'So, I'm not being sent as a companion for my aunt after all?' This sass was unfamiliar to all present.

'Of course, Lena will be delighted to have your company. You two are much alike,' Mother cajoled. 'But your father's right. Your health needs to be improved. And I've always regarded Talbingo as the family sanatorium – I always feel better after a stay there.'

With a new dress & hat and a small bag containing not just clothes but books & pencils, I was to take your place.

'Fortune has smiled upon you, Linda,' you told me on the first evening we spent sharing our room again. As I recall, you looked as if you knew fortune's smile – your hair was glossy and arranged in a grown-up fashion, your fingernails unusually clean, and your pale rose dress was compactly but robustly filled with good health.

'You are not unfortunate yourself,' I replied. 'I like your plan. I think it's wise.'

'My plan?' You uncoiled your plait and proceeded to brush out the waves, which fuzzed reddish in the candlelight.

'The teaching and nursing.'

'Oh, that.' You seemed genuinely unmoved by what I saw as an adult sort of success. 'Well, better than slaving for our own family. And better to be living at home with everyone – everyone but you, I mean – after my long exile.'

'Now I am to be exiled,' I cut in, making you laugh.

'Oh no, you're not. Yours is a reward, not an exile. You'll be pampered like a horse at pasture. I hear they've been working you like a horse here, and that it's time for a rest. You've become very thin, Linda.'

I chose not to answer the personal remark, but instead asked about the nursing.

'I fancy acquiring a real skill. I'm not an impractical person, not to the degree that my aspirations might suggest. While I'm handy on a farm, I know little about people and would like to be more use in that regard. As a teacher, I feel I would too easily stagnate – listening to only my own voice day in, day out and hearing my words parroted back from young throats. No, better to learn to administer medicines and staunch bleeding. As Grannie says, the humility nursing will bring should do me good.'

Should I become a nurse too? was the question that occupied me during the journey to Talbingo. Whenever I felt I had found my way into the groove you'd made for yourself, you seemed to disappear, leaving me alone on a path of your making, uncertain of my purpose. I was so preoccupied with this worry that I only managed to smile blindly at Charles Graham as the carriage passed him in Thornford & he waved with a charming grin. I didn't even lift a finger to return the wave, despite having pristine new cream gloves, which would have looked very well indeed.

Aunt Lena noticed the gloves immediately, as she had the same pair herself, though in white. 'Perhaps we might swap from time to time if we are bored with our own?' she suggested, smiling. 'Our hands seem about the same size.'

A fey young woman, our aunt was a balm that soothed any concerns I'd been harbouring about being unable to follow in your footsteps. I hadn't seen her since I was a young child, when she had appeared adult. Now, almost adult myself, we met as near equals. I was refreshingly unchallenged by her conversation, her looks, her manner. Whereas you, Mother, and even to an extent Mae Gillespie, left me feeling wanting in some manner, Lena reflected myself back at me favourably. For the first few weeks it was comforting indeed to be agreed with daily, to be praised and treated to whatever I desired. It seemed that Lena was Fortune herself, smiling upon me.

When we took breakfast with the French doors open so that we could watch the cockatoos cracking walnuts on the lawn, she did not comment on how little I ate, which I found made me inclined to eat a little more. Fresh, hot toast was added to the rack in the middle of the table by a girl my age called Hilary. During this meal, we would discuss our plans for the day. While Grannie's were often managerial, thorough, and involved bossing a number of people about, Lena's & my own plans were fluid, significant only to ourselves.

But while this lack of importance was at first relaxing, it became steadily more oppressive. It did not appear to bother Lena at all, though I began to distrust the honesty of this appearance. How, I wondered, could a woman of at least eight and twenty be so content to simply read and sew in the morning, walk her Cavalier King Charles spaniel after lunch, collect flowers or fruit before dinner, and break this routine only with weekly attendances at church, occasional visits from the neighbours, and even less frequent sartorial expeditions to a larger centre?

'Do you ever wonder,' I ventured after several weeks of observing my perplexing young aunt, 'whether you are doing the right thing? Not you personally – I mean *one*, generally. Really, I mean *me*.

Perhaps it's just being this age, but I can't help but compare myself with Stella and I never seem to measure up. She's just made from a completely different pattern to me, I think.'

'Shall we sit?' We were walking the spaniel, Timothy, along the edge of the creek and there were willows against which we could rest. Easing herself to the ground, Lena let the dog loose from his lead & he scampered to the edge of the water to sniff. 'If you see a snake in the creek, tell me. Timothy is not sensible.'

I couldn't imagine what my aunt would do with a snake, but nodded.

'I believe I understand what you are feeling,' she said. 'I felt it myself with your mother when she abandoned me to marry your father. Her life in Brindabella seemed, from this safe distance, almost Arcadian – certainly the sort to which I should aspire. But there was no charming stockman interested in marrying me.'

'Really?' I was genuinely surprised. Our aunt, as you know, is beautiful – highly wifely, I would have thought.

'What a dear you are.'

'Do you wish you had married? I mean, do you intend to? You still could.'

I sensed our aunt stiffen slightly. 'Of course, I would not rule out such an agreement, but you are a sensible girl – you must see that there is a paucity of society in Talbingo. It is unlikely that I will cross paths with anyone suitable.'

'What about in Sydney? You are not forced to stay in Talbingo all your life, are you?'

'No, not forced, Linda. I choose to stay here. I have a pleasurable, comfortable and meaningful life with your grandmother.'

'Yes, I see.' I had offended her.

'I am at leisure to pursue my own interests.' What were these, really, I wanted to ask. Yes, our aunt read & sewed & drew, like other ladies, but her main interest seemed to be her little dog. 'Anyhow, you were asking not about me but about yourself. I apologise for going on in this tedious manner. Would you like to hear what I think will become of you?'

'Yes!' For that is exactly what someone of almost sixteen wants to hear.

'I believe you will marry a handsome and dependable gentleman and become a beautiful, capable wife and mother.'

I beamed without understanding why. But I was not satisfied. 'What do you think will happen to Stella?'

Lena laughed. 'Oh, Stella is a more difficult story. If she became a schoolmistress, a jillaroo, or ran away and joined the circus I would be equally unsurprised.'

A reasonable answer, but I realised then that nothing she could say would ease my sense of inferiority. With a shrewdness she saw my discomfort and soothed it. Perhaps she was in fact a silent philosopher.

'Linda, there are many ways of being good and of being happy. You and Stella need not be the same. In fact, that is the beauty of siblings for parents, I hear: they are seldom the same despite being equally loved. You are like honey to your sister's marmalade, jasmine to her magnolia, or lace to leather. To me, neither half of each of these pairs is any more or less appealing than the other. Do you see my meaning?'

I nodded.

Encouraged by my reaction, she went straight to the heart of it all. 'Linda, do not feel that you need to be a performer or writer or rodeo rider, or anything that does not seem natural. You are a lovely specimen of your own making, not an imitation of your sister.'

'Thank you,' I said, wondering at how little I'd understood of Lena until now.

She put a thin arm around my shoulders & pulled me close, kissing the curls at my temple with her cool, dry lips.

Burning Love and Cold Respect

Lena's advice calmed me as we entered adulthood; I returned repeatedly to her words. I was honey, jasmine, lace – all worthy things. You too were worthy, just of a different nature.

Our country federated and we came together as sisters, despite not having lived under the same roof for more than a few weeks in a row. We were becoming content to fulfil different purposes; or, rather, I was acclimatising to not being like you.

'He's normal,' I remember you saying when I enquired about your opinion of Charles. Not a compliment or censure, mere fact. 'I like him of course, but I am not him. He is not I. If anything, he is you.' The implication, of course, was that you were rare. You were turning, in our father's words, into a 'little firebrand', destined for politics or the stage (both to Mother's dismay), whereas I was growing, or shrinking, into the correct shape of young Australian womanhood.

I believe Charles must have enjoyed lace as much as leather, honey & marmalade, for to our mother's trepidation, he appeared to be courting us both – visiting me, writing missives to you; visiting you, writing missives to me.

Having mastered the art of suppressing my feelings, it was not at all taxing to pretend that his attentions towards you were of no consequence to me; I was too young for marriage, I told myself and others, and as a devotee of Austen's, I knew it was only right for the elder sister to be married before the younger. As I exhibited a dishonest indifference towards Charles's indecision, you displayed what I now think of as an equally dishonest competitiveness. The object of the competition held no genuine interest to you, it was merely rivalry for rivalry's sake. Wasn't it? Perhaps, too, there was a twinge of doubt at shunning the life we'd been conditioned to want to lead. Or possibly a flair of old jealousy at the perfection with which I wore the costume that never suited you.

It is difficult to distinguish between what I thought at the time and what I think now, in hindsight. Before reading your book, I don't know whether I was as insightful and aware of your – how shall I put it? – anxieties. That is how I put it to the family as the scandal of your novel spread, ripping through every residence and business in Thornford. Father, who had called you 'little firebrand' with a degree of warm amusement, was silenced. I, or rather the caricature doll of me, Gertie, was incapable of feeling – what was it? – an ounce of what you felt. I paraphrase badly.

I bit down on the words for days, deciding how to defend myself. That my clever older sister was so stupid – yes, stupid – as to confuse continence with lack, charade with truth, was the deepest disappointment of my life to date, second only perhaps to my wedding night. How dare she, I thought of you, how dare she parade herself about the country, indeed the globe, as a representative of the little Australian bush girl, when she knows not a single crumb, not a mote of dust about us. She knows only about herself. She cares only about herself. Grannie was right when she feared you would never marry, as there was no one on God's green earth that you could prefer to yourself. Opinions so high that the rest of us resembled ants going about our meaningless toil. Did you ever once consider who was heating the water for your bath while you wrote, who made the tallow candle whose light you wrote by, who baked the bread you would eat hastily before running out the door, who swept up the crumbs, who pretended to find needlework soothing & would mend your unravelling hems as you thumped at the piano? Oh, but you did see me – us, all those female people you were not akin to – you just didn't care to wonder how I smoothed your passage through each day.

If you do not like it, then do not do it, you might say. Well, I am done with one chore. I will not ingratiate myself to you anymore. 'What a lovely, *lovely* present, sister.' Ugh. 'How good of you to give me what I could never return to you.' Ugh. 'What a thrill to be the sister of such an esteemed authoress.' No. No more of that. Seek your approval elsewhere. The embers of my respect for you died at the final page. And yet I used the ashes to write you that letter of lies, didn't I? And you read it straight, didn't you? Because that was what suited you, and you have always done what has suited you.

I cooled and mellowed, as I do, until my mood fit my words and I saw fit to celebrate my clever sister. Uncle George's vitriol helped; if he was angry, I needn't be. 'Her audacity,' he wrote. 'How dare she?'

Then you told me of Mother's accident to her fingers, which was not due to the veranda door swinging shut. You were reading your letters in the living room when you heard her fist strike the kitchen wall and the plate smash. She yelped rather than yelled. You went to her. She was biting her lip, eyes closed, right knuckles tightly held in left fist, dough forgotten. A dent in the wallpaper next to where the willow pattern had been hanging. You swept up the shards of the heirloom, asked if they should be kept & mended, and were met with just a shake of the head; you fetched Father, who took her to the doctor in Thornford. She'd broken the index & middle fingers so badly they needed to be cut open and realigned. For the next two months she wore a sling and you had to help with everything. You did so without complaint because you felt it was your hand that had slammed Mother's into the wall. Your writing hand.

What a Day May Bring Forth

Fame was not all fair winds for you, I knew. Recall my gentle concern, urging you to give the writing a rest for a bit and join us at the Tumut Show. You're right that I was, or am, hare and hound both. In the same way that I was and was not Gertie, and you were and were not Sybylla, the Franklins were and were not the Melvins. *My Brilliant Career* was and was not your brilliant career. It must have been brilliant for a time, certainly.

I suffered the false edges of the attention. Did I ever tell you about the lady on the platform at Coolah who came rushing after me, touching my arm to ask, breathless, if I were the famous authoress? She'd seen our surname on my luggage. Oh no, if only, that is my sister; yes, immensely proud, how lovely you enjoyed it, I'll be sure to pass it on, really must rush now, thank you, yes, goodbye. Women of the world were after you, wanting to tell you how well you knew them. But a man was after me and that, for reasons I now can't fathom, was enough to balance the scales, tip them in fact in my favour.

I never told you about the proposal because you didn't ask. The hare in me wanted to protect you from envy, the hound was afraid you'd ruin my moment by saying something like, *Is that all? Was that really all he could come up with?*

He called at Talbingo, took me walking through Grannie's garden. We had walked together, what, a dozen times by then – enough for me to have lost some timidity with him. He invited me to sit on his jacket with my back against an apple tree, quite possibly the one you jumped from into his arms. He sat close to me, so our shoulders warmed each other's. He turned his face to examine mine, told me there wasn't a finer-featured girl to his knowledge, nor sweeter tempered, nor better suited to being his wife. Did I agree? I leaned into his shoulder and felt a sort of pride of possession that I can only compare with owning a pony. That body, heated with blood, muscled & clothed as it ought to be, strong enough to carry me, would belong to me.

So distracted was I by the prospect of ownership, my inference that he was offering himself as my husband rather than taking me as his wife, that I neglected to notice his shoulder leaning just as heavily into mine, which had a little extra flesh on it. The medicine seemed to be working and I'd gained four pounds, some colour; possibly I looked the best I ever had or would in my life, was the weightiest I would ever be, aside from while carrying Ted.

This despite the drought and heat, the way the lack of rain seemed to tighten the tendons running down the backs of my legs and make all movement a pain.

Really, Stella, I felt that summer the world was coming to an end, and yet, or perhaps because of this fear, I said yes. I accepted the proposal to share my life with that man. The contradictions were as thrilling as swimming in the Stillwater dams during a storm, or galloping Mischief with reins knotted, legs strong against the animal's sides, arms stretched out, a flying angel.

I didn't question the dizziness of instant success, the best porcelain; promises of lacy, lisle-thread stockings, almost like silk; a position centre-stage in the family. I had done it. I would marry. Any doubt that flickered, those thoughts of throwing the whole thing over, could be sat out, ridden through. I never once let Mischief buck me off, did I? I would lean back and laugh, because the laughter calmed me and in turn her, and that is what I did for myself in those moments of kicking against rationality. The prospect of property soothed me. The knowledge that I would never have to be a maid or a nurse, as you might, soothed me. The sweet affection, for it did exist during our engagement, when we really did feel engaged, was soothing too. What was it to be tied to this man, bound by his name and my new role as his spouse? He was (is) a good man, to be sure. It would be, has been, a fine use of my energies, making his life comfortable, surely?

But the ache in my legs & back lingered as the rain failed to arrive. You ignored my pleas to come to play with us at the Show, ride the Ferris wheel, put your career aside for an afternoon at least. And in the Goulburn Town Hall I listened to your glamorous friend Vida Goldstein unpick the work I'd done to make sense of my life. Women should not have to marry to be assured of a home, she declared. Marriage should be the last resort, in cases of serious love only. We were enfranchised to vote by the Commonwealth constitution.

The rains still did not come. Mother's fingers did not heal. I was newly engaged but the elation was wearing off. Or perhaps instead of wearing off, it tapered abruptly when I found a letter while visiting Stillwater – a letter addressed to you, in a hand I recognised, using words I didn't; a letter I oughtn't have read, which called you the best and truest girl he knew. Best and truest. Friend, too. But what does that word mean? I have only known family, since Edie Paton decided she preferred you.

But the day is here now, absolutely. Ted points to the caramel cattle grazing. It is still the bush out here. Perhaps Charles is right & I'm simply too ill to make fine distinctions, to distinguish between good land and bad, a financially judicious new home and our old life. If I resisted it less fervently, all of it, I would find life easier, he suggested one morning when I could not rise. He looks at me now, stroking our son's hair off his forehead, as if trying to place me. Or perhaps he is doing sums & letting his eyes rest on mine as if they were just another fixture of the carriage.

'What are you thinking?' he asks. I am shocked.

'I am remembering.'

'What are you remembering?'

'Our engagement, and Paterson's futile courting of Stella.'

'Any man, even a poet, would be wasting his time there. She's wed to herself.'

'Quite true.'

But you did not want to be, did you? It was a purist perfectionism, a fear that outside forces might interfere with the delicate calibration of mood and mind that allowed you to write. You protected that element of yourself, and I suspect will continue to do so until your dying breath, & I admire you for it, sister, I really do. Has it been at the expense of certain pleasures, or do you have it both ways via some Bohemian metaphysics beyond the simplicity of an ordinary little woman like me? Have you had your throat kissed? I wonder. Or your tired eyelids? Has a finger stroked the inside of your wrist, following the veins' river down under your gloves? Have your hips been held by hands whose want you do not question because the action makes you forget you are owned and feel, fleetingly, in control? Have you had your chin tilted gently, your jaw traced in a way that sends waves of power down the fabric of skin that you wear every day but which suddenly is foreign? Or had a thumb held over your lower lip? I have had all this & sadly became too sick to like any of it, but the summer the crops died, & horses showed their ribs, & gums dropped branches, & Lawson pestered you to distraction, & you failed to meet me at the Show – that summer I knew those pleasures. If you haven't known them and wish to, I've no doubt there are people in Chicago who would oblige you. The secret is to submit. Submit yourself wholly to all of it. I'm not sure that behaviour is in your nature, nor if it would be wise to cultivate it, for of course it comes at a cost.

Boast Not Thyself of Tomorrow

Despite the publication of your book and promise of a brilliant career, you still had to work. As a governess, a nurse, a maid, and you made most of it look jolly – a ruse to gather material, always aesthetic rather than ascetic. Independently earnt money, yes, but research too. What did you call yourself? Sarah Frankling the slavey? Mary Anne Smith? You took to pseudonyms so well that Mother wondered if you would one day become a confidence trickster.

I basked in the thin, cool light cast by my ring, felt the warmth of women's fingers holding my hand to look at the simple band, enjoyed Charlie's arm at the small of my back & whispers between the curls at my ear. It was free & it was easy.

Laurel died. What more is there to say? Mother and father moved from Stillwater to the smallholding in Penrith. The best of each of us, our darling little version, brimming with beauty, quick wit, brave spirit, & kindness, succumbed to pneumonia – the illness

I have now. Will I see her? You would say no. I would want to slap you for your certainty, robbing me of my only consolation. If I can't watch and feel my Teddy grow, if Teddy soon won't have my neck to reach his arms around, if I cannot see you or Mother, or Grannie or Lena again, then why shouldn't I hope for a reunion with Laurel? I have been, in my actions at least, if not my thoughts, good. There is nothing the Church could fault me on. It depends on how much thought hurts one's chances, I suppose. My thoughts are rotten, hellish things. Laurel was nothing but perfection; yet, of course, I could never know what she was thinking. If we do meet, it should be somewhere cleared of all sensation but a soft scent of bay and jasmine, and a warm breeze.

My Journey

I do feel I'm finally still, though technically I'm travelling further and faster than ever before, in the belly of this train. Charles keeps referring to the new home where we'll live. I see it differently & worry that my view is self-fulfilling; if I could only imagine living there, then I would live. If I could only be happy, then I would be. If I could only stop coughing, then I would cough no more. It is quite simple, Linda, he would say (has said). Heaven knows why you don't just do it.

When I was oddly still and calm, on the eve of my wedding, I felt a false propulsion, a sense of progress instilled by generations of ritual. Transfixed like a fox by firelight, allowing the velvety night of the Franklin and Graham women to wrap around me tight, I let my married self be planned into being. Linda Franklin did not turn into Linda Graham by magic. It was a process of ordering patterns for dresses & veils, selecting flowers, securing a bridesmaid. You really were a miserable failure on that front. Comically sullen, crow-like. Black humour accenting the white of my gown. I hated you for it then but was also triumphant, as I thought your sulking resembled envy, rather than – I see it now – fear for me, disappointment in me. At least smiles were unfashionable that season. Your mood was *de rigueur*.

'Don't forget to vote!' I urged all the women I met in the weeks leading up to my wedding. It is a sign of something, I told myself, to be marrying on this day of unprecedented female freedom in our state, it is an omen. I chose to view it as evidence of my marriage being a source of freedom, but later I came to see it as an odd sort of bargain – personal liberty in exchange for social liberty. If I'd said this to your friend Vida she would've lambasted its wrong-headedness, its self-aggrandisement, passivity, and excuse for conventionality tangled up in an illogical knot. Our votes were counted as we posed for the photographer. One leather glove on Charles's left hand, his right naked, ready to hold mine, but mine full of a spray of jasmine, roses, gypsophila & camellias. The Progressives won easily in both our electorates as I was driven to my new home in Penrith – near Mother and Father, but never again with them.

To Life

You weren't the one privy to Charles's obsession with mosquitoes, clapping & slapping at the elusive whining in the corners of our bedroom. You weren't strangely amused & relieved when he leapt out of the bed to slaughter the offending insects. You weren't subject to his languorous attentions, nor expected to reciprocate with meek yet psychic ministrations. You didn't send me a letter saying you wished you were dead; I meant it when I sent such a letter to you. In the same post I sent Grannie a mosquito I'd caught & killed myself, my immediate job description being to remove my husband's tormentors. Grannie knows all about all, so I thought it worthwhile & found the absurdity a bit of a balm for the rawness of my message to you. Would that the oversized falsetto mosquito bite me in the night & infect me with a disease from which I wouldn't wake. Note that I didn't wish this upon Charles. That's something, no? It wasn't his fault I'd made a poor choice. If anything, it was your fault for illuminating my life's narrowness.

A Bust-up

Have you ever fought with a man? What a stupid question. You fight with everyone. I'm not given to fighting as a rule, but there is I think a temperature which, once reached, makes battle inevitable. I was so hot I felt my scalp lift off when he said to me, 'You're not conceiving because you don't really want a baby, do you?'

Why is it that truth makes one most furious? You're a novelist & student of the human condition; I'd like to know your answer. You'd perhaps say that those truths flow in the deepest runnels of the self, a sort of magma that the crust of propriety sits atop until volcanic activity causes a venting of lava which scalds all in the vicinity. Love is a sort of lava. Passion behaves as such. But it was not love or passion that made me erupt at Charles; it was shame at his accuracy, & raging pity at the fact that he'd wielded the idea as a bludgeon, unaware of its truth.

'Finally you understand me,' I said. He slapped my left cheek so its inside was cut against my teeth & I tasted for the next week the iron I was lacking. If I hadn't already been pregnant, unbeknownst to either of us, I might have been free.

Back at Talbingo

I wanted to go with you to America, but instead I went back to Grannie's and took to bed.

If you'd really wanted to come too, you would've, you might reply. Not everyone has a will like yours, a will that ensures destinies.

'You will live long and attain success,' an old Indian woman at the Peak Hill Show told you on your twenty-sixth birthday. You were disappointed she couldn't tell you what you didn't already know.

Dear, sweet cousin Edwin, Mother's favourite nephew, thought he was going to marry you the following year, but you knew he wasn't part of your successful longevity. Why did you let him believe you'd bring a little Chicago snow back to irrigate his land? How close were you to becoming a farmer's wife? You houndish hare, every bit as much a liar as I've been. Either you sailed right to the edge of the notion of returning and becoming Mrs Bridle & never let me know it, or you pretended to be seduced & never let Edwin know it. I'd wager you couldn't tell me which it was, as you never knew yourself.

Absent Friends Are Soon Forgot

I received a postcard as recompense for losing a second sister. An ugly ship docked in Auckland, surrounded by your illegible scrawl. You suggested I add it to my collection. I did. It's in my trunk as I think.

Do you know what Mother said after you'd gone? She confessed to having once considered doing something similar. I was astounded. This woman rooted to the house & home, growing vast branches of children, shading & sheltering all who passed – she'd thought about moving too. Then Father proposed, & here we all are. We've Father to thank for our existences. Easy to forget this detail.

You missed seeing me broad with child, hobbling about, advertising for a maid because the work was too much for me even before I began retching each morning and evening. You missed my failings as a wife, & for that I'm grateful. You missed Mrs Graham's initially tacit, increasingly explicit acknowledgements of my failings as her son's wife, & for that I'm regretful; you might've punished her in written caricature. You missed my weeks of bedrest, during which

I wished mostly for you to be there, reading to me, entertaining me, telling me stories, & listening to mine. For that I blame you.

And then a pertinent joke of a brochure came from San Francisco. *An Eden of repose for the nervous woman*, it promised. 'Sounds like just your sort of place, join me here,' you wrote, knowing full well I was stuck. For a student of the human condition, you were startlingly blind sometimes, careless, callous, & then so gustily kind that cruelties would be forgotten. I did amuse myself in bed: instead of feeling for the little fish of Ted quickening under my navel, I imagined what it would take to escape in my state. Rising to go to the lavatory was enough to blank out my vision, let alone putting clothes in a trunk, dragging it to the door, driving a carriage to the station, boarding a train to Sydney, catching a ship to Auckland, then Honolulu, then finally showing up, ready to burst with baby in San Francisco & asking to be taken to Eden.

Once Upon a Time When the Days Were Long and Hot

Late winter but the fire was fed up to its fullest & bowls of boiled water steamed & my face was lit with what you'll never know, I hope, my hairline melting down my cheek into my collarbone. 'How did you do this so many times?' I asked Mother.

'Stop thinking so much,' she said, mopping my head. Bite on this. Squeeze this. It is all quite normal. For a purpose. A reason. So I crawled into the cobwebs, the cracks around the ceiling rose, wished myself into an ant's body, wondered how much torture the queens suffer when they lay their eggs, surely not this much, & if so then how could we see ourselves as the victors, the superior species? I was waiting to be squashed, once & for all stood on by God, who saw fit to wring me out like a cloth, tear the material he'd made me from, all for the sake of his new creation, which would've hurt less if I'd felt it was my creation. My baby. No. I was the broken shell. Couldn't even feed him. Too sick. The milk dried, but not before it came in, turning me to stone, but not the kind impervious to pain. I told the doctor I believed even the granite had feelings & he responded by reducing my laudanum, afraid I was losing my mind. A woman's good sense is anchored by pain, I learned that day. She needs a certain weight of it to keep her from flying off, floating away. You escaped with your madness intact, & for that I congratulate you. That is truly brilliant.

'Cheer up, Linda, it will get better.' Mother knew there was no forcing stoicism upon a person like me. Her face seemed to show worry more than did her words.

'I knew that poor child would not cope; she has always been sickly. This was too much.' Grannie's voice travelled.

'Shh.'

'Just hold your baby boy, it will help.'

I did not wish to.

'It's hard for me to breathe when I hold him,' I told Charles. He didn't appear to hear or had no words to give in reply.

Ted had no breast & hated the bottle & so shrank before he grew. 'Count your lucky stars it isn't an old pickle jar fitted with a lamb's teat,' I told him, remembering watching Aunt Lena feed a baby at Talbingo that way & thinking it looked appealing, oh so easy and natural, right and simple, to give milk to a child.

He that Despiseth Little Things Shall Fail Little by Little

It shouldn't have annoyed me so, such a trifle. I believe you meant no malice & were indeed simply sending your best wishes from Chicago, a much more important place in the world. Your best, in this case, was meagre – two lines & a glamorous photograph of yourself wearing a wide-brimmed Mexican hat. You said you were glad to hear of your nephew's safe arrival & to know that I'd survived the ordeal. Had you any knowledge of 'the ordeal', which frankly none of us possesses who's not been through it, despite witnessing our mothers and aunts and friends submit to the fate, you would have written more, I think, your words would have been less flippant. Now I understand that it wasn't the silver sombrero or your cockeyed assumption that I'd be well enough to care about your holiday that peeved me. No, it was the fact that you weren't here to see me suffering from something that you'd not achieved. I missed you, & I missed the opportunity to lord it over you – to turn the agony into success, for we were both collectors of experiences and this was one that you'd eschewed quite deliberately, sensible woman.

Cows and horses either die after giving birth or return to their four legs & manage to walk. I wished I was at either extreme of this spectrum rather than stuck to my sheets by fluids I found foreign but all too familiar; one doesn't reach twenty-four in a farming town without knowing about milk, blood, sick, urine & scourings. It's preparation, I suppose, for dealing with the child's leakages. Caring for my baby boy – keeping him clean, well fed, warm & somehow dry despite the humid world he'd entered, as if bringing the atmosphere of the womb with him – was all I wanted to do, I told myself at the time, silencing any voice that asked me to care for myself, to sluice dried fluids out of crusted hair, to gingerly stretch weakening muscles, to eat a little bread soaked in cow's milk, and above all, to sleep an oblivious sleep. The smallest tasks – plaiting my hair & rinsing my face, walking out onto the veranda & smelling the viburnum, bathing – were not hateful or despised so much as ignored, brushed aside.

'You must take care of yourself so as to care for your baby,' our mother told me. This was something she must've done behind her closed bedroom door in the small hours of the morning, for I never remember her caring for herself instead of us.

Teddy has been a small task in some ways & an enormous one in others. I have felt above all else love for him. But I did on occasion wonder when it would be over, the rising every two hours to be sucked, clawed, stared at, bellowed at, clung to. Surely it couldn't last forever. It did not, but then those little things that irked & whose permanence I feared were replaced by other little things – little teeth, and little stitches in little clothes, for instance – that made me feel as if life were shrinking, contracting like the baby's pupils in the morning sunlight that striped the curtains and bleached the cot.

Charles was never a little thing – big heavy boots, big voice, big black hairs shaved into the basin – but after the baby arrived his conversation became smaller than ever before. Between us there were no words that didn't involve Teddy, livestock or property. I realise now that he was concerned about the farm's finances, about providing for his new family; and after Father's destitution, I ought to have appreciated his frugality & taken more interest in his plans to protect us. I would try to count the hairs on Teddy's head while Charles read aloud from a pamphlet he'd acquired from the Bank of New South Wales; the little particulars, you see, escaped me. No, that suggests I was pursuing them; really, they just flew past like cabbage butterflies, my net lying abandoned in long grass.

'What's your opinion?' he asked once & I was startled to be expected to possess such a thing. Perhaps, I thought, I ought to have an opinion. You, my clever sister, would have an opinion on all aspects of my life, including the dull matter of how to afford to eat & to clothe ourselves; you would protect me against fading into insignificance.

'My opinion,' I ventured. 'My opinion is pending until I've read more on the matter myself.'

'But I've just explained it to you in detail,' Charles replied.

'Yes,' I said, not wanting to reveal that I hadn't been listening. 'But I would prefer to read the material firsthand.'

'Do you distrust me?'

'No. I just find that I grasp the particulars more easily if investigating by myself.'

'I see.' Charles did not seem to believe me. 'As you will.' He slid the pamphlet across the dining table. 'I am glad you are feeling well enough to read now.'

'Yes, thank you – a little better today.'

Idylls of Youth

According to Charles, I became listless. That is another reason why our new home will be in Dalveen. A change of scene. A reason for lists. So much to do to settle in. I listed into his shoulder as we switched trains in Wallangarra for the change in gauge.

'Do you want me to hold him?' he asked.

'Yes, please.' I passed Ted over. The child arched & wept to be in his father's firm grasp, but I felt mostly relief, for there are ribs that seem to be digging into my right lung. I've been trying to take small sips of breath just from the left, but the body does not work that way. Not mine at least.

Charles means well & a new start is wise, no doubt. The climate, fresh as it is now, may help me cough whatever is wrong out of me. 'The key,' a doctor recently advised, 'is to stop coughing. You see, coughing will make you cough more. If you could just train yourself to not cough, you will stop coughing.' Incompetent woman that I am, I cannot stop coughing.

My husband wants me to be happy, he says. But happiness is not a person or a place. We are on our way to a home without friends; we will have all the ennui of familiarity & none of the comfort. I hate the prospect. I hate that he will not see, or admit at least, to the mistake he has made. Perhaps it was not a mistake; perhaps it was a test. If she cannot be happy here, she cannot be happy. Happy used to mean lucky, did it not? All I want is for Ted to be happy. This may be a lucky place for him.

A Tale that is Told and a Day that is Done

The furniture was dispatched here ahead. All I want is my bed. The nearest neighbour, Mrs Turner, has sent her eldest girls to help with the unpacking, and to amuse Ted. Dark-eyed Violet reminds me of Laurel.

Why do we name girls after flowers? I worry for Violet's health, because it seems to me a miracle that any of us survive long in this life. If I had Mother's strength I would not simply sit & watch that flock of black sheep clotting on the plains. I would at the very least stand up straight & dust the cobwebs from that high corner. There's a broom somewhere. There's also a huntsman that can no doubt deal with the daddy-long-legs on my behalf. Delegation is all I'm good for.

Where is Ted? Hoots & coos from the yard. We've not checked for snakes under the veranda, but it's August & we're only just across the border. Queensland: this is as far as I've been from Brindabella. Thornford, Talbingo, Penrith, and now Dalveen. You have seen Chicago, granted, but not Dalveen. Seeing is the extent of what I do now. Looking at the shapes on hills & deciding if they are sheep or roos & caring neither way. Looking at land uninterrupted by a single dam as far as my eye can see. I thought, when Charlie said Queensland, it might mean the sea. I thought, when he said Penrith, it might mean the sea. I knew, when you mentioned the sanatorium in San Francisco, that I'd never sail that far.

You've put oceans between us, sister. You may say they were always there; I'm just now understanding what an earthbound creature I am. I expect your feet have been in it, the ocean? Or perhaps in that lake so vast it looks like sea, and which spreads its mist over your new city so that the tops of the tallest buildings cannot be seen. I should like to bathe my own sore toes in a body of water. The last time I did was in the dams at Stillwater. Nibbled by yabbies. Sinking into the silt. If I bothered to walk around this new property, investigate the plentiful chicken pens, I'd no doubt find water. But my ribs want me to lie as still as possible. Lie still until it all stops. The pools are inside me.

Truth will out, you were fond of saying. Has honesty been your elixir of life? The secret to eternal youth? Because, Stella, you know you're living forever, don't you? Give the world a few years & I'll be a faint, unhappy memory for Charlie, Teddy, you, Mother, our brothers & Father. A portrait in profile, hair haloed. The wedding photograph with you scowling like a bored harpy to my left. Oh Stella dear, your expression in that picture – but I mustn't laugh. I hope you never know what it is to lose your breath. This knowledge is at the farthest edge from that which we share. In the middle are horses, dogs, books. At my side are birth, domestic labour, death; at yours, sea-bathing, freedom, success. Between us, we've lived a real life.

Three

STELLA

To Swim

I learned not to drown in the lagoon at Ocean Beach, I told her. Like this: I rolled onto my front, palms flat against the porcelain base of the enormous tub, legs floating out behind.

The sea now carries that same body to the sand. It's rough and numbing. I'm mottled. Nobody is here but me. It wouldn't matter if they were. This beach is for nudists these days. Wouldn't matter if it weren't. I have no fear of my body. Or rather, I've no fear of what others think of it.

'What's your fantasy?' I'd asked her, and she sent me a link to the video for Björk's 'All is Full of Love'. A feminine android is being assembled by a machine and is singing of the need to trust that love is all around us. Sparks fountain, water rinses her smooth panels, and she is introduced to her double – another human-faced creature with shining white limbs and mechanical fingers, which beckon. The two kneel and press their faces together in a mouthless yet tender kiss. They stroke each other's metallic curves as machines continue working on the pair, welding and refining.

I left the door to my hotel room unlocked and told her to find me in the bath. It still lives in my nerves, but faint and changed, like sugar held in the mouth so long it turns from sweet to savoury. Her thumb on my jaw. Heel of hand tilting my chin. Our four hips. Four thighs. Four lips. Four eyes. Four arms. Four palms. Our hair. Our skin.

I rinse sand off myself, rub warmth back and pull on clothes – hand-knitted socks and hat from my writer friend Ana, oatmeal linen pants, T-shirt claiming *He Mahi Toi Tēnei: This is a Work of Art.* I stop short of the mittens because I want to smoke.

I roll, light with a shivering match and drag, sitting on the deck-chair facing seal-coloured waves. The beach has disappeared, and without the waves' breath I'd feel unmoored as a star in space, a bright thing held at the edges by darkness.

It's time to heat soup. I leave the sea to itself, drop the butt in the enamel mug, and close the glass door after me. The kitchen has shrunk as I've grown, even though its original limits have expanded. I remember my parents preferring the barbecue they'd made outside – a hotplate balanced on bricks, driftwood underneath – to the stove. I open a can of lentil and vegetable soup and slosh it into the saucepan.

As lovers, we fitted together snug and temporary as a puzzle. Outside of those hours she wasn't mine. The idea of anyone belonging to anyone is repulsive and yet I snatched her from my rival as a five-year-old would the first piece of cake, and stuffed her into my mouth, lips and cheeks sticky with greed.

I wipe my bowl with wholemeal bread, eat the soupy slice, rinse the dishes, boil the kettle and make tea. The last of my loose-leaf sencha, bought in Kyoto on a later leg of the tour, along with the mug and teapot that look alive. The pottery resembles my skin in the sea, subtle blotches of pink and purple spreading like bruises. To me they are beautiful. I take the tea things to the coffee table and lie on the sofa, my legs hanging over one arm, head resting on the other. I pick up my book. The poet writes in such a way about the ocean that its snoring out the window loses volume, the words on the page dissolve, and all that's left is other salt, a different type of rolling swell.

This will not do. If it weren't dark, I'd swim again. But being naked is no good. I put down the book, sip tea, pick up my guitar and play a bit. But even the notes are wet, moving around like blood, deep inside what is conscious. The poet calls fate a failure of the will.

If I hadn't tossed my phone into the lagoon this morning, I might call her, or send a message. I mustn't even think of using the laptop, otherwise that'll end up in the drink too. I've already wasted the phone's precious metals, letting them leach into the silt.

I must keep swimming away from her; or better still, evolve into something with legs that walks on dry land. Stop falling back into that warm body of water. But I feel like my teenaged self, letting all the breath out of my lungs and anchoring my weight to the floor of the pool, daring myself to stay there.

It has been three weeks since her last email. Three weeks is like three lengths under water, my limit before rising to the surface for a breath.

To Burn

Ana calls me a bridge-burner. I write straight back (my break from the laptop lasted two and a half days) and say that if I'd burnt all my bridges, she wouldn't be emailing me still. She says she's a bridge-builder, and that I move in such a way that requires never looking back. It's true that in any good friendship, as in a good song, for every action there's an equal and opposite reaction, a balance.

I think of the scooters in Hanoi without rear-view mirrors; the rule is to focus forwards, and if everyone follows it then accidents are avoided.

'Moving forwards,' she replies with an immediacy that warms me, 'doesn't preclude retracing your steps. Your life's shape might be a lemniscate.'

I hate that she's used a word I don't know but am grateful I can look it up. A figure 8. Why not just say that? Perhaps it doesn't adequately convey the grandeur of infinity. Does it bother me, the idea of returning here every decade?

Out the window it's drizzling. Thirty years ago, I would've been playing Scrabble and eating Belgian biscuits. Now I'm sitting cross-legged on the shag rug (odd choice for a bach, like having a dog that can't shake the sand off itself), spine against the sofa. The rug and sofa don't belong to me, nor does the coffee table or the walls or the floorboards or the sandy earth underneath them, the draught that flows up between them, the pōhutakawa trees out the window, or the window or the sky or the waves. But all of it feels like mine. I know I've become awfully confused and possessive. This is now the property of the Pukepuke Tangiora Estate, land which has always been the local iwi's. I paid in cash to rent the bach (that is, I remind myself, *borrow* it) and had only to arrive with my suitcase, guitar case and keyboard, the extent of my actual belongings. The layered view (dove grey, slate grey – the colours of my limbal rings – grass blue, grey brown, pale brown, tussock ochre, and the bone-white brown of sunburnt timber), like a cross-section of earth, is one of my earliest memories. The biscuity smell hasn't changed despite the coats of paint and different furniture. The house used to belong to my parents. In my first year I must've crawled over these floorboards, minus the rug; my knees and palms know it. Part of me burns bridges, but not my body. My body holds tight.

I ask Ana if she'd just like to Zoom instead of all this back and forth with the email.

'Sorry,' she types, 'I'm working.'

'I should be too,' I type. 'Thanks for the session. I think it was very helpful. Will be careful with the matches.'

'Don't burn the beach down.'

There is work to be done, but I need a quick stroll and a smoke. First, though, I use my laptop to Google 'smartphone metals disposal poison'. Mostly aluminium (body), iron (speakers and mic) and copper (wiring), a bit of gold (connectors) and neodymium and praseodymium (motors and magnets responsible for the buzz), and terbium and dysprosium (screen). No lead. The small quantities of each probably won't do much damage as they gradually break up in the sand, but I mustn't get another. If I do, then the pollutants, the exploitation, the waste of finite matter, will be that much worse. Ana is right – I am a bridge-burner. I've burnt my bridge with the smartphone and all it stands for, allows, requires, endorses, does. I do not need it. My hands are busy enough with cigarettes, instruments, Japanese pottery and seawater.

I don't even miss the music on the phone, I realise as I stride along the hard tideline in my mother's gumboots. The sea is the best drummer for the gulls' vocals; I let my footsteps and breath act as a subtle backing track. When I reach the surf-lifesaving carpark, another sound braids itself into the beach's song, thin and fly-away through tinny speakers. A mother is dressing a small child in a wetsuit. A dog is whining on its stomach behind her. She's not holding its lead, but it doesn't seem to realise. It's stuck until she permits it to go. The child is whining too.

'It's too cold!'

'You want to swim, don't you? So, you need your wetsuit.'

'The wetsuit is too cold!'

'Your body will warm it up.'

'I don't want to! I don't want to!'

The woman has left her car engine running and the song is still playing. I hum along. At the chorus, my whole face sings, emptying lungs of smoke into the air. I thought I'd come to loathe it, as I do with popular things, but hearing it for the first time in months, the sonic quality as faint and pale as the made-up saint it's named after, I feel affection. I want this mother to turn away from her child, spot the lone woman belting out the chart-topper and recognise her as the artist herself. Ready to perform in gumboots and handknitted ensemble.

She glances at me but doesn't register who I am. It's tempting to reel in her attention with a cartwheel. But pulling on her son's wetsuit now is holding her in place. If she's chosen to keep the motor running so she can hear my song to the end, it's a watered-down sort of pleasure – a modest nip of consolation in the glass of the quotidian. I settle for a smoke ring.

Initially the hi-hats were too hot, searing off the better textures of the melody, the keys and guitar and my voice. I made her stop and go again and again and again. She was bleach-blond, young and new to the band, and knew me as the matriarch of the group. I was all maternal tantrums.

The woman is throwing a stick for her dog now. It's off its leash and enjoying the pretence of freedom, the kid is paddling where I learnt to swim; the car has been locked and the engine turned off, the radio with it.

'Hey,' I call.

She looks up, slobbery stick in hand.

'The lagoon's polluted. It's not good to swim in anymore.'

She looks at me funny, which is fair enough because I am funny looking.

'It's not just me saying it, there's a sign. There.' I point.

'Oh.' Then to her son, 'Out of there, sweet, it's not safe.'

'I don't want to get out yet.'

'You have to. The lady says it's polluted. Out now.'

Lady. Christ almighty.

She thanks me as if I'm a real pain in the arse.

'The sea's safe,' I say, trying to help. 'Except for the odd rip.'

'Okay, thanks.' She stares at me as if I've suggested drowning her son.

'Enjoy your swim,' I tell the kid, giving him a big crazy grin.

I continue wandering, humming my melody louder now, like a machine about to overheat. I close my eyes and use the dark pink underside of my eyelids (like that famous red Rothko) as a screen. I've only seen the apartment she shares with my rival in photos. Segments of bedroom and bookshelf. Enough to know what they read and the colour of the sheets they sleep between, some psychedelic pattern, not crisp or white, but soft and lived in. They've been together a decade. When I put their faces on my eyelid screen they're not copied and pasted from my own memories but from the *Rolling Stone* cover. My rival is staring down the barrel of the camera, underneath a wire fence of silver eyeliner painted long and strong across each lid. Her hair is slicked back, sleek as if combed after a swim. Her features are small and clean as a cat's. I have seen her tongue when she sings. It's a similar pink to the tailored suit she wears on that cover. And behind her, the band: a competent drummer, beard and glasses, bored mien; and an ethereal bass player, red hair to the waist and falling over her guitar, eyes glazed in a pleasant thought, maybe of me?

In their apartment, the rival would receive tea in bed delivered by my lover. Some days, for some reason, the rival might throw the cup at the avocado-coloured wall. 'She isn't easy to live with,' my lover told me. 'But who is?'

In my projection, their apartment has an open fire. They watch the fire from opposite ends of their couch. They don't touch much anymore. My rival posts to Instagram and my love reads Rilke. If I want to burn myself up, I'll rewind five years to when they'd fuck on the rug by the fire, mouths wide, tongues black with red wine.

To Mother

I am my mother's only child. She knows that I'll never be the woman who wrestles a child into a wetsuit; that she will never have a grandchild. My mother knows that her grandchild is carried on soundwaves instead of in arms. In place of birthdays, this child has launches; rather than one name, many titles. The latest of which is the album *My Brilliant Career*.

The Milky Way and Andromeda will eventually collide and form Milkdromeda ... I am reading the internet when I should be working, feeding my baby. Ana once described to me the way her boobs would become like middens overnight, stony with blocked milk ducts if her daughter hadn't suckled in a while. To feed, for Ana, was to relieve, to ease pain, to do the essential. Working is sometimes like that for me, I suppose. Maybe right now I'm just not full enough of whatever it is I need to express. But the fact that I'm thinking about it suggests a building of pressure. I'm here, aren't I? Back in the bach, sitting at this formica table, staring at my laptop, absentmindedly fingering my guitar, waiting … Held in place by some rule that borders on a sort of mothering.

My own mother mothered me this morning. How humiliating to require it. I had locked myself out of the bach, a dwelling that seems so flimsy and porous that the breeze might break in by accident. And yet I couldn't. Returning from my walk, cigarette butts leaking an ashy stain in my breast pocket as the rain set in, I felt ready to relisten to the cover, sign off on the final version, write something new, read something to deepen the album, talk to the director about the video; the potential productivity was brimming, seeping out to meet the rain. Everything was soaked with possibility. Until I couldn't open the sliding door. Or the back door. Or any window. My fringe was glued to my forehead and a shiver had set in. I reached for my fucking phone. The only number I know by heart is my mother's. So I showed up on the neighbour's doorstep, dripping wet.

Mum was there in an hour, by which point the clouds had cleared and it felt less eccentric to be sitting on the deck, learning the waves, learned by the gulls.

'Darling, what are you doing?' Her hands like sparrows, a performance of fluster. I do something to her blood pressure, I'm sure, even now, more than three and a half decades since her body first objected to me in the early weeks of pregnancy. I once asked her if she thought I still made her sick – a sort of helpless, immune response to my presence. She said it was an interesting thought.

'Sitting. Thanks for coming.'

'Of course. Now, let's get you inside and dry.'

She had brought a crowbar, a credit card and a coathanger. She is my mother.

'What do you have in mind?' I asked.

'Jimmying.' Unintentionally comical.

'Jimmying?' Unintentionally sullen.

'Just let me try, ye of little faith.' So much fluttering.

She jimmied for fifteen minutes in such a way that would've been hilarious if she weren't my mother. As it was, I found the experience insufferable. Her slight body ineffectually levering at the structure. Puffs of expletive. A mirror to my own incompetence.

'Oh for fucksake, give it here.'

She passed me the crowbar. I held it like a baseball bat and smashed the window of the double door. 'There we are.'

'Sweetheart, you should've chosen a smaller window. That's going to cost a fortune.'

'I didn't choose it, it chose me.' She was right, though.

'You could've done that an hour ago with a rock.'

'Yes. But then we wouldn't have bonded.'

I offered to make her a pot of tea. She dithered momentarily, clearly tempted, but excused herself to go to a yoga class. It is a necessity of the adult daughter–adult mother relationship to set boundaries to limit co-dependence. To each function as separate entities in the world. That my mother's face and mine, our bodies and our minds, overlap so much is an awkward indication of the time we spent as one, but that has passed now. And eventually there will be just one of us again. And then none of us. Just the music. And then not even the music. Unless the music is learned by other species, but I am struggling to think of a species that will outlive humans and which sings.

As she rattled the lock with the coathanger, before I solved the problem in my own way, Mum told me that she'd heard on the radio while driving here that scientists were trying to use algorithms to decode the clicks of sperm whales.

'They referred to it as speech,' she said. 'Why must animals speak? And why should we eavesdrop?'

'People like to know, don't they? And we miss being animals.' I watched my mother, who looked very much like a primate that had only recently imagined the coathanger as a tool.

'Yes. I think that's right.'

Are attempts at communication intrusive? I didn't ask, but wondered, pulling the thought up around me like a blanket, a respite from the absurdity of the moment. What do I know about whales? Sperm whales are matriarchal, brainy and loud. Their clicks, I think, are a kind of metronome. Sometimes language measures, at others it mothers.

My mother helped me clean up the broken glass before she left. Her hands were already lacerated from gardening (those vicious roses), but I worried she'd cut herself on my behalf and of course I didn't have a plaster to offer. Perhaps she had one in her glovebox, or up her sleeve with the tribe of tissues. I looked at her arms. They didn't bulge. The pandemic might've put a stop to this hoarding.

'There,' she said when the last of the glass was in the bin. 'That's better. Bye, darling.'

I hugged my bird mother and thanked her in a quiet, teenaged way. As soon as I heard her ignite the engine, I started writing.

Maracas don't click. Castanets click in a small voice, a whale's whisper. My finger and thumb click too slowly and leave a pain in my knuckles after a minute. I like the quiet of being alone but desire the volume that only comes from a band. I put on headphones and play the recording the producer sent last week for feedback, at such a level that it becomes the space in my head: it smokes out the thoughts, they scamper off like foxes to be shot. It's a landscape, hilly and surprising, crags balanced by abysses. I listen again and again, until I recognise the repetition as happiness. Contentment. The next one must be as good; this knowledge swells under the skin of my chest, inflates me with purpose, gives me a rhythm to follow.

'The days are all the same and yet new,' Ana had said after having her daughter.

'You're living in a song,' I replied.

'Yes,' she said. 'These days are the chorus that gets stuck in your head.'

'It's a good pop song, isn't it? Motherhood?'

I want to be catchy rather than caught.

To Marry

My hands have learned now, nearly, to reach only for my cigarettes or guitar (two weeks without the phone). The laptop is quiet. She is alive, I presume, wandering from room to room in their LA apartment, sleeping when I wake, waking when I sleep, making things, thinking about me, perhaps. But the part of her made of words – messages, emails – is dead, or dormant, gone for now. I imagine turning her into a song, and play with what I remember, and what I predict or fear, to ward it off. She is hard on my fingertips, steel-stringed, leaving calluses; she is deep in my ears, resonant ash; wet between my tongue and palate as I sing, but mostly glowing blood-pink behind my eyes.

The state of reaching returns once you're sated, according to Ana. Marriage, she says, is not bereft of desire, but contentment and marriage are not synonymous. 'I never have quite what I want, she tells me, 'I'm always still reaching.'

I performed at Ana's wedding nearly a decade ago. The morning before, we had tea together and I asked her why she was getting married. It wasn't that I had anything against Simon; he seemed, continues to seem, as decent and kind a person as one could wish to be locked into a life with.

She laughed the question off at first. 'That's classic you, such a tactless agitator. So provocative.' Then she stopped and stared into her tea. I waited through the quiet, holding her in place with my gaze. 'Actually,' she said, 'I don't know, other than that it feels right. Sometimes it doesn't, sometimes I'm of a mind to throw the whole business over. But I feel that way about everything – my job, whether to have a baby. I don't know.'

My fingernails are bitten and bad for picking, so I use the plastic tag from the bread bag as a plectrum. Sometimes (often) I enjoy a wrong sound, a bit like writing with a pen that's nearly out of ink, or dancing with a broken toe – the ugliness made of honest strain. But I'd prefer honest ease, to be honestly clean and confident, in sound and mind. Even my voice is frayed with a croak. More tea is the answer. Fewer cigarettes.

I can imagine writing vows, performing the vows, even believing the vows. For a time, at least. I can imagine spending every waking minute with her: walking with her, sitting side by side on the plane (when that sort of thing happens again), doing a crossword together, or watching a film or sleeping with our skulls touching. I imagine her playing bass for me, me singing for her, as we've in fact done. I can even imagine introducing her to my mother and meeting hers. I can imagine Ana saying something like, 'You two are just perfect together,' and having no understanding of how that is the very problem. I wish to be perfect alone. It's not that I wouldn't want to care for her if she were ill, or have her care for me, I'd like both those things very much. It's not even that I'm afraid of being tied to her and relinquishing the freedom to be with others, it's more that love songs are boring and politically incorrect. I have never aspired to write one, and now – for the last two months, at least, maybe four – they're all I listen to.

My mother emails me a link to my great-great-grandmother's coronial inquest, published in an 1890 issue of the *Nelson Gazette.* My great-great-grandmother cut her throat with her husband's razor when she was thirty. She had been married for eight years, had six children, and was a regular at the local asylum. I eat my last can of soup and try to imagine what an asylum in nineteenth-century

Nelson would have been like. The doctor, in his statement to the inquest, didn't think she was answerable for her actions, although she never showed any defect of intellect, or delusion whilst in hospital. What a thing, to never show any defect of intellect, or delusion. It inspires me to work in a way I haven't felt for the past three weeks.

But first, I write a letter to my lover:

> I miss you like the proverbial deserts miss the proverbial rain. By disposition, I am dry. You make me other than what I ought to be. Too elated. Too wet. ('Yes, darling,' I can hear you say, 'but what if you were in fact supposed to be the world's lushest desert? What if I am the one to make you that?') I dreamt about you last night. I dreamt I walked through deserted, locked-down streets to your apartment, which was shabby and cold. An imaginary, symbolic place. We sat together on the brown patterned carpet and cut pieces of paper into important strips. Gradually we stripped. The task of the collage that absorbed us so, and at which we clearly excelled, merged with the love we made led by our bodies. It was our minds in pieces on the floor, or pinned decoratively on the wall. This could be the rest of my life, I thought, and woke feeling more rested than I have all year. It was a quiet dream. We didn't really speak. Mostly we just looked and lay and touched and worked, reading and making. The room was fairly bare. There might've been a cat somewhere.
>
> This is all to say, I love you and respect you and have no notion of what those verbs really mean when I know I have hurt you by leaving and failing to write. I hope you are safe and well, happy in your way, productive and healthy, loved and cared for. I desire only good things for you, and for myself, and yet have this sense that despite the dream we

could not provide them for each other. Heaven is too much to live with; it's something to hope for. If I had what I hoped for, where would that leave me? I'm not ready to die yet.
Nor are you.
Love,
Stella

It joins the document of letters I mustn't send. I start tinkering. Singing. 'She never showed any defect of intellect,/ she never showed any delusion,/ she never showed any defect …'

The thing to remember is that she is married, essentially. Not literally. Though as a band they go by the name Wives. The word 'rival' comes from the Latin for stream, and refers to someone attempting to swim in the same stream as oneself. In the past I have livestreamed my rival. She might not be as strong a swimmer as me. Or she might be stronger, I have no idea. She is anomalous and impressive. Sometimes I wonder if it is her I desire. She is the moon that moves the tides of the audience, the sun around which her band orbits, she is a real star, a true artist. Her success is an exquisitely maintained balance, always on the brink of collapsing. Too much adulation in LA and she takes residence in a remote Scottish hermitage for twelve months to craft ceramic shoes, or she opens a yoga studio in Madrid. Too little domesticity on tour – months of hungover eyeliner left on hotel pillowcases – and she plants an espaliered orchard in the walled garden of her apartment block's courtyard. She insists upon time away from you and time with you. You have been together ten years and she is ten years your senior but is ageless. She is five years older than me and has released an album every two years of her adult life. A book has been written about her, released by an American music media outlet.

I hope it is not in my nature to compare myself with others, to envy, to aspire, to idolise.

Once I jumped from a riverbank, against a friend's advice, and landed on a submerged tree. A little to the left and its sharpest branch would've fucked me, ripped a hole in my togs and given me a taste of birth. As it was, the stick punctured the skin between my toes. Others skinned my shin and scratched the back of my thigh. I wanted to vomit. I was afraid of sinking, I was trembling; shaking with the pain, my stupidity and luck, and the need to swim back across the rapids to where we were camping. When I emerged from the water, silt clinging to the hair on my legs, I walked on my heel and left a trail of blood. The wound became infected. Now it is healed and there is a raised scar I could feel when she licked my sole.

To Work

I work best when I'm happy. Is that not true of everyone? She does not make me happy.

When Ana and I Zoom, she tells me her four-year-old, Hera, said she thought she might be feeling love.

'What did she say it felt like?' I asked.

'Happy and a bit sore and very colourful and sort of sad.'

Work is a predominantly human pursuit. It is unfortunate that I seem to be turning into a porpoise. My particular affliction of love makes me slippery, capable of diving and spiralling rather than walking, forgetful of how my fingers felt on the cold keys as I wrote a quick song during soundcheck, or replied to the email from the engineer asking me to sign off on a cover version our label asked us to record at the soft tail of the tour, before all the world was told to hurry home.

I picture 'work' and 'home' as if written in stone under two metres of seawater (like those poetry plinths around Wellington that tourists are photographed obscuring), the letters rippling and stretching. I once read that prawns make a sound like this: *eeeeee*, the printed representation of which resembles their small bodies dancing in a line.

A journalist once asked me, 'Who is the real you? Are you the speaker of your songs, I mean? How much is performance?'

I had to pause for a solid minute, tugging at my fringe, chewing my lower lip, staring into the middle distance and grimacing. The poor interviewer probably thought I was having a stroke.

'Well, it's all performance, isn't it?' I finally said. 'That's what my work is. I try to be honest. Always. But there's no such thing, is there, really? Beyond the performance? Because we're always performing.' I believed that when I said it but am less sure now. If what I'm doing now is a performance, it's a weird one.

The bread-tag plectrum has gone into the recycling, but might end up in the sea, swallowed by one of the turtles whose ancestors were not killed for their shells to be turned into plectrums. What animal would I kill to get a good sound or look? What was the shellac we used to glaze our paintings at school made of? Cockroaches? Or was that cochineal? Wikipedia says it's a resin secreted by the female lac bug. It seems the bug doesn't have to die to make our paintings (or fingernails) shine – shining from lack sounds about right.

I suddenly realise which animal I must kill to make my music. The one that is me with her, its needs creaturely with immediacy, its sense of the world deep but narrow. I'd kill that porpoise self in order to work.

It's a cold day but I pull off my clothes and walk out onto the deck. The sun reflects white off my autumn pakeha skin and a breeze gives it texture. I walk down the path edged with pink pigface and pelargoniums, climb over the stile onto dry sand. Once I reach the wet sand, I run, letting the loose bits of me swing. When the sea holds my hips I dive. Before surfacing, I sing – a vocal exhalation at least. Eyes closed; sensing, not seeing, the bubbles of noise. When I surface, I gasp. My feet reach for ground but I'm out of my depth.

I swim with strength towards the shore, but feel sure that I'm being carried away.

'You've got me,' I say to the ocean. 'That's okay. You can have me for now.' I float on my back, relax my jaw, trying not to shiver; I listen to the sky, which speaks the sea's grey language. A wave will come soon and take me where I must go. I laugh at the thought of that and salt splutters at the back of my throat. I face the horizon, treading water, and see a flat, rolling swell that stirs rather than sends me anywhere. I turn and look for the bach, which is fox-terrier sized now and waiting obediently.

Float supine again and look at my long toes, like E.T.'s fingers, flecks of black polish on the nails. Clouds are flying fast above shadows in the fist of water that's got me; there's a silhouette of a walker or two on the beach, perhaps a dog. I could yell. I choose not to. Some people flip coins to make decisions, others read the stars, others pray, others reason. This is what it is to be at sea. This is what it is to be in love. This is what it is to write a song. This is what it is to be alive.

I am freezing. But that is the sort of thought John Cage wouldn't countenance, so I try not to either. This part of the universe that is me – not a self, just a portion of the whole – is cold. Very cold. Stupid too. Very stupid. If it's washed back to shore, then it will improve in every sense. It is not praying. No, it isn't praying, it's just thinking. Considering. Setting an intention. Shivering. Now it's drifting closer to where it wants to be. Now it's carried up like a raft on the giant ringlet of the wave that's suddenly appeared. Now it's thrashing the ice out of its limbs, paddling and kicking to propel itself, numbly edgeless, and is shot to the sand, only fifty metres or so to the north of the bach.

Elation. But I must sit for a minute. Must nod to the dog walker who asks if I'm alright.

'Where's your towel?'

'Back at the bach. Don't worry. I live just there.'

I can see she thinks I'm some sort of taniwha. 'Thank you for caring,' I add.

She looks at me as if she's sure I'm not alright. The man with her busies himself throwing a stick for the dog. He doesn't want to be seen watching my naked body.

'Take care of yourself,' she says, as if I've been borrowing my self from someone else, possibly her, and using it rashly.

I nod and try to stand, but find my legs are more of a tail. I fall.

'Let me help you to your house,' she says.

'It's okay, I'll be fine, thank you.'

'I'm sorry, I won't leave you here like this. Let me.' She puts an arm around my waist. 'Actually,' she says, unzipping her firetruck-coloured jacket, 'put this on.'

'No, please, I'm fine.'

'Just put it on.'

'Leave her, dear.' The man is uncomfortable with the direction this is taking.

'We can't leave her. She could be hypothermic.'

The jacket is an undignified length, not quite covering my pubes. I pull it around me tight. There's something lumpy in the pockets. Dog treats? I don't put my hands in to find out.

'There, that's better,' she says. 'Now, which bach was it?'

I point.

'The black one? Okay.' She walks me to the stile.

'Thank you, this is fine here,' I say, as if she's a taxi driver. I start to take off the jacket.

'No, all the way to the door.'

Leaving her companion behind we awkwardly straddle the stile in tandem, my legs still jellied. But she doesn't stop at the door, she enters, surveys my living quarters, sees a blanket and a mug. I stand, a placid horse, as she slides her jacket down my arms and wraps the blanket around my shoulders. Would you like me to boil the jug? A cup of tea?

I manage to convince her that I really am fine, but once she's gone I can imagine her saying, next time she's walking on the beach with a friend, 'This is where the crazy woman lives.'

To Meddle

I don't tell my mother about the incident. She would only meddle. I do tell Ana, and my agent, my producer, my sound engineer, my saxophonist. From a bed nest I write screeds, which in itself isn't unusual, but there's something strange about how suddenly and intensely I crave contact. I reply to old emails, so old that a reply is now not only superfluous but odd. I read promotional materials advertising clothing and stationery. I click on links. I watch a wild-born orca attempting to beach herself on the edge of her tank at Loro Parque zoo in the Canary Islands. In another email a New York pop psychologist writes in a dispatch that we – humans? all life forms? – require a balance of security and freedom, inviting me to 'turn the lens' on myself. Am I balanced? Am I too secure, or too free? I'm in bed, under a feather duvet borrowed from my mother, at nearly lunchtime on a Wednesday morning, with a view of the sea out the window, the sea that took a bit too much of the warmth from my blood, which I'm trying to replace now. The bare facts of my day align entirely with what I aspired to as a nine-year-old when asked what I wanted to be when I grew up. I didn't know about the what so much as where and with whom. I wanted to live by the sea with a dog and a donkey and to make music. The idea of children and a husband hadn't occurred to me. I was a child. I am a child. Do children require a different balance of security and freedom? Or somehow greater quantities of both?

My eyes just opened, which indicates they've been closed. The laptop is not on my lap, but next to me, open at a louche 45-degree angle. I shut her lid and my eyes again, lie back and listen to my freedom, which is not distinct from security after all. That's the problem, lady, I tell the pop psychologist. Thought of that?

Drifting into a waking dream now, I remember discovering that my chin is an erogenous zone and finding it a sublime surprise. There's matching hosiery. Not a faithful memory of the original encounter, but a poetic flourish from my unconscious. There are so many legs and fingers. Mine knobbled, papery and fragrant. I'm certainly dreaming when my vagina is confused with the inside of a whale, hollowed out and furnished for visitors to take tea in, its plush red borrowed, I suspect, from the rows of seats at La Cigale. 'She has a startlingly human expression,' my lover says, wearing surgical scrubs and staring into my eyes.

Dreams meddle with waking life. She meddles with me. My mother meddles with everything. We're all just meddling along. But I feel clearer for the nap, and a safer temperature. A hot shower and fresh outfit, make-up – eyeliner, lipstick – car keys. I will drive to eat something substantial at a cafe. I should feel lucky to be allowed to move as far as I can, unmasked. This bolthole backyard to the world where I live is a boon. I will tune the car radio and listen to the news; it will crisp into sense as I crest the steep hill up from the beach and descend the gravel road on the other side between the thoroughbred paddocks, heading towards the little bridge over the river. Everything's little here. I feel little; no one would ever call me an old soul. I loathe the tone of such a label but still wish it were applicable to me. Grow up, woman.

To Play

I play for a living. Guitar and keyboard, and my role, Miles. I like how spacious the name Miles sounds. Stella Miles Franklin went by this to hide her gender, and I borrowed it. Truthfully, I dislike that novel, but I admire Sybylla's pluck. A friend and I handprinted figure 8s made of my stage name onto T-shirts so that they encircled the breasts – 'milesmilesmiles' slurring into 'smiles'.

To play is to pretend, but it's also real. To play is to trick yourself into entering the real by appearing to escape from it, but of course the best songs don't draw anyone's attention to their trapdoors.

The car radio does not play the news bulletin I expected, an antidote to playfulness, adult reality; instead a musician is being interviewed about her recent performance in an Elvis biopic. She was accustomed to playing rhythm guitar, but for the movie had to play lead guitar and sing at the same time, which she says is like patting your head and rubbing your belly, except more complex and in front of cameras for fifteen hours a day.

Sheep are being herded across the road ahead, so I slow to a stop and watch them jostling away from the keen-eyed dog, its spine rigid. It might work fifteen-hour days too sometimes; who's to say when a dog is off duty? The farmer is a woman who could be my age, wearing a black cap and sunglasses, an oilskin vest, jeans and Blundstone boots.

I'm inclined to assume that everyone doing real work is older than me, but it's true that I'm not young anymore. On stage I am ageless, or every age. Looked down on from the gods (a flatteringly high angle) I'm a glowing child bandaged in off-white calico, all eyes, cheekbones, lips and hands. A porcelain vessel for a voice. The sort of clown that would draw a crowd on *Antiques Roadshow* – an exquisite and rare toy. But looking up from the front row, the low-angle lights find my face haggard; the lines from the corners of my nose to the quivering seams of my mouth are gouged deep, a fright mask. My body is a well-made marionette that jerks and sways to the music; who is playing whom? As I perform, I am the joke I am not necessarily in on; it is a kind of madness that clenches around an audience for ninety minutes and keeps me cloaked.

In the last show, at La Cigale, as I retuned my guitar between songs, fussy and unhurried, a woman's voice yelled that they loved me, all of them in the crowd. How could she know? I smiled because I can't help enjoying being loved. A man's voice demanded banter. I stopped smiling. I pulled the mic closer to my mouth but I gave him nothing. I played. In the fabric of the song, I was safe. Banter was the kind of nakedness that he sought. A personal word provoked by himself, and I would not give it. Not even a breath in his direction. It's all a game and I never lose; the audience doesn't want me to. I know the power of silence. Cage calls silence a choice; I feel it chooses me. This year has been an exaggeration of my notorious interview silences.

I don't ever play alone. Behind me there's a mouth over a reed, fingers on keys, fists holding drumsticks. And my lover with the bass line, my blood in her hands, reverberating against her stomach. She needed so little instruction.

The sheep passed some time ago, they're scattered across the hillside. No one's behind me now; no one knows I've just been parked on the road, thinking. Golden poplars, the range's seams indecently green, sky bright as a Siamese cat's eyes. A different day to the one on which the sea nearly ate me. I'm so hungry. Just drive to get some food, I tell myself.

I park between SUVs in a supermarket carpark in the village. It's still called that even though it's a large, well-heeled suburb of a city. Every person I can see through the windscreen is a woman, and every woman is wearing white pants. I look down at my long cotton dress, more oatmeal than white, somewhat sheer, revealing the red-and-grey-striped leggings underneath. A Swanndri of my father's from the seventies over the top and a hat that was also his. A Russian thing made of faux fur. When he died, I took my seven-year-old self to my parents' wardrobe and looked at, smelled and touched his things. Eventually I wore them.

My fringe is flattened over my forehead by the hat, it tangles with my eyelashes. I put on sunglasses, triangular, black. Smear on hand sanitiser. If I weren't so hungry I would sit in the car for a few minutes before opening the door, to tend to my threshold anxiety.

I want a particular lunch, from the bakery my mother and I used to go to. It's still where it's always been, with tables under red umbrellas on the footpath. The warmer is almost empty, but my guess that whatever's left is likely to be vegetarian is correct. I take a carton of chocolate milk from the fridge and put it needlessly on a plastic tray, slide the tray along the stainless-steel ledge, deciding whether to add a cake. I choose a pink lamington with whipped cream and jam. It's almost too fat for the tongs but I manage to lever it onto a plate.

'Just that?' the girl behind the cash register asks.

'No, I'd like a vegetable pie too, please.'

The tray of food is immensely cheering. I sit at the table of my choice on the footpath, lift the lid of my pie and burst sauce into its steam, like a gory pimple in reverse. Of course it burns my palate because I'm impatient. I fumble the straw into the foil hole in the milk carton then suck as if inhaling. I pause to roll and light, then turn to the lamington. Cream gets on my cheek. I grin to no one in particular. The table next to me is taken by teenagers, which reminds me that this is the place where I had my first cigarette. I indulge in that vertiginous feeling of fast-forwarding through the many intimidating places I've been and the things I've achieved since I was thirteen until I land back in the present.

'This is the right way up,' a girl's voice, obnoxiously sure, says.

'There is no right way up,' her friend or foe replies. I'm immediately on this girl's side.

'No, there is. See?'

I want to see too, but that would involve turning and drawing attention to myself. They probably wouldn't know who I was, or even notice me at all; I'm about sixteen years beyond the limit of their vision. So I do turn, and see that they're playing a game of cards. Maybe Hearts? They're examining the queen. Rotating her – both of her – around and around, trying to choose which one deserves to be the right way up.

'This is the right way up,' the annoying girl says, 'because this queen is more detailed.'

'Stella?'

I look up from where I'd frozen, holding my cigarette and listening. The face is familiar instantly but takes a moment to align with a name.

'Linda? Hello.' It's eighteen years since I've seen her, but I could recite her family's old phone number.

'Wow!' She leans down and I half stand. We hug awkwardly. Her body seems surprisingly unchanged. I wonder if mine does too. 'How are you?'

'Not bad. How are you surviving all this?' I mean the pandemic, but the way I gesture vaguely could suggest the village – our hometown.

'Getting by. Busy. Pretty lucky, all things considered. I'm actually running late for a thing at my kid's school, but could we catch up properly?'

'Sure, yes, I'd like that.' I try to remember how many children she has, from the flashes of her life I've glimpsed on social media. Two? Maybe three?

She gets out her phone. 'What's your number?'

I begin to tell her before remembering my phone is in the lagoon. I tell her it's not working right now. and she looks at me with an affectionate impatience that's familiar from when we were kids.

'What are you doing tonight?' she asks.

'Tonight? Nothing much.'

She suggests a place that used to be easy to get into under-age, where we'd drink lurid pink cocktails. Apparently it's a bit nicer now. We arrange to meet at seven-thirty.

When I drive into my mother's driveway, I find her tangled in the mutabilis rose. She seems oblivious to the way the vine has hooked its thorns into the back of her old grey jersey, until she turns to wave and the plant claws her cheek. I wind down the window.

'Mum, may I have a bath?'

'Of course, darling. Help yourself.'

'Is that rose bothering you?'

'Nothing I can't handle.'

Inside, I check the digital radio next to her bed. It's four. I intend to spend the next two hours soaking in my isolation chamber, my sensory limitation tank.

This is the longest I've been away from my laptop since I threw my phone in the lagoon. I shouldn't smoke in the bath but do, with the window open, and lots of lavender bubbles, enjoying being held by water of a different texture and temperature than this morning's sea. I close my eyes, wet the flannel and use it as a mask, hold my rollie with my right hand.

'Are you alright in there, dear?'

'Mmm, good.'

'Want a cup of tea?'

'Yes please.'

The tea adds scents of lemon and ginger to the lavender and smoke. 'Use this as an ashtray.' Mum puts a heavy glass item from the seventies on the edge of the tub, next to the William Morris cup.

'It *is* an ashtray.'

'Yes,' she says, as if at the same time it isn't quite. She probably means that it hasn't been used as one for thirty years, not since I watered her cigarettes to try to improve her longevity. I'm lucky she hasn't played that nasty trick on me.

'What's the matter, dear?'

'What do you mean?'

'Why are you here? In the bath?'

'I just felt like a bath.'

'Oh.' She's hovering in the doorway, away from my line of sight. 'I came into the village for lunch, and bumped into Linda.'

'Linda from school?'

'Yes. We're going for a drink tonight. So I thought I'd come here to get ready, rather than going back to the bach.'

'Oh.' Then, 'But you don't drink anymore, do you?'

To Lie

I arrive early and take a table in the cordoned-off area outside, intending to get in a cigarette before Linda gets here. She hated it when I smoked at school. But she's early too; I recognise her gait as she approaches.

'We don't have to sit here, let's go inside,' I say, guilty.

'Nah, this is fine. Being inside without a mask still doesn't feel right.' She sits opposite me and scans the QR code with her phone to look at the menu. 'I think I'll get a glass of bubbles. What would you like?'

'Just a Coke, please,' I say, feeling childish. 'I was going to order at the bar when we went in. But we haven't gone in.' I fish in my wallet for a note.

'Don't be silly. You can get the next ones.'

It's all pleasant, flat small talk as we sip. I ask after her kids, she asks after my music. I watch the fish and chip shop across the road, behind Linda's shoulder, expecting each adult to look like overgrown memories, but I don't know anyone, and no one looks at me.

Two drinks in, her intonation becomes choppy. 'I know it's silly,' she says, 'but I feel most alive when I'm vacuuming or scrubbing the shower with my earbuds in. I'm singing along, pretending I'm not where or who I am. I won't pretend to know what your songs are about – is it gauche to assume they're about anything, rather than just existing as themselves?'

I remember when we started using the word 'gauche'. We must've been fourteen or so, mimicking our severe English teacher's vocabulary. 'Try not to be too gauche or provincial,' she told us on an excursion to the theatre. We loved that phrase.

'You're never gauche,' I say, confident in my ability to fill the gap that is our entire adult life until now. My best friend from intermediate and high school, who I've messaged once or twice since I left school aged seventeen, is still known to me, surely.

'I don't know how it happens,' she goes on. 'But I notice more while your voice is in my head. It's silly, like I say, but while I'm listening and singing along, I feel harder and shinier – do you know what I mean?'

I shake my head. 'Not really, tell me.'

She says she means those chestnuts we used to collect from under my parents' tree. 'Do you remember? We'd peel off the spiky husk and reveal the nut that made you realise for the first time why fox-coloured horses are called chestnuts. Anyway, that's how I feel as I clean and listen, as if the layers are coming off me. I feel closer to the world for an hour or two, and it's because of your music. Is that strange?'

Not strange so much as tipsy, I think. She pauses to sip. I consider responding but sense she's not finished. It's an odd compulsion that I follow when I reach my hand across the table and holds hers. My hand is performing its own ritual. My sandpaper skin and fingertip calluses meet hers. Her eyes brim and glow, blue as ever. Mine mimic in a greener way. We become younger and closer.

'Thanks, Stella. What I mean is, in a way you've been there and I'm grateful. Thank you.'

What I hear her say is that in most ways I haven't been there. In most ways, I upped and left. I want to apologise, but it's difficult. So instead I thank her for listening.

'Do you,' she begins, cooler now, not heated by her own experience, 'feel something like that when you listen to your music?'

'No. I've never heard Miles, not the way you have. I'm glad there's that power for you, but it's not there for me.'

'What about when you perform?'

'Performing is different, you're right. I don't feel what you've described every night I play. I'm distant.'

'I see that in your eyes when I watch videos of you.' She stops, perhaps embarrassed at this admission. 'You're absent.'

'I am and I'm not.'

'That's how I feel when I clean.' Linda pulls my hand, which is still holding hers, to her mouth and kisses it, her lips a little wet with prosecco.

To Comfort

I stay the night at my mother's and in the morning she wants to know how Linda is. I tell her Linda is well, it was a pleasant night.

'Melissa from the year above us has two sets of twins.'

'Oh yes, I know,' my mother says.

'And Billie is running for council.'

'Yes, I saw that in the paper.'

'And Anna has a conviction for drug dealing.'

'Which Anna?'

'Just teasing.'

She doesn't like my tone. Takes her coffee mug to the sink, rinses it. 'I'm off to the library now; will you be here when I get back?'

'Back to the bach,' I say, enjoying how this sounds. 'I've work to do. And I don't want to cramp your style.'

I borrow an outfit from my mother. A polyester shirt she wore in the seventies, baggy jeans and a black peacoat. I keep my father's Russian hat. I wonder if all daughters are as parasitic as me, and whether mothers itch to still be fed from, even once their offspring approach middle age.

I indicate right rather than left at the driveway: first, a visit to Linda's house before work at the beach. Last night as we parted she said she had something to give me.

Linda's waiting at her window when I arrive, holding a small child, or large baby, a human of newly bipedal age head to toe in rainbow-hued handknitted wool. She comes out to open the picket gate.

'You came! Two days in a row after eighteen years apart.'

'Of course, I came,' I say. Then, addressing the small one, 'Hello, are you Leonora?'

Linda's youngest stares at me before pressing her face against her mother's neck.

The house is so tidy it seems to throb with organisation. Baskets and boxes of sorted toys. Slices of cake steam on the plate that Linda places on the table, wooden, extendable, with a view from the bay window out to ferns and a trampoline.

'Are you happy here, Linda?'

'Mostly happy.' It's as if our conversation the night before was rinsed down the shower drain when she washed her hair this morning. She deposits Leonora in a white plastic highchair between us and puts a piece of cake and a beaker of water on the chair's tray. Then she brings two cups and saucers, a teapot, milk jug and sugar bowl to the table. 'I'll be mother,' she says. As she pours the tea, two cats enter at speed. The first halts on the lino so abruptly it slides until it's completely still except for its tail, which swishes side to side like an instrument.

'They're brother and sister. They do this every few weeks, I guess when she's in heat. They're only playing. Do say if they're annoying you, though.'

'Of course not. I love animals.'

'Sorry, it's just weird – both knowing and not knowing you, if you get what I mean?'

I nod. 'I reckon we're not that different to how we were as teenagers. Not really.' I bite my warm cake. Butter, cinnamon and orange rind on my tongue; a sultana swollen in the heat releases its juice into the mouthful. The fat and sugar, spice and tang, lightness and weight are held in perfect balance. 'This is *good* cake.'

'It's just the usual, nothing special. The kids gobble it up after school.'

'Do you still sing?'

'Ha!' A wet crumb flies from her mouth across the table and hits the teapot. 'Only in a choir.'

'That's singing.'

'Not like you.'

'I sang with a choir for my last album.' I regret it as soon as I say it; we both know it isn't the same at all. There's a pause, during which we watch Leonora eating.

'Do you think you'll have children one day?' she asks.

No, I think about saying. Yes, I think about saying. I'm not sure, I think about saying. I hesitate so long that uncertainty must be the answer, which is surprising.

'Sorry, that was rude.'

'No, it wasn't.' Though, really, I think it was. Or, if not rude, then at least defensive. 'It's a good question. I'm just thinking about what my most accurate answer would be.' I'm unsure why it's so hard to articulate. I'd assumed that 'no' was a fact of my life. 'I think probably not,' I say in the end, watching Leonora letting her cake drop like sand out of her fist onto the floor, taking comfort in watching it fall.

'Good,' Linda says.

'What do you mean?'

'It wouldn't be right for you. You'd hate it.'

I'm shocked by the offence I've taken at this. The peacoat is far too warm, ridiculous to be wearing it indoors, sitting by the double-glazed, north-facing window, all the autumn sun with the wind filtered out. As I free my arms from the sleeves, a button on the polyester shirt pops undone. I decide to leave it. 'Is it right for anyone?' I say. 'Is it right for you?'

'What kind of question is that for someone who's done it three times?'

'It's just that last night you didn't seem all that happy.'

'Didn't you used to wear that shirt at school?'

'Maybe? I think so?'

'You did. I remember it.'

'It was Mum's. Is Mum's. From her youth.'

'And your youth.'

'We're still young, Linda.'

'Nearly forty.'

'Not for four years.'

A phone rings somewhere in the house, the first landline I've encountered in years, other than my mother's.

'Can you watch her, please?' Linda asks me. Or possibly she's asking Leonora.

'Good cake, isn't it?' I say to the child. 'Want some more?'

Leonora seems keen to follow her mother, or maybe she's suspicious of me, so I cut her another small piece and put it on her highchair tray. The fat fists crumb it again.

'Don't do that,' I say. 'Such a waste. Your mum made it.'

Leonora reaches her arms out and up, and *ba-ba-da*s to get down, or so I presume.

'Alright, why not.' I unclip the belt and try to hoist her, but her creased thighs stick in the gap between the tray and the seat. The highchair rises with her. She howls. 'It's okay, just straighten your legs and it'll be grand.' I extricate the child's limbs from the plastic trap but her back is arched now and she's refusing to be comforted. I pat her and sway and sing a bit. At the singing, she relaxes. 'You know this one, do you?'

'Sorry about that. I needed to take it. Plumber's coming this afternoon. Oh Stella, she's sucking your hair!'

'Shouldn't she be?'

'No, I mean she's getting crumbs and saliva all over you.' Linda retrieves her daughter brusquely, as if I've let the child sully her expensive curtains instead of my appearance.

I look at the lock that hangs against my shoulder after being in Leonora's mouth. 'I don't mind at all.'

To Conform

There seem to me two ways of being: one comfortable and dishonest, the other honest and uncomfortable. To be comfortable in the world is a lie – a denial of its discomfort. It is to ignore what hurts you and others in favour of a quiet, perhaps even successful, life. Or maybe this is a decision inherited from a pattern begun generations before. The uncomfortable way of being is to admit that the world is ill-fitting.

It's been exhaustingly self-absorbed, my failure to conform. At primary school I sang too loudly and in a strange, husky voice but I wouldn't stop, especially when Mrs Jones told me to. I had no aptitude for choreographed dancing, or team sports, or the forming of alliances. It was not a blindness to what could be done to ameliorate my situation; no, I could see quite easily how my splintered edges might be smoothed off and friends made and kept. I could've started shaving my legs like the other eleven-year-old girls who were taunted for their hair by the boys who had less. I could've begged my mother for bootlegged, stonewashed, hipster, red-tag Levi's instead of black leggings. I could've read *Girlfriend* instead of *Tess of the D'Urbervilles*. I could've painted faces instead of fenceposts in sixth-form art classes. I could've taken biology instead of art. I could've stayed at school for seventh form instead of going to uni a year earlier than my peers. I could've stayed at uni instead of dropping out. I could've kept working at the library. I could've stayed with my boyfriend and occasionally performed in his post-punk band, banging some sort of ironic tambourine behind his Mark E. Smith impersonation; a dead-eyed Nico. I could've had a baby and a husband, and a job and a student loan, not quite or at all paid off, and maybe even a mortgage.

But yes, of course there are many forms. Am I not conforming to a different shape? Look at my sunglasses, my impulsive near-drowning, my broken heart. That is still a type. However much I may feel as though I am, I'm not outside of anything.

Except the trampoline. I am outside the net while Leonora rolls about inside it, holding her round knees and chortling.

'That looks like good fun,' I tell her.

'Have a go – you know you want to,' Linda says. She unzips the portal to the child's undulating world.

Why not? I unlace my boots and kick them off, climb the ladder in my socked feet and feel my weight stretch the trampoline's material. Leonora rolls into my leg.

'Is that fun? Do you like that?' I ask, palms down, bouncing gently. She pulls herself up using my shoulders. She seems to want me to stand too, so I do. I hold her hands and bend and straighten my knees. We laugh in the same deep way, the pleasure sitting in our stomachs. I sing 'Ring a Ring o' Rosie' and fall down, double-bouncing her higher than intended. Her face meets my knee as she lands and the laugh stretches into a wail.

'Oh shit, sorry.'

'It's okay.' Linda reaches in and pulls out her daughter, inspects her mouth, the lower lip welling red. 'She's used to it.'

'I'm too big to be a child,' I say.

I take Leonora's injury as a sign for me to leave. After we've said our goodbyes and I'm about to reverse out of her drive, Linda calls, 'Wait!' She runs back into the house and returns with a cassette. Her neat young handwriting on the sticker reads, *Linda & Stella*.

'Are you sure?'

'Yep, it's your turn to caretake our magnum opus.'

'Thank you. I'll treasure it.'

'I want it back in eighteen years!'

'Sooner. I promise.'

The old car has a cassette player. I listen on the way back to the bach. Our rough and tender renditions of Alanis Morrissette and The Pixies and Hole. Then something we tried to write ourselves.

'The customs of man are like footholds carved into inhumanity,' I read in Jenny Erpenbeck's *The End of Days* when I'm back at the beach, away from Linda and her daughter, away from my mother and my daughter self. Taking my time over a sentence that pleases me. I have moved the formica table into the puddle of sunlight next to the broken door, facing the sea, which is teal green with white edges today, the colours of the old Air New Zealand uniform. Further down by the livesaving club, where the breakers are cleaner, there will be surfers, floating like ducks, hoping to be flown into shore. I have no desire to walk today, to go away from this place that is temporarily mine; I've an open novel, a notebook, a 6B pencil for drawing carved footholds made of the inhuman. A guitar with a proper plectrum at last, perfectly tuned, ready to make sounds like customs; a keyboard in case my fingers need to trace different shapes. These are the conditions for forming rather than conforming, for turning the inhumanity over and over before deciding how or whether to sculpt it.

I stare at the beloved sentence until I disagree with its implication that customs must be humane. I feel least human when participating in mass formalities, rituals steeped in animal urges to be safe or to procreate. Perhaps it's because these compulsions are like vestigial organs, designed to grow the human population, when really, we are too many. I love a large audience of course, I just don't enjoy being in the crowd.

My ex, the boyfriend who came after the Mark E. Smith acolyte, is a DJ. He thought raves were a secular religion and invited me to pray with him. I would do all of what was offered to me back then, stride into whatever underground carpark or cathedral was the venue of the night, and feel my self as the cell of a larger dancing beast, moving in unison with all the other cells. It was a relief, a release of the tension of the ego, to be one with a mass, he believed. His calling was to conduct the massive puppet whose many limbs were tied to the beats. It had to build and build and build and build, he claimed, unbearably slowly, until there was no breath left in a lung, no light in an eye, until it was at such a height, such a speed, that everything blurred into nothing. 'Like a frozen heat, the something that is not, and then,' he mimed, 'it drops. And the blood flows fast around the body that is everyone in the room going *ahh*.'

'You're fucking the dancefloor?'

'I'm making love,' he said seriously.

My chart-topper has been listened to millions of times on Spotify. This ex has remixed it. I've performed it every night for sixteen weeks straight, with one rest night a week, to four thousand bodies at each theatre. I have a hundred thousand Instagram followers, who scold each other below the photos of one-legged ducks, or schools of fish, or my nostrils, or my mother's gardening outfits, which I used to offer as absurd sacrifices to the god of myself, before killing my phone.

'This is such a witty consent metaphor. So deep.'

'She doesn't like people analysing her lyrics!! Fuck off.'

'Do your research, shes obvs a Pisces.'

'If you listened to the acoustic version, you'd understand.'

'She's asexual.'

'Really none of your businesses. I'm sorry you had to read that, Miles. xo'

'YOU are transcendental.'

'The Artiste/Priestess is Present.'

'Give me your beauty!'

'Liminal goddess!'

'I just discovered you! Thanks for being what I need.'

'Are you magic?'

'That kind of androgynous energy does things to me.'

'Your hair is so uniquely you.'

'I have never loved a human being more.'

'Miles is my religion. That is all.'

If I were a sandcastle and their words were waves, then I'd be flattened in a day. I let them lick me every now and then if I feel craggy, turrets of angst growing too tall and crooked, threatening to fall, needing a push. But all in all, people threaten my edges. They turn me off at the mains and leave me useless. No, a dancefloor is not for me. I like the definition that comes with a single downlight. I like to be blinded and blinding. I like to wear white.

'Ethereal. That is the word. Are you even human?'

I pressed the heart shape under that one, then a second later pressed it again. I wonder if anyone saw it pulse.

To Buy

Of course I buy things, and I take pleasure in materials. I like my Japanese mug. I like my clothes. My guitar. I'll fondle these items to distract myself from the fact that I am running out of money. I don't know when I'll be allowed to tour again, or how much I'd make from it. While I'm on the road my possessions are neither here nor there. I choose a single outfit for the shows and take several sets, so that every city gets the same photos, and the work neutralises any desire for what can be bought. I'm much more interested in what I can sell, which makes me a hypocrite. Still, I'd never play at a farmers' market, and I don't DJ.

There's a rainbow out the back window burying its brightest stripes in the hillside I climbed as a five-year-old in the dark. Actually, I didn't climb it, I lay in bed listening to the older kids climbing it and hating them for being older. Hating my mother for being cautious. Hating myself for being younger. Or did I climb it? And was I afraid of the dark? Did I cling to the arm of a boy eight years older who held a torch and warned me when we had to squeeze through an unseen barbed-wire fence? Did my bare foot brush a dead sheep's inflated side as we approached the peak and did I scream? Or perhaps I'm conflating that memory with the time we found a swollen-bellied cow in the stream leading to the polluted lagoon …

To Walk

It's lucky I went straight back to work after seeing Linda. It's lucky I saw Linda, because she has helped me go back to work. The following week, my manager takes up most of the screen. He's in his kitchen in London, sitting where I've sat, with his back to the stovetop and his cherry-coloured Moka pot.

'I'm sorry,' I say straight off, because up in the top right corner above the coffee maker is an icon warning me my laptop is nearly out of battery. It's running on red. 'I just have to plug my computer in.' I reach behind me, trying to find the socket. Something in my shoulder twinges.

'You have the power to do things differently,' my manager is saying, 'you just need to move.'

'Sorry, it's fixed now.'

'This stagnation doesn't suit you. You need to move to a city.'

I don't reply.

'Stella, I'm worried about you.'

'No need. I love the beach. It's a holiday, which you were saying I deserved, remember? I'd been working too hard?'

'A year-long hermitage isn't what I meant.'

Has it been a whole year? I try to count back but the months bleed into each other. 'What have you been doing for the last year? Isn't everyone on forced leave?'

He downs his Mondrian demitasse and laughs. 'Darling, others are poking their noses out of hibernation now. Have you been vaxed yet?'

'No, they're not up to my tier. My mother has.'

'That's good. I've had mine. You should get onto that. Tell them you need to tour by the end of the year. They'll understand.'

'Tell who?' I imagine the needle sinking into the eye of the bird tattooed on his shoulder.

'Ask Ange or your tour manager or someone to sort it for you if you can't be arsed. You thrive when you're busy, and your present scenario doesn't sound busy. What've you been up to?'

I remember the recording he sent me a few weeks back. I listened but neglected to reply.

'Writing a bit, actually.'

'Oh, really? Any demos?'

'They're coming along. You'll be the first to hear them when they're ready.'

'At least show me the view. Show me where you've been twiddling your thumbs for eleven months.'

'Eleven? My lease is up soon.'

'Good – get thee to a city!'

'I'm not ready.' I'm not speaking to him now so much as to myself.

'Of course you are.'

'I'm sorry but I've got to go.'

I close the laptop. It feels mean, not showing him the sea, not speaking to him for so many weeks. Not giving him anything. It is mean. But it's beyond my agency. I wouldn't choose to be so ungenerous.

I put on Mum's gumboots and Dad's Swanndri and begin to cry. Outside there's the sort of wind that would be called a squall. I run; I don't know if it's as therapeutic as walking, but sometimes my body demands that I go faster. I run until I hit the trunk of the macrocarpa tree that fell about thirty years ago. I still myself against it, lungs hot and tight, feeling the novelty of the wheeze, amused by my body's reaction to its own suggestion. I breathe in through my nose for four counts and out through my mouth for five. Then in for five and out for six. And so on until I'm inhaling for eight seconds. A singer's trick. The inhaled air is the temperature that the sea looks to be. I watch the yellow collar of foam quivering in the wind and wonder which of my innards it would most resemble. Is there a part of me under my belly skin that could be described as tripe?

Calmer, I walk back slowly, looking for memento shells. Instead I find a piece of driftwood the length of my lover's forearm and just as pale and smooth. I treat it as if it were a bone of hers.

To Drive

There's my mother digging again. The tines of her new garden fork sink the length of a ruler, maybe more, with the small force of her body driven through her foot. She has on the headphones I bought her, to allow her to hear my music properly – is listening to National Radio probably, oblivious to who is parked in her driveway. I'm impressed by her physical power: seventy-two and wielding the fork in a way that could kill a man. Perhaps that should be a medical measure of physical ability – instead of squeezing a doctor's finger, could you thrust a garden implement through an attacker's sternum?

We're all, to vastly varied degrees, at risk of violence, that is the nature of being alive, but there's no need to watch one's mother gardening and imagine her killing a man. Some would call this an intrusive thought, but I welcome it in. It now wants to leave and I'm holding it captive, perhaps to ward off other thoughts.

She's using the fork like cutlery, twisting the matted layer of grass in a circle around the tines, then anchoring the sharp ends in the soil and levering the bundle back towards her, getting purchase to tear up a broader layer.

When I tried to teach myself to knit, like everyone early on in the pandemic, the voice over the top of YouTube video, the voice of the glittering fingernails and chunky, even rows, referred to 'the anatomy of a stitch'. To neatly seam the edges of the hat, I must understand the anatomy of the stitch and use my tapestry needle to burrow in and find a tiny cross-bar of yarn. I did not do this. My stitches were inevitably visible, that's just who I am. I liked the word 'seam' so much that I looked it up and saw that its Dutch origin is *zoom*. Thinking of this now reminds me of the room I left my manager in, which makes my flaws more visible. Gauge. Tension. Tense. Text. Past. Present. Future. Right side. Wrong side. Warp. Weft. Not yet. Soon. Cast off. Measure. Block. Try on. Learn. It's only a metaphor. It is also worn. Bespoke.

A knock on my window jolts me.

'Where were you?' my mother asks.

'Just thinking.'

'In the driveway?'

'At first I was watching you work. You're impressive, you know. I was thinking, If Mum wanted to kill someone with that fork, she really could.'

'Thank you, dear.'

'Are you ready for a break?'

'Yes, I'm exhausted. Morning tea, I think.'

There are still signs of upheaval under her fingernails when she sits at the dining table. I've boiled the kettle and scooped coffee grinds into the plunger. I look for biscuits in the cupboard. Only digestives of course. I put four on a pretty plate, knowing we will each eat only one.

'Did this belong to your grandmother?'

'No, that was Great-aunt Mamie's.'

'I like it.'

'Have it if you want.' She always says this. 'It'll all be yours soon enough anyway.'

'Maybe I will.'

We surprise each other today. My mother eats three biscuits. When I've eaten the remaining one I put the plate in my bag.

'Rinse it!'

'It's fine.'

'Your bag will be full of crumbs.'

'That's just who I am.'

'Don't be so defeatist.'

'If crumbs are defeat, then what's the battle?'

She looks at me as if to say, You well know what you're losing and it's not to do with crumbs, or visible stitches. It is to do with a lack of resolution. Who is really the stagnant one? I've just dug up six square metres of turf to plant a grove of kōwhai and improve the biodiversity of the area. What have you done? Filled your car up with petrol? She says none of this.

'You've disappeared again, darling.'

'No, I'm here. I was just listening to your thinking. You're right, I'm not essentially crumby.' I take my bag to the sink, and rinse and dry the plate, polishing the cracks across the pale teal pattern of a horse and carriage. She would like this plate, I think; it's her colour. She drives me crazy, I might say. 'Crazy' means full of cracks, in one of its old meanings. The urge to get in touch with her (touch her) is so great that I'm constantly threatening to break. I have not only cracks, I realise, but structural damage. A threatened disintegration. A falling apart.

I wrap the plate in a tea towel I like, printed with lemons, shake my bag out over the sink, dust away the crumbs. Put the receipts and other detritus in the kitchen bin. Rescue my driver's licence from the plughole. Replace all that I need, including the plate, in my now clean bag.

'Mum, it's time for me to go.'

'Are you taking my tea towel too?'

'Do you mind?'

'No, I suppose not. Do you mean that your lease is up soon?'

'Yes.'

'Do you have a plan?'

'Enough of a plan.'

'Which is?'

'Wellington.'

'Good. That'll be good.'

'I hope so.'

'I'll miss having you here, dear girl, but it's best you go.'

That's another sort of digging: weeding out the small talk to provide space for words that don't grow naturally.

To Ride

I rode a plane to Wellington after following the short queue of passengers across the tarmac to the narrow metal steps, finding my window seat, and watching my mother standing frozen at the terminal window, hand raised like a maneki-neko cat, handkerchief in her fist, feeling the usual well rise up in me as the wheels began to move. It settled back down deep in my abdomen as we left the ground, only to return as the plane quaked across the surface of Lyall Bay and landed to inane applause in Wellington.

I should stop using the pakeha names. The Māori name for Lyall Bay is Huetepara, meaning ripe gourd. The gourd-shaped peninsula to the south has been officially known as Hue tē Taka for a decade, and is tied to the land as a fishhook is tied to a line.

I take a taxi to Ana's house, ten minutes from the airport. There are Hera's thunderous four-year-old feet on the floorboards, and then Ana's face, which has never failed to put me at ease in the twenty years we've known each other. I am staying in Wellington for a few nights, to do an interview and reacclimatise to people, before flying on to Auckland. I could afford a hotel, but Ana has insisted. Simon is away for the week at a conference, and she'd appreciate the adult company, she said. She doesn't ask why it's taken me all year to visit – why I haven't seen her since Hera was a baby.

We embrace and I hold on longer than ever before. She doesn't let go of my arms when she steps back to examine me. It's the sort of action I always wanted my mother to perform when I was a child. My face loses its usual self-awareness and stretches into whatever shape relief chooses to make it.

Hera appears jealous of this interaction. Her bare feet thunder down the corridor again and in through a doorway second on the left. Her room. I follow her down.

There's a rocking horse in the room. She mounts it and immediately pushes the pretend animal to its limit, galloping in such a way that it seems to achieve the suspension of four real hooves levitating at once. Hera rocks like a deranged jockey until she abruptly stops and says, 'I'm hungry.'

'Let's make some afternoon tea. Stella might be hungry too,' Ana says. 'Come on,' she tells me. 'Don't get stuck in here.' While she boils the kettle and puts shortbread, rice crackers and vegetable sticks on a plate, we begin to catch up gently. I ask after Simon. She asks after my mother. Hera interrupts, asking me if I've ever ridden a real horse.

'Just once.'

'Were you scared?'

'No, I was ashamed.'

'Why?'

'I didn't have her permission.'

The child starts to laugh. 'Horses can't talk!'

'Exactly.'

'That doesn't make any sense.'

'I mean that the horse couldn't say to me, Hop on my back, Stella, I'd be happy to carry you up and down the beach. But I rode her anyway and felt bad afterwards. Do you see now?'

The child looks annoyed.

To Perform

My friend sits on the couch with her feet on the coffee table, the cat on her lap. I sit on the rug with Hera. There's a lot I want to tell and ask Ana, but instead I'm compelled to follow Hera's instructions. We're making a train track.

'What's my job?' I ask Hera.

'You can keep building this track, so it curves around here.' She passes me some pieces and draws a line with her finger.

'That won't work,' I tell her. 'See, it's too narrow for the train to go through.'

'Oh.' Hera takes this constructive criticism well but has trouble breaking what she's started. I sense she wants to work alone now, so I lie back. My vertebrae rearrange themselves with a series of clicks.

'Look!' Hera says. It is as if I've been in Narnia. I thought I was lying with my eyes closed, feeling my back pressing into the carpet for only a moment, but the track is suddenly finished and entirely different.

'Wow! It's like a spiral.'

'It *is* a spiral.' Hera sends the train around the loop. 'Once they hop on, they can't hop off,' she sings.

I look to Ana, to see if she's heard. She has, and smiles.

I tell her about the dream I had just before waking. I was standing in a queue, somewhere with the same palette as my imaginings of East Germany, but it was Aotearoa. When I got to the table with an official woman in a uniform I didn't recognise, I understood I needed to have my photo taken. 'But this isn't going to work,' she said pointing at my face. I thought perhaps I was still wearing a mask and reached to remove it, but there was only skin. 'What's the matter?' I asked.

'The colours are not right. Here, under your eyes. It's a very dark aubergine.'

'That's just what I look like.' It was then I knew I wasn't queuing for a passport photo, but for a group shot that would be titled 'Endless Women'. Something about the bags under my eyes made me ineligible to pose as one of them.

'What do you think it means?' Ana asks, massaging the cat's sides.

'I think I'm feeling my mortality. I think this is commonly known as a midlife crisis.'

'That sounds right. We're the right age, after all.' She presses her thumbs into the cat's eye sockets. The volume of the purring increases.

'You'll decide eventually,' she adds.

'I'm in a morass,' I tell her. 'A boggy patch.'

She gets it immediately. 'You're lost on the moors. Or is it the fire swamp? Are there rodents of unusual size?' We've watched *The Princess Bride* together many times.

'There's sinking sand, certainly. But I believe I'm the only rodent.'

Ana looks at me closely. 'Stella, you're alright. Everything is alright. You are yourself and I love you.' She kisses me on the head, and if it weren't so hopelessly self-indulgent to tell her about two dreams in a row, I would tell her that this moment reminds me of another recent dream. I was in the bathroom of the Warehouse Hotel in Singapore, looking at my reflection, underdressed for whatever event was taking place in the function room. A woman's reflection grew in the mirror. I recognised her. She recognised me. 'Your hair,' she said, taking a piece between thumb and finger. 'I love it.' Hers was red, mine was blond. She was me. She hugged me. I felt like *myself*, in a way I never had before. I woke comforted.

The sound check for my show in Singapore went badly. By that stage of the tour, I ought to have been surging with energy, but that afternoon I was distracted by the cables under my feet. Inside each there should have been three pieces woven together: two signal wires passing the sound from my gear to the audience, and a third wire shielding the sound from electromagnetic interference. According to the technician, there was a problem with the microphone cable and the way it was carrying my voice.

'Can't we just swap the leads?' I asked.

He was squatting like a black-clad toad at my feet, muttering. 'You want your guitar to sound muddy?' he scowled at me.

'I don't think the vocals sound muddy.'

'Fuzzy, then.'

'Not fuzzy either.'

'Look, with respect, this isn't your area. I can get it sorted out, just be patient.'

My lips held each other tight while my eyes held his, as they had the first time a session musician offered to play my guitar for me in the studio so that I could concentrate on singing; as they had at the glossy-magazine interview when my eyelashes were curled, fringe straightened, and body draped in garments resembling ill-fitting straitjackets; as they had when my post-punk boyfriend laughed at my suggestion that I could speak a poem over his guitarist's messy shredding; as they had when my first producer responded to my request for an extra vocal track with 'You are *my* instrument, remember.'

'Listen,' I told the technician, and I sang without amplification, into the theatre. It was a deep, clear pool of sound. My dam. His damnation. My power. He stopped sulking then and at last looked at me the way he should.

'Leave that cable and listen again.' I turned on the mic and sang into it. The pool was still deep and clear, but with a ripple on the surface this time. I explained the texture to him.

'It's your show,' he said.

'It is.'

It is a truth that I always enjoy myself when I play (also a truth that I often cry on the way home from a gig). Once, a few years before her daughter existed and a couple of years after I'd stopped drinking, Ana helped me smuggle myself, disguised in tears, out the back of the Michael Fowler Centre and into the whirlwind fridge of the night.

'Let's go to Happy,' she suggested. Ana had been at Happy for my first performance there. It wasn't called that anymore but was still downstairs from a yoga studio. That teary night, there were no kids playing Korgs or cans of Double Brown for four dollars. Ana returned from the bar with two glasses of Coke just as a young woman who'd been setting up an amp and microphone started to howl.

'Do you like this?' I asked, nodding at the stage. 'You agree she's good?' Ana nods back.

'I love how you keep it real!' a voice called between songs.

The singer stopped sucking her lip and looked out into the small mass of bodies in the dark, all breathing in each other's air. 'No,' she said. 'Don't think that for a moment. There's nothing real about this.'

To Balance

I'm old enough to know my own terrain, the peaks and troughs, the weather pattern, but this knowledge provides no escape; there's no avoiding the lows. That middle zone of either descent or ascension is not what I think of as balance, even though it's in between. I can never remember the difference between average, median and mean, but I do recognise balance and I understand that it requires time.

Thinking about it now, in Ana's shower, the glass cubicle filling with steam, I'm reminded of a singer-songwriter who was our support act in the UK. She was witty and cool generally but on stage she made the mistake of chatting, and it was self-conscious and embarrassingly stiff, like a generally attractive person whose face tenses for a photograph as if they've stopped breathing, dropped everything to look a particular way. One night, she started monologuing about colour wheels. 'Creatively, *creatively*,' she said, 'colour wheels turn me on. I just love, or a better word might be desire, I just *desire* that sensation of trying to hold every colour at once in my eyes, getting the pure white light that has swallowed a rainbow just by looking. Is that weird? I also,' she went on without pausing for an answer, 'love meditating on opposites, the tension between red and green, violet and yellow, orange and blue. It relaxes me like I've *come* to some truth if you know what I mean.'

'Oh my fucking lord,' I remember saying. 'She hasn't even picked up her instrument.'

But in the white steam of the shower I suddenly sense what she means and feel guilty for being ungenerous. I imagine the colour wheel as a paint palette. My mother took up painting in her retirement. Her method is to cut long, narrow rectangles of cotton-fibre paper and drip thin strips of colour into the centre of each, letting it dry before dripping another layer of a subtly paler colour. She does this over the course of a week, beginning with a heavy, dark tone and ending with just water. The effect is a layered stain, a palimpsest of fluids that leaves lines where the edges dry differently each day.

'They're landscapes,' she said defensively when I commented that she'd maybe been inspired by her time as a midwife.

'They look exactly like pads.'

'That interpretation is in the eye of the beholder.'

'I think they're amazing, Mum, I love them. But they definitely look like they've been bled.'

'Tidal, perhaps.'

'They're like origin myths,' I suggested. 'Like the borders of the world, the coastlines and riverbanks and mountain ranges, might've been menstruated by some goddess.'

'Good grief.'

She thought I was having her on.

'I'm just saying they balance out the hard boundaries of countries, drawn mostly by men. These images to me are a woman's stains as sources of creativity, rather than shameful waste to be disposed of.'

'I never saw it as shameful. Women can't help what they secrete.'

I asked to borrow her materials. While my mother worked, I watched my page bubble into its own shape. With each squeeze of the sponge, lines ran according to the paper's contours, sometimes together, sometimes apart, two powers pulling the one substance in different directions. Two currents with an occasional confluence, reminding me of that undertow.

When the drops threatened to breach the border of my figure 8 shape, I mopped them with a clean sponge. The dried image wasn't as close to what I'd envisaged with the wet. The colours regressed to rust, the textures were chalky. Still, I flattened the page under a pile of books and waited to see if the result might be worthy of an album cover design.

'You're forgetting you're not a painter, you're a musician,' my mother said when I sulked about the failure. 'You're not trained to make a decent painting. You can't expect to be skilful from just dabbling. Why not just get the rights to a nice Georgia O'Keeffe?'

It's a misstep to assume your mother knows what you mean.

Wrapped in a towel, I head out of the bathroom. My life right now feels like I'm sitting alone on a seesaw, making myself bounce up and down to appear independently happy. Really, my knee is sore and I'm lonely. I know the answer is to swap to the swing instead, or dig in the sandpit. That's how I coped as a child. Without siblings or friends, I anthropomorphised a bag of marbles, divided them into kingdoms and devised a saga of love and betrayal.

To Plant

The birds' colour shifts from dark to light, like flipped leaves, their flock buffeted by the coastal gusts. It's as good a day for gardening as any in Lyall Bay, and Ana and Hera and I are in the backyard.

'Digging will help you,' she says to me.

'It will help me too,' says the child.

'Yes, it will help us all.'

'Not the pussen.' The cat is stretched out in the sun on the deck, a paw over her eyes.

Ana hands me the good spade to use. She has a shovel with the wobbly wooden handle, her daughter has a blue trowel. 'Our task is to finish the plot,' says Ana.

'Is it like writing a story?' I ask as I sink my implement into the corner of lawn that will soon be a bed of edible and floral things.

'Tell us a story, Mama,' Hera says.

'Okay.' Ana assumes a storytelling voice. 'Once there was a lawn. Every Saturday a man would mow the lawn, and his hands would smell of petrol right into the evening when he lit his barbecue, which sat on the paving next to the freshly mown lawn. While the meat cooked, the man's sons kicked a ball to each other.

'This lawn knew it was a symbol. And when a woman came with her hoe and started to hack at it, it tightened its many-fingered fists on the sandy soil. She began in the corner closest to the barbecue, intending to leave a strip of turf for her sons to play on, and she had her headphones on.'

'What was she listening to?' I ask.

'Hole.'

I smile.

'The music drove her to break every one of the lawn's fingers. She levered up clods the size of her torso and flung them into a corner, until there was a mound as tall as herself and an expanse of earth as inviting as chocolate pudding. She aerated the soil with her fork, as if testing a cake, turning and stirring the impacted clay. Destroying the lawn took two hours. She did it without pause. Once the violence of preparing the soil was completed, she allowed herself a rest, during which she considered what to plant where. She had been raising kōwhai and pōhutukawa, mānuka and poor knight's lily, puka and hebe, coprosma and flax. And so she planted a grove for the birds and for herself. The end.'

Hera and I clap, the sound muffled by our gardening gloves.

I'm not a natural at manual labour, and I end up contributing what I'm best at. I sing. I hand Ana the good spade and sing for the hour that she digs the lawn. Sometimes Hera sings too. Then I make lunch. I heat leftovers of the vegetable lasagne I made the night before and boil the kettle for tea.

As we eat, Hera says, 'You can stay as long as you like in my room.' My mouth twitches involuntarily at the edges, like an over-tired eye. I thank her and say that'd be nice, while knowing that I will leave the day after tomorrow.

'Have you heard of the Vertical Earth Kilometer?' Ana asks, seeing that I am closer to crying than I want to be.

I haven't.

'It's an artwork that seems to me the opposite of your art,' she tells me. 'Yours soars up while it burrows down. Yours adds space, it takes up space.'

'Yes, but what is it?'

'A massive brass pole that a man drilled into the earth in this park in Germany. The whole thing is buried, with just the flat top showing.'

'Ugh.'

'It reminds me of a kind of hidden pouwhenua.'

'What's pouwhenua again?' I don't recognise the word at all; 'again' is a feint, a shameful saving of face.

'You know, those carved posts at marae? They mark territories and suggest the relationship between the tāngata and the whenua.'

Does she mean between the people and the land? I think so, but my memories of fourth-form Te Reo Māori lessons are faint. How long have I been away from home? Touring sporadically for two years, and before that mostly based in the UK. Can it have been more than a decade since I've lived here? Touring here doesn't count. I've done that a few times, but never for more than week or two. Is a decade enough time to lose an accent or forget a language?

'What are you thinking?' she asks. I've paused for too long.

'It's just hitting me how long I've been away.'

'Do you miss England?'

'No, I miss home.'

'Here or there?'

'I don't know. I think that's a big part of my trouble. I thought it was here. But I've forgotten most of the Māori I learnt at school.'

'So stay longer and learn.'

The house is sleeping, even the nocturnal cat. I creep out onto the deck, stand in the quiet black wind. I want to see the moon, see how close she is, watching over the garden. The clouds are blown aside and she's revealed, on the cusp of her super blood self that will follow a solar eclipse tomorrow. Her light holds the traumatised young leaves and roughed up soil from the morning's work. I breathe in cold salt air through my nose and breathe out warm bed breath through my mouth.

To Doubt

'Stella?'

'Yes?' Hera and I are sitting on the deck, where I'd stood with the moon last night. The day is clear and unusually still now. We are drinking black Milo (milkless, grown-up).

'Imagine if there was no two.'

'What do you mean?'

'Imagine if there was just zero and one.'

Delivered like a punchline rather than philosophy. I am coming to regard this child as an oracle. I hold up the index finger on each of my hands.

'In your world of only zero and one, how many fingers would I be holding up.'

Her laughter brews deep in her belly. 'One, of course! One and one would be one. It would be so easy to count in that world, wouldn't it?'

I'm compelled to stroke her back, which shudders with laughing. It isn't a good reason to procreate, my sudden desire to make an oracle, but right now it feels good.

'And you and me sitting here,' I ask, 'would we be one?'

'Yes.' She headbutts my arm, pushing her fine curls into my armpit, wanting to be tickled. I could like this, I think, providing a child with what they want and wanting it too. But such care would swell up to fill the space I've been guarding since I was smaller than her.

'How did you not expect it to be hard?' I asked Ana when Hera was a few months old and Ana hadn't slept more than half an hour at a time in weeks, and was sick with mastitis and the realisation that Simon would never feel the same burden she did.

Ana was offended by the question. Of course she'd expected it to be hard. The difference, she told me, between an expectation and the reality that follows is the difference between a shadow and what casts it. She didn't say that I didn't know what I was talking about but I got the sense she wanted to. All I'd really meant was that mothering had always looked like agony to me. I did not understand how women willingly lost themselves in marriage and birthing.

Yet now, sitting here on the deck is a counter-argument with Milo on the tip of her nose, small fingers with broken nails holding her cup carefully.

There is always both something and nothing. I consider trying to articulate this thought when I'm interviewed later in the day at the Radio New Zealand studio. The presenter is maternal and familiar in a way that provokes me to behave like a shy teenager.

'You'll be doing your first live performance in more than a year next month, in Auckland – how are you feeling about that?'

Would it be true to say I'm feeling damaged, punctured, porous, unsure? Am I missing that part of me that only appears on stage and which I believe is the essential part?

'Eager,' I say finally. 'I'm feeling eager.'

'So am I. I was there in the audience when you last toured New Zealand – at your Wellington show – and I don't want to embarrass you, but I must say it was one of the most moving performances I've ever had the pleasure of seeing.'

'Thank you. That means a lot.' Does it? Or am I being compliant and polite? I say, 'I feel like when I speak it's from the bottom of a pool, and it's a miracle if anyone hears. But when I'm singing I'm floating above the ground.'

The interviewer looks triumphant. As if she's taught me to do a trick. 'Gosh, I have to say, it's *nice* to hear you speak. Do you find it difficult to contemplate performing, to connect with your public, after a hiatus?'

'Well, it does feel like it's been longer than a year. The virus has infected time; everyone I know agrees on that. But I don't know if I've ever really connected with my public, or if they're even mine. Do you mean the people who listen to my songs? The songs have a public, I think.'

My songs are to me physical things, that exist in space and have the capacity to touch a person. I don't touch anyone much anymore. It's at this point that I consider articulating my something and nothing idea, but don't.

'Touring takes a toll, and you'd been touring seriously before Covid. A lot of shows, not a lot of rest. How did you cope? How did you take care of yourself on the road?'

I think about the word 'care' and have an image of women with corpses. Washing them, dressing them, anointing them, singing over them. I suppose I did versions of those things for myself as I was carried from continent to continent, illuminated and amplified six nights of the week. 'Care is also a kind of song,' I say. 'Maybe a lament that more could be done, which is always true. I take care of the music quite well on tour, usually. Perhaps the parts of me that seem less essential to that don't get cared for so well.'

I'm squeezing my left hand with my right. The presenter makes some new comment but I'm distracted by an old box in the corner of the studio, now being used for paper recycling. On its side is the promise that it once held 'transducers that deliver the truth'. That, I think, is one way to define music.

We go back and forth for a little longer, until she says, 'It's been so good to talk to you at last, Miles. What a treat to have you in the studio with us. Best of luck for your upcoming show and I hope to be in the audience again.'

Ana is waiting for me outside the studio.

'Effusive?' she asks.

'Yes.'

'Good questions?'

'Yes, no, I don't know. I got distracted.'

'You always get distracted. Did she ask about your personal life?'

'What personal life?'

To Learn

Thinking about the interview, and what I should or should not have said, reminds me of the public speaking I did the week before I left the bach. I had been invited back to my former high school to speak at a Friday assembly.

'But I don't like speaking in public,' I told my mother when she asked if she might pass on my email address to the assistant principal, who'd heard I was home.

'It'll be good for you, though.'

'Why?'

'You'll have to come up with something. Wisdom for the teenagers. Might be just what you need for yourself.'

She had a point. I was wallowing in her bath (again) at the time, had been for more than an hour; the skin of my fingers frowned as I used the toes of my right foot to turn on the hot tap, to delay the inevitable.

'My wisdom is opaque if it exists at all.'

'Well, they think you have something to say, so I think you should try.'

'They should go through my manager.'

'Stella, you're home now, not in London.'

'That doesn't matter. I'm still busy.'

My mother raised her eyebrows at me.

'Alright, I'll do it.'

I don't remember what I said at the assembly exactly. I wore crushed-velvet leggings in midnight blue with a mustard-coloured linen shirt, cherry-red silk scarf around my hair and a lot of matching lipstick. 'Good grief,' Mum said when she met me afterwards. 'Loud.' I took my guitar too, in case words failed me.

'Hello,' I remember saying. Repeatedly. To people I met and remet. I'd parked the car where I used to park twenty years ago, just in front of the curb I popped a tyre on while turning over a Pixies cassette and driving too fast. I skulked to the front desk. 'Hello,' I said to the woman behind the desk. She knew who I was. A bell rang. I detest bells. This one was more of a siren, actually, the sort that makes your body stop and consider how to get underground as soon as possible. It didn't sound as I recalled it sounding when I was a student; then it was a modern, dystopian sort of honking goose signalling recess or lunch.

'Stella!' An adult I didn't recognise approached. Narrow spectacles gave her eyes a judgemental expression. A quantity of equine teeth were exposed in a smile that, had it seemed sincere, might've cancelled out the implicit criticism of the squint. She proved to be the assistant principal.

'Hello,' I said. Once again.

'I nearly called you Miles! How embarrassing. Do you get that a lot?'

'Sometimes. It's alright. I answer to it. I chose it.'

'I'll take you to the theatre now, before it gets too crowded. Is this the first time you've been back to the school since you left?'

'Yes.' She must have seen me staring into the windows of the woodwork room, and at the tree a ginger cat fell out of when a boy called Bronson threw stones at it and broke its leg. Familiar shady corners, blue and burgundy paint.

The theatre was where I first played for an audience. A smudged line of yellow chalk on the concrete floor could have been the exact position of the stool on which I'd perched, looking like Joni Mitchell and sounding like Courtney Love if she were folky, Bob Dylan if he could sing, Marianne Faithfull if she were a teenager, Patti Smith if she were less sincere, PJ Harvey if she were Kiwi, Björk if she were Kiwi – sounding like the start of Miles.

Other sixteen-year-olds – real, current, not just remembered – were walking in packs through the dried-blood-coloured double doors. I breathed shallowly, trying not to inhale too much of them, and looked for the ones who might have last stood on that chalk mark, perched on the stool. A kid arrived alone, swimming in his clothes, retro canvas satchel covered in pins. Another two walked together but didn't talk; each held a book that didn't look like a set text (*The Master and Margarita*, *Anna Karenina*). She – that younger me – was in the theatre somewhere and I'd never find her. I hadn't worn midnight blue, mustard and red back then; I was very quiet.

The assistant principal introduced me to the school captains, who she said would introduce me to the assembly. They were sporty, amenable sorts with badges rather than pins – lapels shining with praise. All-rounders doubtless up to date with their physics homework and happy with their cameos in the school musical. Wholesome young people with friends, boyfriends and girlfriends.

Who knows, they might marry each other one day and have two children.

While the boy spoke at the mic, the girl whispered to me, 'I really love your latest album. I listen to it *all* the time.'

She might have been saying what she knew would set me at ease, I couldn't tell. Still, it wasn't her flattery so much as her whispering while her counterpart was addressing the school – her brief lifting of the school-captain mask, a gentle flouting of politeness to declare herself an acolyte of mine and not what she appeared to be – that won me.

'Hello,' I said when it was my turn to stand on the chalk mark. The rest, as I say, I can't recall. But if I were to give this talk in my head now, it might go something like this: Tēnā koutou, tēnā koutou, Tēnā koutou katoa. It feels strange to be back here. Strange to be telling you what I've learned, because honestly, I feel less authoritative than I have in my whole adult life. Less adult.

Then I might've licked my lipstick teeth before continuing: I don't like speaking particularly. Playing music is easier for me. I like advising even less, unless it's something very specific. But I'll try, because you look a bit bored. What have I learnt? I've learnt not to skinny-dip in April in a rip. I've learnt that my mother was right about some things. She told me once to have lots of friends rather than boyfriends or girlfriends. I thought she was just worried I'd get pregnant. But now, at thirty-six, I understand. Friendship is golden. Most of you probably desire danger – skinny-dipping in rips – I know. Obsessions can distract from what we're good at. I never thought I'd be very good at anything until I taught myself to play guitar. I learned that music would always remind me of who I am and what I might offer. Find your version of that and hold it like the raw egg we had to keep safe for a week at primary school. Is that something you're still made to do? School is absurd, right? I think I remember cellotaping my egg when it got cracked. Sometimes I feel like my gift is cracking. A bit crazed and leaky, by a love that feels like an infection. It's sort of comforting to know that what I'm suffering hasn't changed since Sappho described it. It's a bit like an emotional version of the bubonic plague – do you know that the plague may have been in Europe three thousand years before Christ? And the disease is still around today. Impressive, in a way. I've had problems with most addictive substances, but this is the first time the substance has been human. She blurred my edges and I was scared I'd run away from myself. You know when you paint with watercolours and load too much water onto your brush and the pigment races beyond the edge of the line you're intending to make? It's something like that. I'm losing control of the lines of myself because of her; she is water. I can't afford to dissolve or be at all softened. Does that make sense? Probably not. But look, some of you are nodding. That's kind. Thank you.

You need calluses to play guitar well, I would tell them. Calluses take practice. I've been learning to cultivate tougher skin. To treat music as my first love, my only love, my child, my purpose. What a thing to decide when I could have been a nurse or a contact tracer or even a teacher, heavens. I have had to teach myself this – that what I can make is enough to offer in return for what I take from the world; it has value.

Then I maybe would have pulled my lips between my teeth, as I do when the words have dried up. How about a song now? How about I start with the song I first performed here when I was your age? Would you like that? Yes? You probably haven't heard it before, but anyway. Okay. Here we go.

To Sustain

I walk slowly through the rich-person's supermarket in the middle of the city. A boy in a high-vis vest and heavy boots grabs a bag of white bread rolls. He's moving too quickly, with too much purpose, I hope, to notice me standing in front of the shelves of hummus, dumbstruck as I conduct analyses of price, packaging, quantities, colour, texture, branding, ingredients and their origins, seasonality, my mood and hunger (which often come to the pessimistic sum that the best approach would be to buy nothing, eat nothing, take off my shoes and coat, leave them at an op-shop, then walk to the harbour and jump in). I dither beside the dehydrated seaweed snacks and listen to the boy ordering something at the deli to put in his rolls.

'Could I get three dollars of shaved ham, please?'

The attendant tells him there are fifteen types of ham to choose from.

'I'll leave that up to you. Anything's fine.'

I expect he wants whichever ham would give him the most for three dollars.

'Let's say five slices,' he says. 'No, make it six.'

He's matey and flirtatious with the older lady. A late teenager whose confidence might come from having left his peers behind in school two years ago and having a bank account of his own with a full-time wage going into it. I'm not sure how much is going into mine at present. Enough for me not to have to check, but much less, I imagine, than a year ago. I find the crème fraîche and the filo pastry and a bottle of cleanskin riesling and take my basket to the checkout.

I cook well when I follow instructions, but I never quite follow instructions. The recipe does not call for rainbow chard, but spinach. It includes steps I deem unnecessary. The pie, when cooked, smells nice but looks soggy; a green liquid leaks out the bottom of the loose-based quiche dish (not the right kind).

'Delicious!' Ana says, opening the riesling. 'It'll be delicious. Thank you.'

'What is it?' Hera asks.

'Spanakopita.'

'Spana-what-ipa?'

'Kopita. Spinach and cheese pie.'

'I don't like spinach and cheese pie.' She begins to cry.

'You say that about every dinner. If I offered you ice cream and called it dinner, you'd say, "Don't like ice cream!"'

'You don't know that. How could you know that?'

'I make good toast. I could make toast?' I say.

'No, don't make anything else,' Ana says. 'You've cooked something nice and we'll all eat some, won't we?'

'Oh god!' The child runs to our shared bedroom.

Ana and I sit at the table to eat. Hera returns to pick at her pie, most of which Ana ends up scraping into the compost bucket on the bench. 'Best not to think too hard about waste,' she says. 'My worms have a richer diet than a lot of people in this city.'

'Why is it best not to think about that?'

'Because worm thoughts go nowhere good; they're dark and leave you feeling small and dirty.'

'I have them all the time.'

'I know you do. They probably contribute to your basal metabolic rate.'

'What goes in must come out.'

'Or it's just held as excess weight.'

'Am I heavy or light?'

'You're both.'

Hera leaves and returns again, this time with a picture book about black holes. 'How much does a star weigh?'

'Lots,' I say.

'How do you weigh a star?'

'You put it on a seesaw with another star and see which end goes up and which goes down.'

'Don't be silly!'

'I'm not! It is something like that. But it's more like a tug of war between the stars. The one that pulls the other into its orbit is bigger.'

'Does it win?'

'I guess so. Though it depends if it's better to be big or small. Is that right?' I ask Ana, who's looking it up on her phone.

'You're pretty close. The problem is that stars are solitary, they don't like sharing the seesaw or playing tug of war, so they're hard to weigh.'

That night I do what I haven't for almost a year. I go to the dreaded, gridded corner of the internet that I promised myself I wouldn't and I look. I look for two hours that feel like two minutes. I type her name into the search bar. Twelve new followers. Ten new posts. I type my rival's name. This account is not private. The latest post was three hours ago. Feet sucked by the sea. The caption is dull: *This is walking on the sand.* No shit. But three hundred fans have commented on it.

'Where are you exactly?'

'I think you must be very close to me now!'

'I love you! I love you! I love you!'

I can hear their voices overlaid and competing for her attention, affection, respect. I keep scrolling through her posts until I find a photo of them together. *Seven years married.*

'Congratulations!'

'I love you both!'

'I wish you were my mothers!'

'You are such good role models in all you do.'

I study the photo as I was once taught to study a life-drawing model. The angle was severely foreshortened. Turn off the bit of your brain that expects a leg to look a particular way and concentrate instead on the shapes. This is how I look at them now. Elliptical lips. Parenthetical haircuts. Rectangular garments. Shadows. Light. The dispassionate geometry of two bodies together.

To Absorb

It's rained so much that the brown jar that was a vase until yesterday is brimming. (We'd emptied the wilted tarragon flowers out of it to add to the mulch for Ana's new garden.) There's a slick surface reflecting the clouds and spilling over its curved lip are the drops that cannot be admitted. That's how I feel. Impervious by virtue of being full. Not a porous thing, but entirely open – only with no room for anything more.

'More what?' Ana asks. She surprises me because I wasn't aware I'd been speaking.

'For any of it.'

'Any of what, though?'

'I don't know, it's blended in together now. It's like asking me to find a raindrop in that jar. Like everything's just energy really.'

Ana looks disappointed in me, so I try again.

'I'm sad about leaving you. I'm sad about not talking to my mum more, for not trying harder.'

'Harder to do what?'

'To listen to her. To care about her. I think I've got so used to being looked at and listened to in my career that I've forgotten how to do those things for others. I'm sorry.'

Ana puts her arm around me as we look out at her wet garden. There's something calming about it, like watching a fire. 'Why are you saying sorry to me?'

'Because I've been absent and callous, I think.' And, even worse, I realise as I rest my head on Ana's shoulder, because I'm scared that my old strength might be gone. That I won't be able to perform like I used to. And I'm admitting these personal failings now so I can at least try to be someone outside of the performance.

'Well, if you have been then I forgive you. And your mum will too. I'm just happy to have you here now; I'm sure she was too.'

'It's not just you two, though.' I lift my head. Wipe my cheek.

'Who then?'

'There was someone in Paris.' Suddenly I feel exhausted, and go lie on the sofa. Ana sits next to me and puts my feet on her lap. She's alert now. Interested.

'I thought it was just the long tour and then the pandemic – the change in you.'

'What change?'

'You seem agonised. Even your emails did. Love makes sense as a reason. Who is he?'

'She.'

'Who is she?'

'Bass player. An amazing bass player.'

Ana smiles. 'Go on.'

'You know how I'm not good at eye contact? I think I've always been afraid of being caught by a grip that wouldn't loosen. Anyway, I remember when I first said hi to her. And she said hi back. And then we played together so well that I was afraid I wouldn't ever be able to play with anyone else. I just wanted to feel her breath in me and to breathe into her. But I'd got quite superstitious with the quarantine and lockdowns and outbreaks, so we just toured, we worked hard, we barely touched at all, until the last night in Paris before I flew home.'

'Oh Stella.' Ana strokes my shins. 'It sounds like you're in love, that's all.'

'In it as I was in the sea when there was a rip and I had no togs or towel. But I think it's letting me swim back to shore now.'

'Do you want to?'

'Yes.'

'Why?'

'Because I'm coming to admit that I'm a creature of the land and air. This wetness isn't me.'

'Metaphors are helpful, but remember that's all they are. You could be with this woman on land, she doesn't have to drown you.'

I shake my head. 'No, you don't understand.' It's rare that this happens, Ana not understanding.

'Why didn't you tell me about her sooner? All those bullshit messages about whales and fireflies and John Cage when you had something real and serious to tell me.' She's laughing but sounds hurt beneath it.

'I'm sorry. You're right. I should've. But it's like I've been drowning. She's too much for me. I can't sing under water. I'm not a whale.' I feel a cry rising in my throat.

'Oh Stella,' Ana says again, and reaches over and pulls me into a hug.

I lean my ear into her hair and close my eyes. I know what she will understand. 'She doesn't belong to me. She belongs to somebody else.'

'Who does she belong to?'

I tell her, using my rival's real name. Ana and I have written and spoken about her at length. We're both a fan.

'You're kidding?'

'I'm not.'

'Well, that's complicated.'

'Yes.'

'But, you know, no one actually belongs to anyone. Does she want to be with you?'

'Not anymore, I don't think.'

'Why don't you ask her?'

Because I'm not the sort of person to ask that question, even though I don't believe in the concept of sorts of people. That notion robs us of the chance to change. I say, 'What you love comes at the cost of what it makes impossible. That's obvious as any old philosophy.'

'What's obvious to you is completely unclear to me,' Ana says, without frustration or accusation. 'I can't see why what you love should rule out anything else you want. What do you want, Stella?'

'I don't want to care for her,' I say.

'Not what you don't want; what do you want?'

'I want the impossible. I want to be at home and elsewhere all at once. I want lots of lives. Which is horrid greed when other people are satisfied with one life. They're so busy they don't have time to wonder about illusions.'

'Which people? People like me?'

I stare at my friend.

'Multitudes, Stella. As the man said, we all contain them.'

'I don't contain millipedes!' Hera has crept in to eavesdrop.

'Multitudes, not millipedes,' Ana says.

'What are multitudes?'

'Many things, multitudes are many things.'

'I do contain those, then. Blood and bone and water, lots of water.'

Hera crawls onto our laps and we stroke her, praise her brightness. She asks us to read to her.

'Stars,' I read, 'are in a constant state of collapse.'

To Sister

Sometimes I fantasise that my friend is actually my sister. It is unlikely but possible that I did have a sister. A twin I absorbed in utero, who in a way still sustains me. Such thoughts are common for me in flight, the plane a place of possibility, here above the clouds. My sibling and I might've shared our mother's womb for some of the nine months, growing in tandem, so close we didn't know we were two rather than one. Being me, I might've eaten her. I picture a pink, toothless thing sucking vigorously on her twin, but perhaps it was more due to an imbalance in resource distribution; I might've hogged what the placenta had to offer, my limbs lengthening as hers withered. This might've happened so early and gradually that our mother never even knew that for a time she was holding two lives. If she had known, she would've mourned what had been lost, and I would've had to prove myself as precious as two girls. And deep down in the roots of my cells, in the beginnings of my body, my sister would still exist.

She might have been identical. Pieces of what I would've been are hers. We are as close as it is feasible to be, limbs linked, soft skulls butting, tiny hands holding. Fingers entwined once sufficiently defined. When we are born she emerges first – or do I? We are so the same that it doesn't matter in that moment. We emerge. No longer immersed and merged but now two. Twins. We cry in unison, two cries, and the doctor congratulates our mother on our good squawks.

'Two healthy girls, nice and pink,' he says. Mum holds us on her chest briefly, examines us through her large 1980s specs, says hello, before we're carried off to be washed and dressed in our matching knitted outfits. A few days later, when Mum is rested, we are reunited with her, ready to compete, which is to say live our lives.

As I fantasise, I scrawl lyrics: Promise and compromise are twins/ One a collapsing star, distant light/ the other work – toil and strife.

I'm startled by how easy it is to write this account of something that never happened. It worries me that by the time I've imagined my sister up to my (our) present age, I'll struggle to believe she doesn't exist. There's already a flickering of grief, like the start of a fire.

If I did in fact eat her, does she live in the doubts I have about the value of what I do? Or in the rare instances of letting the bath of convention comfort me? The coughing machine of the music industry feeds me – what is my effort actually worth? Nonsense to be worried about a single smartphone after all these years of air travel. I watch the little flap on the wing open. Only the fact that the world got sick with a respiratory illness stopped us flying, cleared the sky and the air temporarily.

Or, if she were whole, a whole sister – who sucked her right thumb and had eyebrows that curled up at the ends and a pigeon-toed gait – what would she have done, how would she have lived? Would she be settled in an easy life? I imagine her sitting in her comfortable living room, perhaps under a blanket she crocheted herself. We'd both enjoy our Zoom conversations but they would be infrequent. I'd ask after her teaching and my niece, she'd ask after my music. These would be our contributions to the world, and we'd openly respect each other for them. But during our conversations I'd nevertheless be distracted by evaluating my lack of generosity, judging the world she'd made for herself, a world softly furnished by a husband and child. This tendency to judge is something she'd notice, and not do herself. Not so as I'd notice, at least.

Her daughter would look edible to me through the screen. 'I'm going to gobble her up, you know. Hear that, little one?'

My niece would giggle as I mimed biting at the laptop camera, eyes wide and bright as a giant's. She would love to be frightened by me, and recognise my playful threats as love.

'We'll see you soon, Stella,' my sister would say.

'Yes, I hope soon,' I'd echo.

And her eyes would mirror mine.

Acknowledgements

This book is largely about how art isn't made alone – every novel or album that might seem to be the work of one person is in fact due to communities who offer support, care, help and inspiration.

Without Miles Franklin's *My Brilliant Career*, *My Brilliant Sister* would not exist. For her wit, her gumption and her legacy, I acknowledge Stella Miles Franklin. Franklin's portraits of Sybylla and Gertie led me to the Mitchell Library to answer a particular question: who was Linda Graham (nee Franklin)? For a thorough, rigorous account of Franklin's life, I recommend Jill Roe's exceptional *Stella Miles Franklin: A Biography* (HarperCollins, 2008). I also owe a debt of gratitude to Roe for her edited collection of Franklin's letters, *My Congenials: Miles Franklin and Friends in Letters, Vol. 1 1879–1938* (Angus & Robertson, 1993), which includes in a much more legible form the letters between Stella and Linda that I struggled to decipher at the Mitchell Library. These letters, particularly that which I quote on page 18, let me hear Linda's voice. Without Linda's own writing, this book would not exist.

Part two of *My Brilliant Sister* adapts the chapter titles in Franklin's novel, and contains letters that I have imagined the sisters might have written to each other. There are references throughout this book to other texts, most of which are credited. The story referred to on page 7, 'Stir Fry', is from Claire Louise Bennett's *Pond* (2015). The poetry Stella is reading on page 182 is from Alice Oswald's *Nobody* (2019). The coronial inquest mentioned on page 192 was published in the *Nelson Evening Mail*, 11 July 1890, regarding my great-great-grandmother, Margaret Wilkins. The phrase 'no defect of intellect and no delusion' was used by the coroner.

Thank you to the many mentors I've been fortunate to have since I started writing: Damien Wilkins, Chris Price, Fergus Barrowman, Ashleigh Young, Tony Birch, Kevin Brophy, Amanda Johnson and Eddie Paterson, to name a few.

Thank you to the brilliant women who read early versions of this book: Chloe Lane, Erin Scudder, Suzie Fraser. Particular thanks to Catherine Bisley for being a brilliant friend and inspiration for more than two decades. Finally, thanks to the extraordinary Joan Fleming for our *affidamento* and for coaxing me on throughout the years of writing and editing.

Thank you to my agent, Clare Forster at Curtis Brown, for invaluable encouragement and guidance – not least for urging me to enter the Victorian Premier's Literary Award for an Unpublished Manuscript. Thank you to the 2023 judging panel: Miles Allinson, Astrid Edwards, Allee Richards, and all involved with the VPLA.

Thank you to my publisher, Ben Ball, for seeing what this book could be and believing in it/ me. Thank you to my editor, Meredith Rose, for being the most astute and sensitive reader my writing has ever had and for helping sculpt the manuscript into the book that it is now. Thank you to Lizzie King, for her expert proofreading. Thank you to Anna O'Grady and everyone at Simon & Schuster who has spent time and energy bringing this book into the world. And thank you to Sandy Cull for the beautiful cover.

Thanks to the generosity of all those who were willing to read this manuscript in advance of its publication. Tony Birch, who's been encouraging my writing since we first spoke over the phone in 2008, before I'd even moved to Melbourne. Emily Bitto, whose guidance and friendship I appreciate so much. Alice Miller, whose own novel about literary sisters I can't wait to see in print. Miles Allinson, for really getting the book (in all its versions). Ceridwen Dovey, of whom I've been a fan for many years. And Emily Perkins, for reading so quickly and kindly (and recommending *The Double Life of Veronique*).

Thank you to my colleagues (particularly Tara and Yvette, who are now more friends than colleagues) and students – I love working in high schools, particularly when I have the chance to spend all day talking with young people about books and writing.

Thank you to dear friends: book club (Phoebe, Holly, Sarah, Alex, Claire, Lyndall, Jules, Steph, Cameo, Di, Kate, Megan); Sass Chat DJs (Ben, Jules, Tim, Steph); Longwood family (Matt, Rastko et al).

Thank you to my family. Anne and David Brown – the best parents a writer/person could have (thank you, Dad, for the proofreading and Mum for sharing your own writing and research about our family with me). Paula Russell and Patrick Fletcher – the best in-laws a writer/person could have (special thanks to Paula for the Miles Franklin literature). Marion – my brilliant sister-in-law. Robin – constant source of joy, love and silliness.

And Nick. In *My Brilliant Career*, when Harold proposes to Sybylla she says, 'If you had any sense you'd have nothing to do with me … I am given to something which a man never pardons in a woman. You will draw away as though I were a snake when you hear.' That something she is given to is 'writing stories'. Thank you, Nick, for not drawing away and for pardoning. This book would not exist without your support, kindness and understanding. Thank you for being there, being who you are, and allowing me to be me.

Finally, this book was written in Merri-bek on the lands of the Wurundjeri Woi-wurrung people, whose sovereignty has never been ceded.

Amy Brown is a New Zealand-Australian writer and teacher who lives in Naarm/Melbourne. She has published three collections of poetry, four children's novels, and completed a PhD at the University of Melbourne. Her poetry, essays and reviews have been published in Australia and New Zealand.